Once Upon A Time In The Black Country

Part Three

Money and Morals.

Thomas J.R. Dearn

Once Upon A Time In The Black Country

Part Three
Money and Morals

Paperback Edition First Published in the United Kingdom in 2021 Amazon KDP Publishing

eBook Edition First Published in the United Kingdom in 2021 Amazon KDP Publishing

Copyright © Thomas J.R. Dearn

Thomas J.R. Dearn has asserted his rights under 'the Copyright Designs and Patents Act 1988' to be identified as the author of this work.

All rights reserved.
No part of this book may be reproduced or transmitted in any form or by any means, electronic, mechanical, photocopying, recording, or otherwise, without prior written permission of the Author.

Disclaimer
This is a work of fiction. All characters and incidents are products of the author's imagination and any resemblance to actual people or events is coincidental or fictionalised.

www.onceuponatimeintheblackcountry.com

Copyright © 2021 Thomas J.R. Dearn
All rights reserved.
ISBN: 9798507795109

October 1830

The relentless rain beat down hard upon the wooden deck that had been scrubbed and polished persistently. The Prison Hulk Ship Dolphin had been moored in Chatham Kent when it set sail for Van Diemen's land on the 26th of June 1830. The four-month voyage had been utterly miserable with a daily grind of cleaning the ship and laundry duties. Many of the Convicts on board did not make it to the other side as disease and sickness was rife and those that did survive knew that they were in for an equally torrid ordeal of hard labour upon their arrival.

The convicts that survived stood on the deck of the ship in neat rows and awaited their fate. Their crimes ranged from minor felonies such as theft to more serious offences such as fraud or even rape, but they were all deemed as being unwelcome to remain in Britain, but not quite unsavoury enough to be hung. As a result, they were transported to the other side of the world.

Van Diemen's land was a large island some 150 miles off the mainland coast of Australia. The territory would later be renamed as Tasmania in an attempt to rid the region of its unsavoury connection to British criminals. Between 1825 and 1853, some 75,000 convicts were transported to Van Diemen's land to bolster the British colony's labour force and Edward Fennel was one of them.

Edward Fennel was born on the 14th of October 1804 in Hope Bagot, Shropshire, a small Hamlet that lies almost directly between Ludlow to the west, Tenbury Wells to the south and Cleobury Mortimer to the east. As a young man, Fennel had moved to the nearby Black Country in order to find work in the industrial region. Here he met and married Susannah Hows from Brierley Hill in 1826. The couple soon had a son John who was just 4 years old when his father stole chickens in desperation to feed his impoverished young family. In 1830, this simple theft was considered a felony and Edward Fennel was sentenced to transportation and 7 years hard labour.

As Edward Fennel stood obediently on the deck, he cast his eyes upon the murky, grey and dismal form of Van Diemen's land which lay ahead of him. He had expected Australia to be hot and bright, but in reality, Van Diemen's land had a relatively cool climate in comparison to the rest of the continent. In the winter months 12 degrees was the maximum daytime temperature, with snowfall still common in October. As he stared and awaited his fate, Fennel's mind was filled with thoughts of his wife Susannah and his young son John who were back home in the Black Country. They were what seemed like a lifetime away and he knew that he would never see them again... *Did he deserve this fate?* He thought to himself sadly. *All he had wanted was to feed his starving child... Was that such an awful crime? Did his son deserve to grow up without a father and in a poor house because he could not bear to see him go hungry?*

Upon completion of his hard labour, Edward Fennel moved to the Australian mainland where he lived out his days in Carlton North, Melbourne City, Victoria. Back home in England, his wife Susannah remarried in 1833 and then later died at the age of 38 in Kingswinford in 1847. Edward Fennel would then go on to marry a fellow convict Ann Mary Harber in 1851, just three years before his death at the age of 49 on the 23rd of January 1854... Back in the Black Country, Fennel's son John would live to the relatively old age of 79 when he died in Dudley on the 8th of January 1905.

Edward Fennel's great, great grandson was born in 1920 and was also christened Edward Fennel. Fennel juniors' crimes would far exceed the severity of his great, great grandfather's, but was he too a victim of the circumstances of his times? Would his endeavour to provide a better life for his wife and child result in a similar fate to that of his long-deceased ancestor? Or would his luck hold out?

****

Chapter 1
June 1944

"The eyes of the World are upon you. The hopes and prayers of Liberty-loving people everywhere march with you." Eddie Fennel hated Americans almost as much as he hated authority and the words of General Dwight D. Eisenhower echoed through his mind as he sat huddled in a landing craft off the coast of Normandy. Shells flew overhead and exploded in the water nearby as the men of the 1st Battalion Worcestershire Regiment dragged on their final cigarettes and checked their weapons. Ahead of him stood a man he had already followed through hell and back in Africa, his commander, Captain William Mucklow who was also a distant relative.

Mucklow casually smoked and did not show an ounce of fear as he sought to bolster the morale of his men. He was a battle-weary soldier and had served in the army since the late 1930s as had his slightly younger second Cousin Eddie Fennel. Mucklow was a stocky, well-built man in his mid-20s with thinning brown hair and intense blue eyes. Lance Corporal Edward Padraig Fennel was similar in appearance but was slightly shorter and had brown eyes. Like Mucklow, Fennel had been incredibly lucky to make it as far in The Second World War as he had and the young man was beginning to wonder when his luck would run out.

Eddie Fennel had joined the army at the age of 18 in 1938 and was quickly sent to the Middle East where on the 7th of September 1939, his fellow Worcestershire 1st Battalion comrade Private Darby became the first British soldier to die from wounds sustained during The Second World War. As the war began to unfold, Fennel and the battalion soon saw action as part of a triumphant campaign in East Africa where the British army fought in hellish desert conditions to defeat the Italians in Abyssinia. It was around this time in 1941 when the then Second Lieutenant William Mucklow transferred from the 2nd battalion who were stationed in India to the 1st in Africa where, by pure coincidence, he was reconciled with his second cousin Eddie Fennel. The British had enjoyed great success against the Italians but when General Erwin Rommel and the Nazis landed in 1941, in the Germans they found considerably tougher opponents.

On the 22nd of June 1942, Mucklow and Fennel fought bravely alongside their regiment to hold their position at Tobruk, however they were eventually overwhelmed and the British surrendered during the disastrous Battle of Gazala. From the original battalion only 68 officers and men remained and Mucklow and Fennel alongside a handful of others had been incredibly fortunate to escape and find their way back to England. It was here that Mucklow gained promotion to Captain for his heroics in Africa before going on to help form a new 1st Battalion around the existing 11th. On the 1st of January 1943, the 1st Battalion reformed and by September of that same year became part of the 214th Infantry brigade which would go on to feature heavily in the D-Day landings in June 1944.

As the landing craft drew closer to the French beach, machine gun fire ripped through the vessel and tore at the flesh of several of Fennel's comrades. The victims screamed whilst the survivors gritted their teeth and prepared to exit the boat and make their way through the final yards of the English Channel, up the beach and towards the machine gun posts that continued to reign countless bullets in their direction. *He should have surrendered at Tobruk with the rest of the 1st Battalion. He may have had to spend the rest of the war as a prisoner, but at least he would be alive!* Captain Mucklow did not share the same viewpoint. He was a man made for violence, as was his father and as the craft grounded to a holt, he screamed the order for his men to depart and the hell began.

As Fennel dropped to the watery ground and the icy cold waves rose above his knees the man to the immediate left of him instantly had his head blown off by a German shell and the remnants of the man's brains decorated Fennel's face and a small segment of blood and raw tissue made its way into his mouth. He instantly spat the cold meat into the crimson-coloured sea and had no time to ponder the revolting horror of the moment as he had no option but to make his way out of the water as quickly as physically possible. Years later he would spend hours thinking about that moment and wondering why it had been the man to his left who had been hit and not himself. He would never even know the man's name...

Commanding officers and NCOs continued to bark orders, but they needn't have bothered, the objectives were already crystal clear. As Fennel ran, the dead, wounded and dying littered the ground that lay before him and at one point he found himself mouthing a silent apology as he trod and stumbled upon the carcass of a colleague. Many of these men were relatively raw recruits and the utter horror and anguish of war was simply nothing they could have prepared for. Eddie Fennel had been involved in many battles, though it never got any easier to stomach. He would often look upon his commanding officer and relative Bill Mucklow with envious eyes as the slightly older man showed no fear in battle, only a blood thirsty desire to drive forwards and fight.

Those that made it up the beach threw themselves into a sandy embankment and as they awaited their next orders, they had a second to comprehend the realisation of what had happened to their fallen friends.

"We need to take out that machine gun post." Mucklow gestured towards a concrete battery that was filled with Germans who continued to spray bullets across the beach and into the hundreds of other British soldiers who were spilling out of their landing craft and onto the beach. "Fennel, get over here." Mucklow often made a habit of selecting his relative for the more dangerous jobs as it was known that the pair were related and he did not want to be accused of any favouritism. Besides, he also knew that Fennel was an excellent and experienced soldier and that he could rely upon him to get the job done.

"Yes sir." Fennel arrived beside his commanding officer and a sinking sense of dread spread through his bones upon realisation of what he was being asked to do.

"Eddie, I want you to run over to that machine gun post as quickly as you can and drop a grenade through the turret. I'll get the lads over there to pepper it with fire in order to create a diversion." In his civilian guise, Bill Mucklow spoke with a broad Black Country accent, but in his position as a British army officer he would adopt the required 'King's English' in order to make himself clearly understood. It made no difference to Fennel, he was a Black Country lad himself and they had both been born and brought up in Cradley Heath. Fennel said nothing. He pulled out a grenade and Mucklow patted him on the back as he flung himself forwards and ran at full pelt towards the battery, bullets splitting through the air and making contact with the ground that surrounded him. He reached his target without time to feel relief, pulled the pin from the grenade and flung it into the concrete enclosure of the battery. He threw himself to the floor and covered his head as the power of the blast scattered German limbs around the crowded concrete tomb. As survivors exited the battery, grasping their bloody wounds and missing limbs, Mucklow and the rest of the battalion sprayed them with bullets before making their way across the beach behind the batteries, embarking upon a ruthless killing spree as they massacred the fleeing Germans mercilessly... Some of the Nazis raised their hands as if to surrender, but little notice was taken. They were slaughtered just the same as the others and although Captain Mucklow did not agree with it, he understood that his men had just witnessed many of their comrades and friends being blown to pieces and now it was time for pay back...

Eddie Fennel would live to fight another day... He went on to fight in Operation Epsom, an offensive that was intended to outflank the Germans and seize the city of Caen, before moving across the Dutch-German border on the 18th of November 1944 during Operation Clipper. It was here that the 1st Battalion Worcestershire regiment would feature in some of the first fighting of British troops on German soil. They quickly took the village of Tripsrath before fighting on deeper into Germany where they supported the US forces. Then, on the 7th and 8th of

May 1945, total and unconditional surrender by the Germans was signed and for Eddie Fennel the war was over. It had been his whole life and for 6 years he had known nothing other than fighting and killing. *What would he do now?* Unlike many of his comrades, he had no sweetheart or loved one to return home to. He had his parents and siblings who were anxious to see him, but apart from that, the end of the war had made him redundant and signalled the end of his relevance and purpose.

Chapter 2
January 1946

"Oh Edward, do stop dawdling. There is so much work to be done." Mrs Thomas owned the Green grocers shop Eddie Fennel had found work at in Cradley Heath after the war and he had been relatively lucky to have found work so quickly after his demobilization in late 1945. It was now January 1946 and Fennel had made the mistake of looking up at the vast array of snow that was falling from the dull winter skies that engulfed the Black Country. He paused and thought about the last time he had seen snow fall in Europe the previous year in vastly different circumstances. *How lucky he was to be living when so many of his friends were not!* Then, inevitably he would think of the man whose head had been blown off to the left of him as they had exited the landing craft at Normandy. After, his mind would always drift to the many, many Germans he had massacred in so many different obscene ways...

The words of his employer cut through him like a rusty knife and her immensely annoying, high-pitched voice was almost enough to draw him back into killing! In his day-to-day activities listening to her order him around like a naughty schoolboy, he often imagined her as a German soldier back in the war. Then, in his tortured vivid imagination he would hack her to pieces mercilessly with his bayonet. In a million years he would never harm an innocent civilian, let alone a woman, but his ultra-violent fantasies would help him pass the time during his miserable time at work. He was the only employee in the small shop and Mrs Thomas relished the power she held over a member of the opposite sex. Her own husband was not particularly nice to her and she would ease her frustrations by taking them out on the young war veteran who served in the shop. Fennel found the entire situation excruciatingly humiliating and he often considered how he would much prefer to be back in the war risking life and limb as opposed to leading this feeble life. He had hoped to get a job at the Austin works over in Longbridge, or at one of the many local factories, but so far he was still waiting. There was no longer a need for the manufacture of tanks, planes and ships so heavy industry was not as desperately in need of new employees as it once was. Sometimes he considered robbing the store and giving Mrs Thomas a damn good slap during the process! But that was really not his style and would be hardly worth the effort. His father was a drunkard who spent most of his own earnings in the various local pubs, so it was vital that Eddie Fennel maintained a regular job and helped his mother to feed the family. He did have two sisters and both had held down jobs in local factories since leaving school at the age of 14; *but it was the least he could do to help contribute towards the family's upkeep.*

Fennel returned to his duties stacking vegetables as he heard the bell on the front door ring to indicate the arrival of a customer. He did not look up to see the man's face but he did notice a sudden change in his employers demeanour as the customer approached the counter.

"Eh, hello Mr Mucklow. I hope that your father was pleased with his groceries?" Mrs Thomas stuttered with fear and Fennel could not help but feel amused at her plight. He looked up at the mention of the man's name and felt immensely happy to see the imposing figure of his former commanding officer Captain Mucklow. "Your father doesn't usually er, collect from businesses such as mine? I believe that it is mainly public houses who pay for that sort of thing?" Mrs Thomas had a Black Country accent just like everybody else in the local area, but her attempts to try and make herself sound more respectable by adopting a 'posh newsreader' accent were somewhat humorous as she still neglected to add the h's at the beginning of words that required that phoneme.

"Oh my father was very happy with his greens, thank you Mrs Thomas. It's Eddie ar'v come to see actually madam." Mucklow smiled politely and made his way towards his former comrade and distant cousin. Fennel quickly stood to attention and saluted his onetime superior officer.

"Fuckin' hell Eddie, we ay in the army no more aer kid!" Mrs Thomas tutted under her breath at the use of such language in her shop and Mucklow instantly regretted having swore 'with ladies present' and he swiftly apologised. Mrs Thomas nodded awkwardly and adjusted her hair pin.

"Well, please do not take too long about it Edward. We have much work to be done." She looked sternly at her employee and marched purposefully out of the room and into a stock area at the rear of the shop.

"She's a barrel of laughs ay her?" Mucklow smirked and gestured towards the doorway where the 'old battle axe' had just disappeared.

"Fuckin' hell sir, ar swear if her was a bloke I'd have lamped her aaht by now!" Fennel shook his head and Mucklow saw the sheer and utter humiliation in his eyes. Mucklow smiled and reached into the pocket of his long black Crombie coat. He was immensely well dressed in a three-piece suit, Crombie overcoat and the obligatory trilby hat.

"Come on Eddie, call me Bill, we'm family ay we?" Fennel smiled and nodded. He was very pleased to see Mucklow and the sight of him reminded him of both happier and far worse times. "Here, get a drop of this daahn yer, its fuckin' freezin' aaht there!" Mucklow lowered his voice so as not to be heard by Mrs Thomas and handed Fennel a hip flask filled with blended whisky. Fennel grasped it gratefully and took a long gulp, the hot liquid immediately warmed his mouth and burnt the back of his throat.

"Hows yer Mrs Sir? I mean Bill! And yer ode mon and yer mother?"

"They're all bostin' thanks Eddie. Hows your family?"

"The usual. Me ode mon's always in the pub and me mother's frettin over her father in Dublin. He ay very well mate." Fennel hardly knew his relatives in Ireland and found it hard to show concern for a grandfather he had never met. His mother was originally from Dublin and would often curse the English and be very vocal in her support for the IRA! She would often tell her husband that "She should never have left her family to come to this awful god forsaken country!" Eddie Fennel's father was English and Fennel had been born in England. As far as he was concerned he was English and much to the disappointment of his mother he had no interest in his Fenian roots on his maternal side.

"Ar'm sorry to hear that Eddie." Mucklow received the hip flask back from his friend and took a swig himself. "How do you fancy doing a spot of extra work? Will pay a damn site better than this aer kid."

"Who for?" Fennel raised his eyebrows in interest. *Anything had to be better than working in this bloody grocery store with that vile woman!*

"Me and me ode mon." Mucklow fixed Fennel with a hard serious gaze and Fennel knew deep down that he should really thank his former commander there and then and turn down the offer. The Mucklow family were notorious criminals. They were fabulously wealthy from their activities in protection rackets, bookmaking and from their various other schemes. Bill Mucklow's father Willie was the local crime lord and his power and influence was legendary. Fennel had been given the opportunity to join up with the Mucklows when he had first come back from the war, his deceased grandmother on his father's side had been a Mucklow and was the sister of Willie's father who had died in a mining accident over forty years ago. Fennel had been anxious not to get into trouble with the law and had turned the opportunity down, but now things were different. *He had put up with four months of working in this god forsaken shop and there had to be more to life!*

"Sure Bill... What can I do for yer?" As he spoke the words, Eddie Fennel could not believe what he was saying and he knew that it was wrong, but he did not feel regret.

"Good lad." Mucklow was genuinely pleased. He hated to see his much respected relative like this and he longed to help him. He also liked the fact that Fennel was a relative and he knew that this would please his father, as Willie Mucklow liked to keep his business associates close and he knew that a family member would show more loyalty to the cause. Loyalty was everything in the Mucklows line of work. They needed to be able to trust their gang members and be sure that they would not 'grass' on them to the Police or work for rival gangsters. It was vital that all associates and potential members be made aware of the consequences of what would happen to anybody who disappointed their trust. "You do know what it takes to work for us though don't you Edward?" A coldness returned to Mucklow's voice and suddenly he was the 'commanding officer' yet again…

"Yes Bill… Ar'm rather fond of me legs mate." Fennel laughed but he knew that his cousin was not a man to take lightly and his father Willie and his Uncle Eli were even more dangerous! "Ar bay a grass Bill. Yow can trust me, yow know that mate."

"Ar know that me mon." Mucklow's warmth returned and he held out his right hand for Fennel to shake. "Yow still gew in The Waggon and Osses daahn Reddal Hill?"

"Ar." Fennell responded.

"Bostin. Ar'll see yer daahn there later. 7 o clock?"

"Yeah ok Sir, ar mean Bill… Thanks mate." Eddie Fennel waved enthusiastically as Billy Mucklow left the shop. He had made a deal with the devil and he knew it…

The Waggon and horses pub stood just off the main road between Cradley Heath town centre and Old Hill. It never got too busy and Eddie Fennel would often go there as he knew that he could have a quiet pint after work and not be disturbed. He was often quite the loner and that was the way he liked it. He had spent the entire war huddled together with friends and comrades and he could not escape the guilt he carried around with him every day. He had survived whilst many of them had not and for that reason he found it particularly difficult to engage with social interactions. Often, he would long for female companionship, *but he did not deserve it! Why should he be enjoying the fruits of life when others had been denied that opportunity? Maybe it was just that he lived a daily humiliation at the grocery shop as punishment for his fortunate survival?* Just like his father, any finances that were not passed on to his mother, Fennel would spend on alcohol and the numbness and oblivion he would obtain would help him to deal with his guilt and anxieties. However, this would often prove to be one big vicious circle as the alcohol would make him feel on edge and paranoid the following day so he would need to repeat the entire process again for just a couple of hours of relief.

"Hello Eddie." Bill Mucklow entered the main bar of the pub and several of the regulars noted his appearance. He was known and respected throughout the area and the drinkers wondered what such a man would want with one of their own? *Eddie Fennel was just a quiet man who stood alone at the bar and made his way through 5-6 pints a night followed by a Johnnie Walker nightcap.*

"Hello Bill." Fennel had remembered to address his former commanding officer as Bill and had refrained from calling him Sir. "Can ar get yow a drink?"

"No, dow be saft Eddie. Ar'll get um." Mucklow insisted on paying for the drinks and the pair retreated to a small table that stood in front of the window and adjacent to the bar.

"What can I help you with Bill?" Fennel went straight to the point as he sipped his beer and took his cigarettes out of his top pocket.

"Do you know the Neptune pub on Powke lane?"

"Ar... The one next to the cut where the ode boatmen gew?" Fennel placed a cigarette in his mouth and lit it carefully.

"I want yow to gew daahn there and meet a fella called Tummy Ducks... He knows the cut like the back of his hand. We gor a shipment coming in ahht of Brum." Mucklow lit a cigarette and studied Fennel's face for a reaction. "I want yow to help Tum load the boxes onto a lorry and then drive um daahn to Bristol where they will be loaded onto a ship." Mucklow took a drag of his cigarette and then exhaled. "Yow can drive a Wagon cor yer Eddie?"

"Yes Bill... But why dow I just drive the Wagon out of Brum? Nobody uses the cut anymore?" Fennel was a little confused. The canals had been in decline for years and were an outdated form of transport. Mucklow lent in closer and lowered his voice to a whisper.

"That's the point Eddie. It's very discrete, the law never monitors the barges on the cut." Mucklow smiled. "Do you know why?" Fennel shook his head. "Because we pay em not too!" Mucklow let out a little laugh and waited for Fennel's reaction.

"Why?" Fennel spoke loudly and then suddenly realised his mistake before dropping back to a whisper. "Why, what's in the boxes?"

"Dow ask questions aer kid, that's one of the conditions of working for me. Load the goods, drive em to Bristol, then yow and Tum come and meet me in the Haden Cross Sunday dinnertime." Mucklow winked and continued to speak in hushed tones. Fennel knew exactly why he had been chosen for this job. *Whatever was in those boxes was obviously highly illegal and Mucklow clearly wanted somebody else to the run the risk of getting caught as he would only be able to guarantee Police protection until the local Police's border.* Fennel could not help but feel a little disappointed, but then what had changed? *Mucklow had always chosen him for the risky missions during the war because he trusted him to get the job done.* Billy Mucklow could see that Fennel was deep in thought. "Eddie, how much do yow meck a week in that grocery shap?" Fennel smiled and raised his eyebrows with embarrassment.

"About 2 pound and 6 shillings." Mucklow smiled and pulled out his wallet.

"There's five quid there." Mucklow placed a crisp five-pound note onto the table. "When yow come back to The Cross on Sunday ar'll have another five quid waiting for yer."

"Fuckin' hell Bill!" fennel had been blinded by the money and as sure as anything, his life in gangland crime had begun right there.

Chapter 3

On Sunday the 27th of January 1946, the first political elections took place in Germany in almost 15 years. It was the beginning of a new era for the war-torn country which had been divided up after the Second World War, but closer to home Eddie Fennel was feeling nervous as he stood at the bar in the Haden Cross and drank beer with his newfound associate Tummy 'Ducks' Hingley.

As he stood and sipped his beer, Fennel could not decide what was more nerve wracking, the haulage of the illegal goods down to Bristol he had just pulled off with Tummy, or the fact that he was about to sit down for a drink with Bill Mucklow, his father Willie and Willie's adopted brother Eli Davis. They were the top villains around and were notoriously dangerous. Fennel had even considered remaining content with the £5 he had already been paid and sending his excuses, but a curiosity and desire to escape the awful grocery shop led him to the rendezvous.

The job itself had been routine and straightforward. Fennel had met Tummy 'Ducks' at 6 AM at the side of the cut next to the Neptune public house on Powke lane and the pair had waited for the barge to emerge out of the dark morning mist, laden with their cargo. As instructed, Fennel asked no questions and he left all the talking to Tummy 'Ducks' who conversed with the sailors at the drop off in Bristol. It occurred to Eddie Fennel that Tum was a gifted communicator and could probably talk his way out of any situation. All Fennel had to do was help load the goods and drive the lorry.

"Yow did well aer kid. Yow day ask no questions and got on with the job." Tummy 'Ducks' was in his mid twenties and had a round face with thick dark hair. He wore a suit that was slightly too small for his rounded beer gut and a black trilby hung from the back of his head exposing a high sweaty brow. The drop off had taken place the previous day and the pair had been late getting back, hence why Bill Mucklow had arranged the meeting for the Sunday. Fennel had made an effort. He wore his army demob suit complete with trilby and a matching overcoat. It was nice to be wearing something other than the tatty rags he wore to the shop and for the first time since he had worn his army uniform, he actually felt respectable and a little bit of inner pride was beginning to return to him. Every so often he would catch a glimpse of himself in the grand mirror that stood behind the bar and would feel slightly impressed. *He had spent too long downtrodden and lamenting the fate of his war colleagues. He owed it to himself and he owed it to them to finally try and make something of his life. They had died so that he could live and the very least he could do was to wake the fuck up and try and make something of his life!*

"Yow will be alright working with us kid. Just do as yum told and keep your mouth shut." Tummy 'Ducks' lit a cigarette and a serious look came over his face. "Willie Mucklow woe tolerate grasses, so unless you wanna end up face daahn in the cut, dow talk to nobody abaaht our business." Fennel nodded, managing to hide any nervousness from his expression.

"Dow worry Tum. Ar'm family, they can trust me. Besides, ar followed enough orders in the army!" Fennel hated authority, but he had a respect for Billy Mucklow that he had not held for other officers. Mucklow was 'down to earth' and had the same tough Black Country roots as himself.

"What yow mean family?" Tummy 'Ducks' was slightly surprised at Fennel's revelation and he felt intrigued.

"Mar grandmother was a Mucklow. Her brother was Willie Mucklow's father." Fennel took a drink of his beer and thought nothing more of it but Tummy 'Ducks' felt envious. He was loyal and desperate to make his way up the hierarchy of the gang, but he knew that the boss, Willie Mucklow would favour 'blood and kin' every time. With Willie's nephew Harry Scriven still away on national service, Tummy 'Ducks' had hoped to make the most of his absence, but now here was another relative to get in his way! 'Ducks' didn't let his disappointment show and he generously ordered another round of drinks for the pair.

"Cheers Tum." Fennel thanked his associate for the drink but it fell on deaf ears as the pub door suddenly flung open and in walked Eli Davis followed by the mighty Willie Mucklow. Both men were of about 50 years of age and had a ferociously intimidating look about them. Davis was about six foot five inches tall with slightly greyish brown hair, a full face and the widest shoulders Fennel had ever seen. Willie Mucklow was shorter. About five foot eleven with a rounded slightly flabby face that had the appearance of a British bulldog. He was a thickset man who was almost gorilla like in appearance and looked remarkably similar to his only son Bill, who was currently nowhere to be seen. Fennel had hoped for the reassuring presence of Bill but as it stood, he was set to meet his new bosses alone.

"How's yer ode mon aer kid?" Willie Mucklow spotted Fennel straight away and recognised his own cousin's son. Bill had already informed him that Eddie Fennel would be doing some work for them and the senior Mucklow was enthusiastic at the prospect of recruiting more family, flesh and blood into his organisation.

"He's ok thanks Mr Mucklow. He drinks too much ale but dow we all?" Fennel felt sheepish and nervous, but he came across as confident and casual.

"Mr Mucklow? Fuck that aer kid. Yow'm family. Yow call me Uncle Willie." Mucklow patted Fennel on the back and Tummy 'Ducks' heart sank. *He had been right.*

Eli Davis collected a tray of beers and pork scratchings from the bar and the four men walked through to a small side room that stood in a secluded area at the far side of the pub. It was Willie Mucklow's private space and was reserved for him and his associates. He took his place at the head of the table with Eli Davis sat alongside him and the other two men opposite.

"Where's the fuckin' Captain?" Davis lit a cigarette and looked to the window at the front of the room that revealed the main road that ran between Halesowen and Old Hill. 'The Captain' was the affectionate nickname Willie Mucklow and Davis had bestowed upon Mucklow's war hero son Bill, who had attained the rank of Captain during the war. Both Willie Mucklow and Eli Davis were also bona fide war heroes who had served with distinction during the 1914-1918 First World War. Willie Mucklow had lost both of his brothers during that conflict, including his twin Stan and consequently the bond between Mucklow and Davis had grown. Eli Davis had been beaten and badly treated as a child by his own father and at the age of 9 he had been unofficially adopted by the Mucklow family who took him in and cared for him. Davis' father had been brutally murdered upon leaving the pub one night in the early twentieth century and the details surrounding this had been a closely guarded secret.

At that moment, the door opened and in walked Billy Mucklow. "Talk of the devil!" Davis tutted in good humour and took a gulp of his beer. Bill instantly recognised Fennel and smiled warmly.

"How bin yer Eddie? Come next door with me for a bit aer kid. Ar gorra settle up with yer." Bill Mucklow gestured towards the door and Fennel stood up. "We'll come back in a bit mate. Ar got yer money and ar want to have a little chat." Bill Mucklow certainly did have Eddie Fennel's money but it was a more generous pay out compared to what they were going to pay Tummy 'Ducks' on account of Fennel being family. He also had other things he wished to talk to Fennel about away from the prying ears of Tummy 'Ducks.'

Fennel followed Mucklow into the crowded main bar on the other side of the pub.

"Nothing like a big crowd for a little privacy Eddie." Mucklow lent against the wooden bar and gestured to the full room. Everyone was busy minding their own business, talking amongst themselves and terrified to even get caught looking at Billy Mucklow. It wasn't that he was cruel and vicious towards ordinary folk, but it paid to stay well out of the Mucklow's business and to not cross them. "Yow did a good job with that delivery aer kid. Kept yer mouth shut and did as yow was asked. Ar like that and so does my ode mon." Mucklow lit a cigarette and offered one to Fennel which he accepted eagerly. "Two large Bushmills please." Mucklow spoke politely to the barman and he promptly stopped serving other customers and quickly poured two huge measures of Irish whiskey for the two men. "Eddie, it was an honour to serve alongside you in Africa and Europe. Ar'm so proud that yow have decided to join us back home now too." Mucklow patted Fennel on the back and Fennel began to wonder what he had gotten himself into. As far as he was concerned, he had done one driving job, *was he now a full-blown member of the gang?* "We saw and did a lot of bad things in the war Eddie." Mucklow picked up his whiskey and urged Fennel to do the same. "But its time we left the past in the past." Mucklow had an inkling that Fennel had been struggling to get over his wartime experiences and he was right. "So lets drink to the boys that day come back, then we look to the future." Mucklow raised his glass in respect to their fallen comrades. "To the regiment and those not present." Fennel copied the gesture and both men swiftly swallowed down the contents of their glasses and banged them down hard on the bar. "Now, lets meck some fuckin' money!" Mucklow laughed and blew smoke into the air. "Ar know I can rely on yow Eddie. It ay that Tummy's a bad kid. He's loyal and he does a good job, but he's all mouth. He knows the cut and he helps us shift stuff but he has his limitations." Fennel listened eagerly and nodded. "You see, the Police know we shift stuff on the canals. We pay them to look the other way and the cut is the perfect way of moving things subtly. That way we dow have to worry about the special breed." Fennel looked confused.

"What's the special breed?"

"Them coppers that cor be bought. They bay interested in money. They'm dedicated to their jobs and upholding the law. Fuckin' losers." Mucklow shook his head in distaste. "The top coppers know we use the cut so they leave us alone, but some of these dedicated bastards cause me problems." Fennel nodded, he understood fully. "This is where ar need help from an Army tough guy like yow." A sly look came over Mucklow's face and he lowered his voice. "Yer see ar got a problem with one of these special breeds… There's a cozzer, well not even a real cozzer, a Special Constable. Do you know what one of them is Eddie?"

Fennel shook his head. He had spent his entire adult life in the army fighting a war and he knew little about civilian Police ranks. "It's a fella who wants to be a copper but he ay up to it so he does it for free, for the fun of it! The only folks who hate um more than us are the actual real coppers! They work for free which means the decent coppers dow get their overtime."

"By decent coppers yow mean the ones who teck back handers from yow?" Fennel smiled but instantly regretted his comment, luckily Mucklow smiled and saw the funny side.

"Anyway, this Special, fella's called Dougie Roberts. He is poking his nose raahnd our boats. He reckons we are moving illegal goods through the cut... The proper coppers have told him to leave our boats alone, but he is like a fuckin' dog with a bone. He woe let gew." Mucklow exhaled more cigarette smoke and shot Fennel a sideways glance. "The cozzers want me to do something about him. Normally we wouldn't touch coppers, its against the rules, but this fella ay a proper cozzer so its ok." Mucklow lent in closer and dropped his voice to a whisper. "This is where yow come in Eddie. Ar need yer to break his fuckin' legs so he cor walk up the cut no more." Fennel raised his eyebrows and looked at his cigarette.

"Ar dow know Bill... Ar thought I was just a driver?"

"We both know yow'm more than that Eddie. Yow fought like a devil in France, a talent for violence is what ar need... I could do it myself, but I want yow on board Eddie. Yow'm family." Fennel looked at the floor and could not decide what to do. His mind went blank and he doubted that he was even capable of saying no to his former commanding officer. "Tummy 'Ducks' will drive you. Roberts drinks in the Old Bush at the top of Powke Lane. Gew in there and do it in front of a packed pub, it will teach people to keep their fuckin' noses aaht of things that dow concern them. Do this for me and yow will be on the payroll. No more taking shit in that fuckin' grocery shap!" Fennel thought about it for all of twenty seconds and then smiled and nodded.

He couldn't face going back to the shop and being humiliated again. He had committed violence for a living before, what was different now?

Chapter 4

The dark red tiled floor had more than likely stood since Victorian times and the deep mahogany bar smelt of kerosene, stale beer and tobacco smoke. As Eddie Fennel stood at the bar in the Neptune public house on Powke Lane he sipped a half pint of ale and steadied his nerves with a single measure of cheap blended Scotch. He wore his demob suit and overcoat and his trilby was pulled down over his brow. The barmaid was in her middle thirties, was generously plump and had a moderately feminine face. She studied Fennel carefully and wondered at his marital availability, but the thoughts were certainly not reciprocated and Fennel wished that she would move away and leave him to his thoughts. He was awaiting the arrival of Tummy 'Ducks' who was to drive him the short distance up the hill to the Old Bush pub, where he would perform his dreadful deed upon the orders of Billy Mucklow. He had certainly carried out more extreme acts of violence for Mucklow in the past, but that was during wartime and against their Germanic foe. He literally had no idea how many men he had killed, *surely a simple beating of some Copper wouldn't make much difference?* He pondered the act as he swallowed down the remnants of his whiskey. *There was no chance of reprisals from the law as it was their wish, alongside that of Billy Mucklow, that the Special Constable be punished. Just like during the war when he (Fennel) was just a soldier, acting on the orders of his superiors. It was not his job to question or pass judgement on their wishes, he was merely there to carry them out. For that reason, he would feel no guilt.*

"Yow ready aer kid?" Tummy 'Ducks' arrived alongside Fennel at the bar and beads of perspiration trickled down his grimy, overweight face. He had obviously been struggling to be on time and the prospect of disappointing Billy Mucklow through his carelessness was not a scenario he wished to contemplate. Fennel downed the dregs of his beer and smiled at the unattractive barmaid, instantly regretting his emittance of false interest.

"Ar Tum. Yow got the motor?"

"Yes mate, it's aahtside." Fennel followed Tummy 'Ducks' out of the pub to a blue 1937 Austin 10/4. Tummy 'Ducks' did not own the car, in 1946, owning a car was a rare luxury that was often only available to the wealthy. Instead, the Austin was part of a small fleet of vehicles that were owned by the Mucklow family for use by their associates for professional, business reasons. Fennel opened the rear door and climbed onto the back seat. He did not want to be seen arriving at the pub and he assumed that he could attain more discretion on the back seat by pushing his head back than by sitting in the front. Tummy 'Ducks' wrongfully mistook this for a pompous act and he assumed that Fennel was trying to assert his family privilege by being chauffeured in the rear seat. *Fennel had been chosen for this job so he was clearly a tough man of violence.* Tummy 'Ducks' doubted his own ability to carry out today's violent job and he chose not to confront Eddie Fennel over his decision to sit in the back.

The car passed over the canal bridge and began the steep incline up Powke Lane towards the Old Bush that stood at the top of the hill.

"We got any tools?" Fennel looked around the car and could not see any potential weapons. *Was he expected to break the guys legs with his bare hands and feet?*

"In the boot." Tummy 'Ducks' muttered his response, still smarting from Fennel's apparent 'overstepping' of him in the gang's hierarchy.

The Austin 10/4 pulled up in a small car park that lay at the side of the pub. The two men got out and Tummy 'Ducks' opened the boot where Fennel cast his eyes over an array tools. There were two crowbars, a cricket bat, a selection of pliers and a rather gruesome looking meat cleaver. Fennel picked up the smaller of the two crowbars and tried to conceal it under his overcoat.

"Yow ul have to point him ahht to me Tum, cus ar bay got a fuckin' clue who this fella is!" Tummy 'Ducks' nodded and led the way into the pub.

The Old Bush was a small pub that was divided into two tiny bars at the front of the building. The pub had originally been owned by a local undertaker and it had a particularly cosy atmosphere on account of its size.

Tummy 'Ducks' and Eddie Fennel went into the main bar area where they were greeted by a roaring open fire and about a dozen regular drinkers who filled the semi crowded space. Dougie Roberts was sat at the bar with his back to the door. He cut a solitary figure as few locals would converse with him on account of his Special Constable status. Tummy 'Ducks' nodded towards the Special and cast a threatening glare around the rest of the room. 'Ducks' was a known member of the Mucklow crew and the locals knew better than to stare and each and every one of them instantly made a conscious effort to 'mind their own business'.

"Dougie Roberts?" Fennel called the name loudly and Roberts instantly turned around, confirming his identity. "Message from Billy Mucklow aer kid!" Fennel pulled Roberts backwards off his bar stool with his left hand and then used his right to crack him in the ribs with the crowbar. Roberts clutched his chest in agony and Tummy 'Ducks' kept a vigil to ensure no bystanders attempted to intervene. He needn't have worried. "Yow were warned Dougie. Yow need to leave Willie Mucklow's canal barges alone!" Fennel raised the crowbar high above his head and continued to rain down blow after vicious blow onto Roberts' right leg. The Special Constable emitted blood curdling noises as his bones splintered and cracked. The shocked clientele in the bar looked on with horror and at one point the concerned landlord spoke to Tummy 'Ducks'.

"Dow you think he's had enough Tum?"

"Yow stay ahht on it, we'll decide when he's had enough." Tummy 'Ducks' responded but was relieved himself when Fennel raised his crowbar for the final time, content that he had caused sufficient damage. As he studied the agonised man who lay upon the floor, again Eddie Fennel felt no guilt. Like during the war, this was the wish of his superiors and he would accept no responsibility. Orders were orders and whether it had been him carrying out this awful crime or somebody else, the outcome would have been the same. *Why shouldn't he collect payment for it?*

When Eddie Fennel returned to his family home in Bannister Street, Cradley Heath, he noted that the house appeared eerily deserted. His father was probably out drinking at one of the many local pubs and his older sisters had long since married and moved out. His mother would usually be found in the back room tending to an Edwardian cooking range that served as both the family's cooking device and source of heating. Unusually for a winter's day, the range was not even lit and an icy cold filled the high ceilinged, Victorian worker's house. The rooms had barely changed since Fennel's childhood in the 1920s and it had been just about enough for the family who were poor on account of Fennel's father's drinking habits. Many other families had made extra coins through small chain shops at the rear of their properties where females slaved away to make small intricate chain for pitiful wages. Fennel's mother had not once entertained the idea of such work. She was not local and had come from a family background where the men worked whilst the women tended to the house. Though her upbringing had been impoverished and she had almost succumbed to working in the famous 'Monto' area in her native Ireland. Monto was an area of Dublin on Montgomery street that became famous as the British Empire's largest red-light district. Eddie Fennel's mother, Mary O'Connor, as she was then known, escaped this potential life of prostitution when she followed her brother Sean to England in 1916. Sean had been a rebel fighter and had fought against the British rule during the Easter uprisings of 1916.

The Easter Rebellion was an armed conflict which was launched by Irish republicans against the British rule in Ireland. The Republicans had hoped to capitalise on the fact that Britain was engaged in war with

Germany at that time and their aim was to establish an independent Irish republic. It was the most significant uprising in Ireland since 1798 and the unsuccessful outcome and the British brutality with which they dealt with the perpetrators would go on to bolster support in Ireland for independence. The revolt only happened for 6 days, but in this time some 485 people were killed.

Following the unconditional surrender of the rebel forces and execution of their leaders, Sean O'Connor had been sent to an internment camp in England under Regulation 14B of the Defence of the Realm Act 1914. Upon his release at the end of the First World War, Sean O'Connor had returned to Ireland but his sister Mary had since fallen in love with a young English chain maker and World War 1 veteran who would subsequently become Fennel's father.

"Mother?" Fennell called out into the cold house and continued to ponder the whereabouts of his parent. The house consisted of just two downstairs rooms and two upstairs and Fennel had spent most of his childhood sleeping downstairs on account of his two sisters who had shared the room upstairs. Since they had grown up and found husbands, Fennel had moved into the upstairs room, though this had only been in the last six months since he had returned from war. Fennel listened hard for his mother's reply but heard nothing.

"Mother?" He called again a little louder and began to feel a little concerned. The front door had been left unlocked and there was no reason as to why his mother should not be home. He moved slowly through the house and opened a door that revealed a steep, narrow staircase that rose to the upper regions of the property. As he climbed the creaky staircase, he thought that he heard a whimpering sound coming from his mother and father's bedroom and when he reached the small landing that stood at the top of the stairs he distinctly heard his mother sobbing. It would not have been proper for him to barge into his parents' room uninvited, so he paused on the landing and knocked on the door.

"Who is it?" Her coarse Dublin accent sounded through the door and it quivered with emotion.

"It's me Eddie. What's gewin on? Why am yow upset?" Fennel heard footsteps within the room and then the door opened to reveal his mother who looked devastated.

"It's your grandfather Edward. He passed away. I got a letter from Ireland this morning." Fennel looked at the floor and tried to show some emotion. He had never met the man and he found it difficult to grieve for a relative he did not know. "I should have been there with him so I should... Not stuck here in this god forsaken heathen hell hole!"

"I'm sorry to hear that mother." Fennel continued to try and feign sympathy.

"Your father won't even come with me to Dublin for the funeral... I will have to go alone." Fennel sensed that his mother was insinuating that he should accompany her in his father's place, but he did not have time for that! *He was only just finding his way in a new career working for the Mucklows and the last thing he needed was time away in an Irish city!* "Or maybe?" Fennel's mother immediately stopped talking and looked away.

"Maybe what?" Fennel asked the question, already aware of what she was about to ask.

"Oh nothing Edward... It doesn't matter."

"What is it mother?"

"Well, I was just wondering. Maybe you could come with me to Ireland? Meet some of your family?" Fennel groaned inwardly but did not have the heart to disappoint her.

"Ok aer mom. Yow can show me yower ode home in Dublin." Fennel's mother smiled through her salty tears and embraced her only son. He would have to make his excuses to Billy Mucklow and explain that he would not be around for a while. *He would also have to use whatever earnings he had to pay for their trip...*

Chapter 5

The funeral passed by with little drama. Despite his mother's efforts, Eddie Fennel had not been brought up as a catholic and the Latin passages during the service made little sense to him. As others grieved he tried to look respectful and thought about what he was missing out on back home with the Mucklows.

After the service, the mourners returned to a small, terraced house in Sheriff Street near the city centre of Dublin, an area known for its high levels of deprivation and crime. Once inside the house, Fennel was surprised by what happened next. There was suddenly an abundance of Irish whiskey to be had and the sombre mood lifted to be replaced by a party atmosphere, a celebration of life. Eddie Fennel was anxious not to speak and give away his English identity, the war of independence had been less than 30 years previously and a lot of bitter ill feeling still remained.

"Edward, come and meet your uncle Sean, the reason I went over to England in the first place. If it hadn't been for him then you wouldn't be here!" Fennel's mother pulled him over to a thickset middle-aged man with black hair and wild brown eyes. Fennel had heard many tales of his uncle's involvement with the IRA and he naturally felt a little wary of how the man would take to a former English soldier!

"It's grand to finally meet yer young man. Here, have some more whisky." The big Irishman filled Fennel's glass generously and Fennel felt surprised at his welcoming attitude. "I hear you were in the army?"

"Eh yes, 1st battalion Worcestershire regiment. I served in Africa and Europe." Sean O'Connor looked impressed.

"I had my run ins with the British army. In 1916 and then again in the early 20s. Now if you were to tell me you were in the Back un Tans, then that would but different. But as you are, yer at least half a good man!" O'Connor laughed and clinked his whiskey glass against Fennels, it was his father's wake and he wanted to drink and celebrate, not fight.

The Black un Tans were a form of Police officer who were recruited into the Royal Irish Constabulary during the Irish war of Independence. Most of them were British soldiers who had fought during World War 1. They were known for their acts of brutality against the Irish people and in September 1920 they famously burned down the town of Balbiggan just north of Dublin. "You should meet my lad Johnny. He's a little bit younger than yourself. He's an IRA man too but don't hold that against him, we're all family here!"

Johnny O'Connor was a skinny man of barely twenty years of age. Like his father, his hair was jet black and he had the same wild staring eyes. He muttered something incomprehensible to Fennel before putting out his right hand for the Englishman to shake. Johnny O'Connor exuded arrogance and he spoke so quickly that Eddie Fennel misunderstood much of what was said. He said something about hating the English and wanting a united Ireland but then he also said something about respecting family loyalties. Fennel wasn't sure whether the young man liked him or not and he didn't really care but when he finally said something about getting a beer at a local bar, Fennel's ears pricked up. He would be in Dublin for a couple of days and the idea of sitting in this dreary little house in the midst of a stinking inner-city slum for the entire time did not appeal to him.

Johnny O'Connor led Eddie Fennel to a rough looking bar called O'Neill's on Pearse Street. By now, Fennel was half drunk from the copious amounts of whiskey he had drank at the wake and he was not concerned about his own safety. An Englishman alone in this part of Dublin was not safe, but with his new friend Johnny O'Connor at his side, Fennel did not feel threatened. Besides, he was a war veteran, a seasoned tough guy who was capable of extreme violence. He was not afraid of anyone.

"Two beers." O'Connor lent against a groggy old wooden bar and the barman poured two pints of Guinness. It was not what Fennel was used to drinking, but he was not about to complain.

"So... We're cousins?" O'Connor had been silent for a good few minutes and then he suddenly blurted out the obvious.

"Yes. Your father is mar mother's brother." Fennel lit a cigarette and cast his eyes around the run-down bar. Working men stood in their overcoats and flat caps and dogs roamed freely throughout. A huge man with greying red hair, intense blue eyes and just about the hugest fists Fennel had ever seen approached the pair and took a seat at their table.

"Who's your friend Johnny? What have I told yer about bringing strangers in here!" The man was in his early 50s and he completely ignored Fennel.

"This is Eddie Fennel, he's over from England for me Daideo's funeral." At the mention of the word England the big man's eyes turned to fire and he ferociously pulled O'Connor into a quiet corner where he proceeded to point his finger and make threatening gestures, but Fennel could not hear what was said. A few minutes later. O'Connor returned looking just as confident and arrogant as before. "Don't worry. I told him you were Irish but been living in England for a while. Just don't speak too loudly!" O'Connor flashed a wicked smile and downed his Guinness.

"Ar dow give a fuck mate." Fennel spoke with alcohol laden bravado and O'Connor shrugged. "Two more beers please mucka." He ordered the next round and he spoke loudly and with pride in his broad Black Country tongue. Suddenly, the immediate area around them went totally silent and Fennel felt eyes upon him throughout the bar.

"Come out ye Black an Tan come out and fight me like a man, show your wife how you won medals down in Flanders, tell her how the IRA made you run like hell away from the green and lovely lanes in Killashandra!" A group of men erupted into song and several of them spat onto the floor in disgust.

"I think we better leave." O'Connor's arrogant confidence was all but gone and he became embarrassed and ashamed of his newfound relative. "I knew we should have gone out in O'Connell Street, it would have cost more a pint but there would have been no trouble!" As the two men made their way to leave, the big man from earlier suddenly appeared in front of them with two younger men at his side.

"You can leave Johnny, you're a loyal brother, but this English pig will have to pay for the crimes of his countrymen." Fennel looked at the big man, grunted and smiled.

"Go fuck yer sister Paddy, yer fat fuckin' bastard!" Fennel gritted his teeth and punched the older man as hard as he could and the entire bar held its breath as the big man fell backwards into his two younger accomplices, his nose bloody from the punch. The two younger men instantly lunged forwards to attack Fennel who had hoped that his cousin would come to his aid, but this did not happen. Fennel put up a brave fight, but against the three men he stood very little chance. They beat him down, spat on him and then continued to beat and kick him until he lay semi-conscious and bleeding on the floor of the bar. Not a single person in the premises was willing to help him. The big man he had struck was Eammon Connelly, a feared and prominent IRA boss and nobody would dare cross him. Eventually, Connelly pulled his two men off Fennel and the big man drew a sharpened blade from his pocket. He walked towards Fennel and knelt behind the Englishman before raising his head by the hair and lowering his blade to Fennel's throat.

"I want it noted that I Eammon Connelly, avenged our leaders of 16 and those massacred on Bloody Sunday here in this bar! If any bastard reports me to the authorities, then it will be their family I come for next!" Connelly was raging and spittle flew from his mouth as he spoke excitedly about the pending execution.

"Eammon, leave him be. He's my cousin. He's from good Irish stock. He's a good friend of my father Sean O'Connor!" Johnny O'Connor eventually began to protest and Connelly paused,

"Is this true?" Connelly spat the question into Fennel's face who's eyes were rolling as he lay barely conscious. Sean O'Connor was a respected member of the IRA and a good friend and associate of Eammon Connelly. Fennel managed to nod his reply and Connelly reluctantly lowered his blade and stood up.

"Come on boys. Let's go and get pissed!" Connelly gestured to his two associates and the three men hastily left the pub leaving Fennel bruised, battered and bleeding on the floor. He tried to move but this caused him to do what he had been fighting so hard against not to do, he passed out.

About two hours later, Fennel came around in one of the rooms above the bar. He was instantly greeted by the smooth sounds of Bebop Jazz and as he became more aware of his surroundings he identified the artist as Charlie Parker. He had been stripped to the waist and his wounds had been bathed and treated in some kind of ointment that was on a small table next to the bed. He tried to move to reach his cigarettes but the pain struck him again so he lay his head back against the soft pillow and looked out at the dark Dublin sky that he could see from out of the window. He assumed that he must have still been in the same bar in which he had been beaten as he could still hear customers downstairs. They laughed, spoke, drank and got on with things as if nothing had happened. *But who had cared for him?*

She returned to the room and was just about the most beautiful woman Eddie Fennel had ever seen. She had light brown shoulder length hair, stunningly attractive brown eyes and a perfect figure that was neither too skinny nor too fat. She wore a skin-tight pencil skirt that accentuated her hips and for a few seconds Fennel forgot that he had taken a massive beating.

"Don't try to move, its gunna hurt." Her soft Dublin accent was as mesmerising as her looks but she had a sultry manner that added to her sheer magnetism.

"Have I died and gone to heaven?" Fennel winked at her but he felt awkward at the corniness of his line, she raised her eyes heavenwards and smiled.

"No. You were beaten up in the bar. I couldn't just leave you there like that. Johnny O'Connor saved your life. He said that you were his cousin?"

"Yes, that's right. His father is my mother's brother."

"I know what a cousin is." She was abrupt, yet she was smiling at the same time and Fennel found her totally irresistible.

"Well, it sure was worth taking a beating to see yow! Mar name's Eddie." She smiled again and took out a cigarette and lit it.

"I'm Teresa." She blew smoke into the air seductively and Fennel became even more desperate for a cigarette.

"Teresa, would you mind passing me mar fakes? Them in mar jacket."

"What the hells a fake?"

"Sorry, mar cigarettes." She picked up his suit jacket and rummaged through the inner pocket until she found a silver-plated cigarette case. She took it out and placed it on his bare chest. He took one out and she lit it for him.

"Maybe I could take you out to thank you for helping me?" Fennel had not always found it easy to ask women out, but he grasped the opportunity whilst he could. She put her cigarette to her lips, raised her eyebrows again and then shrugged.

"Why not? You can buy me a few gins I suppose." Fennel grinned. Maybe he would be staying in Dublin for slightly longer than he had anticipated?

Chapter 6

By the end of February, Eddie Fennel found that he was still in Dublin. His mother had made the trip home alone and Fennel was now spending most of his time making up schemes with his unsavoury cousin Johnny O'Connor and around the ever-beautiful Teresa with whom he had now fallen madly in love.

His money had long run out and he found that he was relying on Teresa, who's family were wealthy, and whatever he could make hustling on the street. Johnny O'Connor had a particular talent for snooker and a favourite scam was for Fennel to identify a weak or intermediate player in a bar and then make a comment along the lines of "I bet you couldn't beat my mate?" Nine times out of ten, the player would take the challenge of a 'cocky Englishman' and O'Connor would deliberately loose the first game. At this point, Fennel would offer a wager. Of course, the player would now fancy his chances of winning some money, only this time O'Connor would play seriously and win the bet. If there was ever any protest, Fennel would apply a bit of 'muscle' and the money would then be paid. It wouldn't last for ever, but for the time being it kept Fennel in beer and cigarettes and allowed him to spend a little more time with Teresa.

"So, you're still fooling around with that eejit cousin of yours are you?" Teresa sat at a circular table for two in a large exclusive bar on O'Connell Street. Eddie Fennel sat opposite and admired her pretty face as she sipped cocktails and smoked expensive cigarettes.

"It's temporary. When I get back to England I will go back into business with my other cousin. He is a very wealthy man." Fennel tried to make his involvement with the Mucklows sound grander than it was. In truth, he had been in Ireland for so long now that he did not even know if he had a position with the Mucklows to go back to.

"Now why would you wanna go back to England when you could stay here with me?" She grabbed him by his tie, pulled his face into hers and kissed him fully and passionately on the lips.

"Because I can't keep fooling around making up schemes with Johnny that's why!"

"You could always get a job working for my father? He is a wealthy man." Teresa took a sip of her drink and looked at Fennel intently. *Was he serious about their relationship or was he just 'fooling around' with her too?*

"Who is your father?" Fennel did not really like the idea of spending the rest of his life in Ireland, but he was desperate to remain with Teresa.

"Eammon Connelly. You met him that night at O'Neill's bar on Pearse Street." Teresa immediately looked away, knowing exactly how Fennel would react.

"Are you fuckin' joking? All this time we have been seeing each other and you didn't even think to tell me that he is yower dad?" Fennel almost spat his beer across the table.

"I'm sorry. I didn't tell you because I thought it might put you off me." Her sexy eyes pleaded with him and he could not feel anger at her. "That was why I had to help you that night at the bar. Because he is my father I felt kind of responsible."

"And you really think that he would give me a job? The guy wants me dead!" Fennel shook his head and looked at the floor. *This place was not safe for him and now he had fallen in love with the daughter of an IRA kingpin!*

"Maybe if I talk to him, he will see sense?" On second thoughts, Teresa knew that her plan would be unlikely to succeed. Her father would not approve of her relationship with Fennel and she knew it. Fennel shook his head.

"Sorry bab, but I ay workin' for no IRA bloke." She crossed her legs seductively and the slit in her skirt revealed her stocking tops.

"Well, I guess we will just have to think of something else then won't we."

"Maybe you could come to England? With me?" Fennel felt a quiver of excitement, *he had found a way for them to be together!* He wondered what she would make of his small, terraced house in Cradley Heath and what would happen once she found out that he was just a small-time enforcer for a local gangster?

"Me? Go to England? But what about my family? My friends? Eddie that really is out of the question." She laughed off his suggestion inconsiderately and Fennel could not help but feel a little hurt. *Did he really mean so little to her that she would not even consider going away with him? He had thought that they were in love, was he just a fool?* She could tell that she had caused offense and she felt bad, but her stubborn, Irish temperament would not allow her to acknowledge it.

The rest of the evening passed by awkwardly. The couple had still strolled back through the streets hand in hand and she had hugged him tightly and kissed him goodnight when he dropped her at the corner of her street, but something did not feel quite right. Fennel desperately loved her and he wanted to find a way of making their future together work, but now he was having doubts as to whether or not she wanted the same thing. He gave her a final wave goodbye and then trudged slowly back towards his grandparent's home in Sheriff Street, pondering his options and his disappointment.

It turned out that Fennel's maternal grandmother was a lovely welcoming old woman and she had made him feel very welcome in her home throughout his duration in Ireland. In reality, she appreciated the company after the death of her husband, and it was a great opportunity for her to become acquainted with her grandson from across the water in England. As Fennell opened the front door he noticed that the house was in darkness and his grandmother, who had become accustomed to waiting up for him was nowhere to be seen. He entered the house cautiously and as he turned to lock the front door behind him he suddenly felt the cold metal of a gun pressed into the back of his head. Suddenly the lights flickered on and Fennel could make out the reflection of two men in the window who were stood behind him. One of them was his uncle Sean, the other man who was holding the gun to his head, he could not see as his own head was obscuring the view.

"Turn around slowly pig! One false move an I'll blow you feckin' head off!" Fennel recognised the voice immediately and he slowly turned around to face the big man. "Do you remember me pig?" Connelly's breath stank of whiskey and tooth decay and Fennel wondered how something so ugly could produce such a beautiful daughter. He nodded and stared hard into Connelly's eyes. "Well, you can thank your cousin Johnny for saving you that night in O'Neill's, but I have since heard that you have been seen out with my daughter!" The big man was breathing heavily with absolute fury and his eyes possessed an intense hatred that Fennell had never seen before in any man. Eddie Fennel did not know what to say, the gun was pointing straight into his face and he could see no escape. "If it was up to me you would be dead already pig, but you can thank your lucky stars for your family! If it wasn't for your uncle here, then you would be finished so you would." It took a lot of will power and all of his self-control for Connelly not to pull the trigger, but out of respect for his friend Sean O'Connor he did not do it.

"It's time you left Ireland Eddie. There is a boat leaving for Liverpool at dawn. If you are not on it then I have given Eammon Connelly my word that I will kill you myself. Don't make me do that Eddie, I would not want my sister to suffer the death of a son. But by god Eddie, if you are not on that boat then I will feckin' kill you." Sean O'Connor's voice did not have the same warmth and friendliness as when Fennel had first met him at his grandfather's funeral and he knew that his time in Dublin had come to an end. He would not see Teresa again and it tore and gnawed at the pit of his stomach, but she had not demonstrated the same affection for him so his love was somewhat unrequited. It was time he went home. He collected his belongings at gunpoint and trudged sadly out of the door. He had not even been able to say a farewell to his grandmother or his cousin Johnny but he was lucky to escape with his life and he knew it.

It was a relatively short walk to the Dublin docks and Fennel spent the entire night walking around the vicinity in order to keep warm. He thought of nothing other than Teresa and he had even considered going to her home to ask her one last time if she would come away with him; *but Eammon Connelly would have been there and if she really did love him then she would not have laughed at his suggestion the first time around!* He had no other reason to stay in Ireland so he figured it was best to simply get on the boat and leave for good. His uncle Sean had already purchased him a ticket, such was his desperation for him to leave so all he would have to do was simply get on the boat and sleep for a couple of hours if he could find a bench on board the ship.

As the gates opened for boarding early the next morning, Fennel found himself first in line. He climbed on board the ship after having spent all night waiting. He walked up the ramp and made his way to the back of the boat where he cast one last sad look at the city of his beloved. He watched the ripples on the murky water as they passed up into the River Liffey and he signed inwardly. Dublin was not a beautiful city, but it had character and he continued to feel saddened that he had not been able to make things work with Teresa Connelly. He had never really been in love before. His adult life until recent months had been all about fighting a war and trying to simply remain alive. Of course, he had known women intimately in several countries, but he had never forged a relationship of any relevant meaning. *Was Teresa a one off? Would he find the same thing again?* He thought about the barmaid at the Neptune pub on Powke Lane and chuckled silently to himself, *No! He would not be that desperate!* The seagulls sounded loudly overhead and Fennel could feel the motion of the waves as the boat slowly began to pull away.

"Well then Mr Fennell. Were you planning to leave without even saying goodbye?" A voice sounded behind him and his heart almost skipped a beat as he recognised it straight away.

"Teresa! What are you doing here?" He turned around and passionately embraced her, unable to believe his eyes and ears.

"You were right Eddie. Why shouldn't I come to England with you? Johnny O'Connor got a message to me. He told me what your uncle and my father were planning to do so I came down here to the docks and bought a ticket… I love you Eddie." He embraced her again and held onto her tightly as the ship began to move out of Ireland. It appeared that he had a lot to thank Johnny O'Connor for. Saving his life and now reacquainting him with the woman that he loved.

Chapter 7
September 1955

Nineteen fifty five was a landmark year in the evolution of the twentieth century. The first McDonalds restaurants were erected in America, the first Disneyland park was opened, the Vietnam War began and the rise of Rock n' Roll went from strength to strength as the first riot at an Elvis Presley concert took place in Jacksonville Florida.

By 1955, Eddie Fennel had a smooth operation running. When he returned from Dublin in 1946, he quickly fell back in with the Mucklows and rose up fast. By the 50s, Willie Mucklow had retired and handed total control of his empire to his son Bill. Business had then continued to go from strength to strength as Mucklow junior had negotiated a partnership with Isiah Boswell and The Brummie Boys and the future was looking very lucrative indeed. Whilst Mucklow was busy selling stolen cars from the Austin factory in Longbridge, his other cousin Harry Scriven collected protection money whilst Fennel was left in charge of some of the less savoury rackets. Fennel had his own crew and as long as he took a case full of money to Billy Mucklow every month, he could do exactly as he wanted. This suited Mucklow well as even though he still had a financial interest in Fennel's activities, there was no direct trail linking him to any illegal doing.

Eddie Fennel had proven to be a particularly good earner. He ran a series of illegal bookies, organised and promoted unlicensed boxing events, but where his real talents lay were in long firm fraud. Basically, Fennel would set up a company under a false name. He would then order a small delivery of electrical goods to a warehouse complete with a secretary and official company letterhead so that everything looked legitimate. Next, he would pay for the goods promptly and then repeat the process until he was able to set up a credit arrangement. Once the credit was in place, Fennel would then proceed to fill the warehouse with unlimited goods which fennel's associates would then sell on for a quarter of the actual retail value. It was a perfect 'Robin Hood' situation. The poor working folk of the Black Country got cut price goods they would otherwise be unable to afford, Eddie Fennel and Billy Mucklow got rich and the electrical suppliers got a nasty surprise when they eventually turned up at a vacant warehouse looking for their money! The Kray twins and the Richardson brothers in London would also go on to have great success with similar scams in the 1960s.

Unlike Billy Mucklow's wife, who was literally left at home to look after the children, Eddie Fennel's wife Teresa played an active role in his business ventures. From playing the role of 'secretary' in the long firm frauds, to sitting besides him ringside at a boxing event; Teresa Fennel took to the roll of gangster's moll like a duck to water. She loved the glamour, the notoriety, the fear and the respect. In fact, it wasn't much different to her childhood in Ireland where she was known for being the daughter of a feared IRA leader and she loved the attention. Her perfect good looks were legendary and her flirty secretary act had been a vital element in closing down many a long firm deal. Eddie Fennel had the perfect life, a beautiful wife, a young daughter who had been born in the Spring of 1952 and enough money to fund a relatively lavish and luxurious life for them. But in 1955, events from outside of Eddie Fennel's control occurred which would have an impact on his operations in the Black Country.

"Looks like we've seen the end of summer mate." Tummy 'Ducks' looked out of the window of the Neptune pub and sighed at the heavy rain that lashed down on the grimy windows and pelted off the roof of Eddie Fennel's 1947 Rover 16. Fennel sat back into a vinyl bench seat and nervously watched a snooker game that was going on in the centre of the room. Billy Mucklow had the Haden Cross and Eddie Fennel used the Neptune or 'The Nep' as it was affectionately known on Powke Lane by the canal bridge. The room at the back was dark and shadowy with a well lit snooker table that stood in the middle. It was where Eddie Fennel and his crew spent much of their time drinking, thinking up scams and interrogating anyone that stepped out of line.

"Ar dow give a fuck about the bloody weather Tum, sit daahn!" Fennel was not nervous about the snooker game. His man was winning and he stood to make a small amount on a wager.

"What's up with yow Eddie?" Tummy 'Ducks' walked back over to Fennel and sat down on a stool opposite his boss.

"What's up with me? What the fucks up with me?" Fennel was exasperated at his colleague's lack of understanding. "We ay seen nor heard nothing from Billy Mucklow, Harry Scriven or Dickie Hickman for fuckin' weeks!"

"So? We've got our own thing gewin on. Why do we need them? Surely this means we dow have to pay Bill every fuckin' month?" Tummy 'Ducks' could see no problem with the disappearance of Bill Mucklow and his naivety was beginning to frustrate Eddie.

"Yow stupid fat fuck!" Fennel spoke through gritted teeth. "With Billy Mucklow gone we pretty much loose everything. Who do you think pays off the cops so that we can do half of the things we do? Who do you think protects us from being taken over by the big boys from Wolverhampton and Brum?" Fennel shook his head and took a long gulp of his beer. "Ar dow just pay Bill aaht on the goodness of my heart or because he's mar bloody cousin. Without Bill we could be taken over by the Boswell's or the Tanner's at any point!"

"Ar thought Brian Tanner had disappeared?"

"Yes, he vanished, but his son Cedric has taken over and he's an even sicker, nastier little fuck then his ode mon!"

"So where is Bill Mucklow?" Tummy's stupidity was starting to seriously annoy Fennel. "Sorry Eddie." Tummy 'Ducks' realised the stupidity of his question and lit a cigarette. "Why dow we just pay off the law ourselves? Skip the middle mon?"

"Dow talk saft Tum. What we gunna do? Turn up at Ode Hill Police Station and say, eh excuse me lads, who do we give this illicit highly illegal bribe too?" Fennel shook his head and laughed in frustration.

"What about Willie? Cor we gew and ask him if he knows where his son is?" Tummy 'Ducks' blew smoke into the air and shrugged and Fennel began to mellow slightly.

"I didn't really wanna do that. Willie's retired and ar dow wanna worry him, but if we dow hear anything soon then we may have to." Fennel drained his glass and placed it back down on the table.

"Want another raahnd Eddie?"

"No thanks Tum… Ar better be getting off. Settle up with these boys after the game and ar'll see yer tomorrow aer kid." Fennel stood up, patted Tummy 'Ducks' on the back and gestured to the two men who were playing snooker. He walked through the main bar that led to the front door and waved goodnight to a number of well-wishers who were gathered in the room. He fumbled in his suit pocket for his keys and went out to his Rover that was parked on a patch of land opposite the pub. The rain still continued to pour down and Fennel cursed as he pulled himself into the driver's seat of the grand car. The engine fired first time despite the wet and Fennel turned on the head lights and windscreen wipers. It was just over two miles from the 'Nep' to Fennel's detached house on Furlong Lane, Colley Gate and he put the Rover into gear and began the short journey.

Eddie Fennel and his wife Teresa had an impressive house that had been built in the 1920s and it stood on Furlong Lane adjacent to the entrance to Spring Street. Fennel pulled the Rover onto the drive and cursed the weather as he sat and pondered whether to make a run for it or sit and wait to see if the rain eased. He switched off the engine and the headlights. As he sat alone in the darkness listening to the thunderous sound of the rain beating down hard on the roof of his car, he thought he saw a shadow move in the rear-view mirror. *What the fuck was that?* He thought to himself. *Probably just a fox.* He lay back his head into the comfortable leather seats and wondered what would happen in the coming days. *Where was Bill Mucklow? What was going on?* Just then he froze as he thought that he heard movement on the pavement outside. He reached into his suit jacket for a trusty set of brass knuckles and prepared himself.

"Hello Eddie!" A familiar voice sounded and Fennel nearly had a heart attack as Billy Mucklow suddenly appeared out of the shadows and jumped into the passenger seat alongside him.

"Fuckin' hell Bill! What yow trying to do!" Fennel quickly tried to compose himself and Mucklow burst into laughter. He looked rough, as if he hadn't shaved for a few days and Fennel instantly noticed that he was not his usual ultra-confident self. He had known Mucklow for many years and had served with him during ultra-dangerous missions in World War 2. There really had been times when their chances of survival had been minimal, but they had always found a way through. On this rainy Saturday night in September, Eddie Fennel noticed a vulnerability in his former commanding officer that he had never seen before and he found it totally unnerving.

"I'm not going to be around for a while Eddie." Mucklow's laugh faded and Fennel could see a sadness in his eyes that Mucklow would never admit too.

"Well, yow ay been abaaht for a few weeks now mate. What's gewin on?"

"Ar cor tell yer too much aer kid. Me, Dick and Scriv did this job daahn Oxford way." Mucklow was nervous and was constantly checking the windows in fear that he had been followed.

"What kind of job?" Fennel was intrigued.

"That dow matter aer kid. Harry's gunna be moving abroad and me and Dick am gunna be doing a bit of porridge."

"Yow'm gewin to jail? Why Bill, what's gewin on? Am I in trouble too?" Fennel could not help but think of his own interests.

"No... Yow should be ok now Eddie. You heard about that kid Cooper getting killed?"

"Ar, I know he was a friend of Harrys?"

"Yes... Harry will be back soon, He will know what to do. Yow got nothing to worry about kid. Some lads ar know from London have sorted things so you and the rest of my family will be safe. My side of the bargain is that I have to gew to jail for a bit. Ar cor tell yer nothing else at the moment mate." Fennel had never seen Mucklow like this before and he did not know what to say. "Ar want yow to oversee things for me whilst me and Harry are away. Yow'm in charge now Eddie. Boswell and The Brummie Boys woe give yer much trouble but stay low key and try to be discreet for a bit."

"Why Bill? What's gewin on?"

"Honestly kid, ar cor tell yer nothing else Eddie. If yow have any problems contact these boys in London." Mucklow pushed a piece of paper into Fennel's hand. "Yow'll be ok. Do us a favour, keep an eye on mar family and my ode mon for me please will yer aer kid?" Mucklow almost seemed emotional as he patted Fennel on the shoulder and then disappeared off into the night as swiftly as he had arrived. Fennel sunk back into the driver's seat again and a million thoughts and questions drifted through his mind. *How would he carry on without Bill Mucklow? What had happened? Why was Bill suddenly so nervous and a shadow of his former self?* He lit a cigarette and tried to gather his thoughts. Billy Mucklow was more than just a business associate, he was a close friend, a former comrade of war and a distant relative. He had genuine concern for the man and hoped that all would be ok. But then he remembered that *Billy Mucklow was the toughest man he had ever known and how he had fought hard and ruthlessly against the Nazi's throughout World War 2. A short term in prison was nothing Bill couldn't handle, and in the meantime, he would keep things going as best as he could. He wasn't short of money and business was booming, he would find a way through and come out of the other side with a smile and a pocket full of money. He was Eddie Fennel, he always found a way, he always came up smelling of roses!* Or so he hoped!

Chapter 8
May 1965

By May 1965, the swinging 60s were in full flow. Both the Beatles and the Rolling Stones had enjoyed successes in the music world, and fashion had evolved to encompass risqué miniskirts, men with long hair and colourful and elaborate new styles that were of a sharp contrast to the decades that had passed.

Eddie Fennel had continued to prosper. Of course, he had needed to 'tone down' his operations in order to attract less attention from the police and rival firms. He ran a protection racket in the immediate vicinity of Cradley Heath and he continued to run a series of illegal bookmakers. The biggest change in his enterprise was that instead of having the freedom to promote big unlicensed boxing events, he now had to rely on small exclusive bouts that were attended by 50-100 spectators as opposed to a couple of thousand. Either way, Fennel found ways to make money. He knew which fighters he could 'get at' and he knew how to manipulate things so that he could control the outcome of each and every fight. Fennel also saw the financial opportunities in the entertainment industry.

With the success of bands like the Beatles, the Stones, the Hollies and the Kinks, they showed the world that ordinary lads from British working-class backgrounds could rule the radio air waves and become famous pop stars. Young kids up and down the country suddenly started forming bands and set out to try and become the next big thing. Like many others, Eddie Fennel saw the potential in this, and he soon set up makeshift music venues in large old pubs where hundreds of screaming young girls could pay to see the local wannabes. He owned several pubs in the Cradley Heath area and would employ various local bands to play for revellers whilst keeping the thirstier 'ode men' happy in other establishments. He balanced it to absolute perfection. This would mean acquiring two pubs that were relatively close to each other, putting bands on in the larger pub thus driving the regular drinkers and 'ode chainmeckers' into the second pub where they could sup beer and complain about the 'other' place and it's 'awful' music. Fennel himself would frequent the second type of pub, *but why not make money from the teeny boppers?* The disappearance of Billy Mucklow may have hindered Fennel to the extent that he wasn't quite making the same money he had been during the early 50s, but he still continued to thrive on a slightly smaller scale.

On Wednesday the 19th of May 1965, West Ham United beat the German side 1860 Munich in a 2-0 evening game at Wembley stadium to become the second British club to win a European trophy. In Cradley Heath, a bright red Jaguar MK 2 sped through the High Street towards The Bell Hotel that was situated in St Anne's Road just off Five Ways. The driver and owner of the car was Eddie Fennel and he was pissed off. He had been enjoying several ales in the Neptune on Powke Lane when he had been disturbed by a phone call from the licensee of the Bell. The Bell Hotel was owned by Eddie Fennel and its relatively large size meant that it was a perfect venue for live music, but on this night, some rather unsavoury events had occurred and Fennel was livid.

Two burly doormen stood on the door and Fennel approached them with fire in his eyes.

"Which one of yow pair of fuckin' clots let that bastard in here?" The doorman on the right panicked.

"It was him Eddie, but he day know!" The doorman pointed to his colleague next to him and before he could protest Fennel grabbed the second doorman and kneed him hard in the groin sending him straight to his knees in agony. Eddie Fennel had spent a lot of time around Bill Mucklow as a young man and he had learnt from the best. He would not suffer fools.

"Where is he now?" Fennel stood back from the doormen and waited for an answer.

"Sid Homer and Frankie Tromans have got him raahnd the back Eddie." The first doorman spoke again and Fennel could not help but feel disappointed at how easily the man had given up his mate. *Maybe he should have given them both a slap?*

Fennel walked around to the back of the pub where he found his employees Sid Homer and Frankie Tromans with a young man of around 25 years of age. He had shoulder length hair and wore a black leather jacket.

"Teck this piece of shit aaht to the Jag. Yow pair sit either side of him in the back and do not let him gew anywhere!" The two men escorted their prisoner to the red Jaguar and Fennel climbed back into the driver's seat. The man said nothing and Fennel started the straight 6 engine. He drove slowly for about 2 miles until he came to a lockup garage on The Brickhouse Estate in Rowley Regis. Fennel got out of the car and opened up the garage door before switching on a solitary light bulb that swung in the middle of the room. Fennel was annoyed. He should have been on his eighth pint of Banks's mild by now and tucking into a nice bag of KVE pork scratchings. Below the lightbulb stood a single wooden chair and Fennel gestured for his two henchmen to bring the prisoner in. Homer and Tromans dutifully led the man to the chair and Fennel pulled down the garage door behind them.

"Please take a seat." Fennel smiled sarcastically and the man in the leather jacket sat down. "Do you know who I am kid?" Fennel lit a cigarette and lent back against the concrete wall. The man nodded smugly and Fennel shrugged. "Ok… Good…" Fennel took off his suit jacket and loosened his tie slowly and purposefully so as to incur maximum tension for his guest. "Ar'm gunna be honest with yow mate. Ar dow like people that sell drugs. Especially bastards who try to push em in mar pubs!" Fennel gritted his teeth and hit the dealer with a back handed slap of such force that he nearly fell out of the chair. The man turned back to face him, fresh blood was running from his mouth and then he half smiled. "Yow think this is fuckin' funny kid? Yer woe be loffin' when ar hang yer up by yer bollocks an use yer carcass for a punch bag yer cocky little shit!" Fennel hit the man again, but this time with a full fist and the chair flew backwards as the man's nose broke on impact.

"Pick him back up." Homer and Tromans were two well-built men in their mid-30s. Homer was bald and Tromans had brown hair with a side parting. They hurried forwards and pulled the long-haired drug dealer back into the chair. "You see, when drug pushers come into mar pub, some poor little 16-year-old wench in a pretty little dress ends up tecking a pill, and she ends up sick or worse... Not only is that very upsetting for me and her family, but it also brings down an awful lot of heat and police interest into my operations and I do not need that!" Fennel pushed his face into that of the drug dealer. "If it comes down to a choice between burying some poor decent kid or burying you, then there is no choice... But dow expect mommy and daddy there crying over yer grave side, cus they woe fuckin' find yer... An it woe be fuckin' quick!" Fennel was trying to scare his prisoner but he meant every word. He had slaughtered many men, their only crime was their Germanic nationality, the prospect of killing a filthy drug-pushing scumbag like this did not faze him one bit. *Decent men had died during the Second World War, his friends and comrades... Why did this cretin who poisoned the bodies and minds of the innocent deserve to live?* Fennel took a drag of his cigarette and then pulled a hip flask from out of his jacket pocket that was hung on a rusty nail. "Would yow like a drink boys?" He took a swig of the Scotch and offered some to his associates. The two men nodded and Fennel flung the flask over to them. He put his cigarette to his lips again and blew smoke across the room. "I understand that yow'm just a pusher and that you represent somebody bigger." Fennel spoke to the drug dealer again. He had made his point and had demonstrated that he was willing to and was capable of hurting him. Now he wanted names. "Who put you up to selling pills in Cradley Heath?" The dealer smiled again and sat back in his chair as blood poured from his broken nose and onto his elaborate floral shirt.

"Somebody a lot bigger and more dangerous than yow, and when he finds out about this he's gunna sort yow out!" The dealer finally spoke and then started to laugh hysterically as he spat his own blood into the air. Fennel shrugged again, took another drag of his cigarette and then sighed.

"Lads, tie his hands together." Homer and Tromans did as they were asked and they used a small piece of chain that hung on the wall to tie the drug dealer's hands as he sat in the chair. The pusher said nothing, he let them do it. In his mind he clung to the comfort that one mention of his bosses' name would deter Fennel from any further violence. Fennel waited until the dealer was secured and that he had his full attention before opening a blue metal toolbox that stood on top of a dusty old wooden cabinet. Inside were a selection of tools and the drug dealer glanced over at the torturous instruments and remembered tales he had heard about Fennel's old leader Billy Mucklow. *Maybe it was time he opened up and explained who he worked for?*

"Ok… Fine. I'm gunna tell you who I work for, but then I demand an apology and a lift home!" The drug dealer had seen enough. Things were about to get nasty and he was ready to talk. *Then they would feel afraid!* Eddie Fennel stubbed out his cigarette on the floor and began to laugh.

"Yow'm ready ter talk?" Fennel continued to laugh. He looked at the man who was secured in the chair and could feel no pity. "Maybe ar bay ready ter listen?" Fennel suddenly stopped laughing and picked up a pair of pliers from the box. "Yeah, Bill Micklow could teck teeth aaht with these things… Or cut off fingers, or toes." Fennel enjoyed the fear he created. He was not an evil man, but he had a strong sense of justice and to him a drug dealer was the lowest of the low. He touched the cold pliers to the dealer's face and slowly traced them around his cheek towards his mouth. Each move was deliberately slow and utterly terrifying. "The only people scarier than Bill were is ode mon Willie and his uncle Eli." Fennel continued to tease the vicious pliers around the dealer's face. As yet he had not used them in anger, but the mere suggestion of what was to come and the way they caressed the entirety of the dealer's face created a tension that was unbearable. Homer and Tromans looked on and wondered what would happen. They were fully aware of their boss's capabilities and they also knew of the implications for themselves if they were to be found as accessories to violence. "I heard that Eli Davis once cut a man's tongue out and then fed it to him until he choked and died on his own blood." The story was true and the dealer still hoped that the mention of his own employer would cause Fennel to be lenient. "Then ar remember hearing how ode Willie Mucklow would tie fellas face daahn in the cut to a barge as it went under Netherton Tunnel. If the chap was still alive when he reached the other side then he always talked." Fennel smiled and genuinely enjoyed the nostalgic tales of his elders. "Oi, yow pair, give me that Scotch back!" Frankie Tromans reached for the hip flask and then flung it back over to his boss. Fennel took a long swig and then returned to the dealer. "So... What yow wanna tell me aer kid? Who put yow up to selling pills in Cradley Heath?" The dealer half smiled and he suddenly felt a little more confident.

"Cedric Tanner..." Fennel suddenly looked away and sighed inwardly. Cedric Tanner from Wolverhampton had inherited his father's business and was fast establishing a narcotics empire that was generating him significant wealth. Eddie Fennel did not like Cedric Tanner. He was a loathsome man who supposedly had a perverted and unnatural interest in young boys. Fennel took another drink of whiskey and pushed his face even closer to the pusher.

"Is that right young man?" Fennel suddenly stood up and moved closer to the main door. The drug dealer smiled with a smug satisfaction. *He was Tanner's boy, he could not be touched!*

"We gunna let him gew boss?" Frankie Tromans asked the question and wondered if he would make last orders at the Nep!

"Pull his fuckin' trousers off and wire him up!" Fennel suddenly started laughing again and the dealer began trying to struggle, but it was no use, he was securely chained. Tromans and Homer then proceeded to pull the man's jeans and underwear off and the two men watched in amusement as the once cocky drug dealer began to sob with fear and self-pity. Fennel then pulled down a cruel looking device that had once been used for boosting the batteries of old military lorries. Sid Homer took the machine and placed a crocodile clip onto each of the man's testicles and then stood back. "Ar want yow to send this message to Cedric Tanner. We dow have drugs araahnd here." Fennel proceeded to plug the torturous machine into the mains and then looked on as he watched the dealer scream, plead and cry in agony…

Cedric Tanner's dealer suffered that night. When Eddie Fennel eventually ended the ordeal, the crazed man bolted out of the lock up without even pausing to collect his trousers or underwear. The three men left in the lockup found this highly amusing and Fennel lit another cigarette as he pondered the future implications of the night's activities.

Chapter 9

The midday warmth of the May sunshine caressed Eddie Fennel's brow as he sat back on a deck chair in his large garden and enjoyed a glass of cider that had become lukewarm in the heat. His teenage daughter lay nearby and listened to pop music on a portable transistor radio. It was not Fennel's sort of music and his daughter had become bored with his constant complaints about the volume of the radio and her apparent lack of clothes. He enjoyed the sun immensely, but other things had been on his mind and had been troubling his sleep in recent nights. He noticed the curvaceous shape of his stunning Irish wife emerge from the house and as she approached, he as ever felt a lucky man and wondered how he had ever been able to attract such a beautiful woman. She was in her early 40s but she still looked good. She wore a fashionable PVC mini skirt with knee high boots and as she walked Fennel noted that she had perfected a trademark 'wiggle' that made her even more alluring.

"I brought you a cup of tea Eddie." Her Irish accent was thick and husky and he loved her deeply.

"Thanks bab, but yow drink it or give it to Tina. Ar'm on the cider."

"It's a bit early for that isn't it Edward?" She looked at the three quarters empty glass of cider in his hand and raised her eye brows.

"It ay never too early bab." Fennel tried to force a smile and slapped her backside playfully.

"What's wrong Eddie? You haven't been yourself for a few days now." She stroked the top of his head affectionately and gave him a smouldering look that never failed to melt him.

"Nothing bab. Ar'm bostin."

"That's a lie Eddie. The last couple of days something has been wrong. You always tell me everything. What's different now?" Teresa was a big part of Eddie Fennel's activities, she made it her business too and he valued her opinion. Fennel 'downed' the last of his cider, sighed and lit a cigarette.

"We caught this fella selling pills in the Bell the other night." Fennel blew smoke across the garden and looked up at his wife who was stood over him. "We bashed him up a bit, tried to make him see the error of his ways. Ar cor have drugs in mar venues bab."

"Fucken' hell Eddie, you didn't kill the bastard did ya?" Teresa Fennel did not necessarily agree with drugs either, but she knew that her husband had a tendency to be a little heavy handed at times.

"No bab, nothing like that…" Fennel was grateful for that much. "Turned out that the guy works for Cedric Tanner."

"Who's Cedric Tanner?" Teresa shrugged and stole a drag of Fennel's cigarette.

"Do you remember Brian Tanner from back in the 50s? He used to run things over Wolverhampton way."

"Yes… Horrible little man, evil eyes."

"Well, Cedric Tanner is his son and he took over his ode mon's empire. He's a nasty piece of work. Worse than his father!"

"Is he threatening you Eddie?"

"No… I haven't heard anything. But he ay gunna be happy abaaht what happened to his dealer." Fennel took his cigarette back and dragged hard.

"Are we in danger?" Teresa's instant thoughts were for the safety of their daughter.

"No. You will be fine." Fennel lied. The Tanner's had a reputation for going after and hurting civilians and getting at their rivals through their families and loved ones. Teresa sat down seductively on his lap and raised her hand to his face.

"Maybe you should go and see this Cedric Tanner? Let him know that you meant no disrespect but you will not have drugs in your venues?"

Fennel thought for a minute. Billy Mucklow had always taught him to stand up to the big boys. *'Never show an ounce of weakness because they will respect you less.'* He placed his hand on Teresa's exposed and particularly curvaceous thigh and slowly caressed it.

"I might. Or I might let him come to me… I haven't decided yet." Drugs were the future of gangland and Fennel knew it. But up until now he had managed to avoid them. Billy Mucklow had dealt in a little bit of cannabis back in the early 50s through his Jamaican friend Robert Murray, but he had pulled out when Murry had expressed a desire to move to cocaine. The Mucklows had never really agreed with drugs and they felt that the recreational 'spliff' was very different to the harder more lucrative narcotics. *Pills were particularly dangerous and there was no way that Eddie Fennel was prepared to let them become a fixture on his patch!*

"Don't worry Eddie. Everything will be fine." Teresa smiled and Fennel kissed her fully on the lips. Their teenage daughter protested in disgust and she quickly took her radio inside to escape her parents outward display of affection.

"Thank fuck for that!" Fennel laughed. "Ar cor listen to that bloody racket no more!"

"Isn't that the sort of music you have in your pubs?" Teresa lent in closely and hugged her husband.

"Yes, but it dow mean ar have to bloody like it." Fennel smiled as he finished his cigarette. Sooner or later he would be hearing from Cedric Tanner and he would just have to wait and see what happened.

That night, when Eddie Fennel returned home from the pub, he was surprised to see a downstairs light on at his Furlong Lane home. It was well past midnight and his wife and daughter would usually be fast asleep in there beds by now. His heart began to race and he fell into a blind panic. He should never have left his family alone knowing what Cedric Tanner was capable of. He quickly pulled out an old German Lugar P08 pistol from his jacket and got out of his car. He didn't usually carry a gun but since the business with Tanner's pusher he felt the need for a little extra protection. He crept swiftly up the garden path and paused at the front door. He felt the adrenaline shoot through his veins and he had the same rush of anticipation that he had felt so many times during the Second World War, but only this time his wife and daughter were at stake. He took a deep breath and then barged into the hallway and then straight through to the living room.

"Hello Eddie, I wasn't expecting this reaction I must say." Teresa was lay out seductively on the sofa, scantily clad in a pair of nylon stockings complete with suspender belt and matching lacy underwear. A Nat King Cole record span softly on the turn table and Fennel instantly felt relieved.

"Ar'm sorry bab. Ar thought somebody had broken in when ar saw the light on so late."

"I hope you don't mind me waiting up for you Eddie?" She purred in her sultry Irish accent and beckoned for him to come closer.

"Not at all bab." He drew closer to her and knelt at her side as she lay on the sofa.

"I've been thinking." She pulled herself up to face him and put her face to his. "It may be against some moral code that you have but I think that you should reconsider your involvement with the drugs business." Fennel shook his head and moved away. "No, listen Eddie, there is a fuck of a lot of money to be made from narcotics. Instead of going up against this Cedric Tanner we should be going into business with the man." She grabbed his tie and pulled him close again, her breath on his face was hypnotic and alluring.

"Ar dow deal in drugs Teresa."

"There's no need to, just sit back and make money from it. All we need to do is put up an investment and allow dealers to work in our pubs. We can pay other people to do the rest." Fennel was not convinced, it went against the grain and he desperately did not want to get involved in narcotics. "I don't see how you have any choice Eddie? All of your rivals will go down this route and once they get stronger they will come after us." Fennel knew that she was probably right, what he wouldn't have given for advice from Billy Mucklow at that time. He half smiled and kissed Teresa on the lips.

"Ar dow like it Teresa, but ar will have a think about it and have a chat with Tummy 'Ducks' tomorrow." He grabbed her forcefully and lifted her off the sofa and she giggled like a naughty schoolgirl as he carried her up to bed.

Two black rover P5s pulled up outside the Neptune on Powke Lane and Tummy 'Ducks' alerted his boss straight away.

"They'm here Eddie." Tummy 'Ducks' came away from the window and sat down alongside Fennel, Sid Homer and Frankie Tromans. They were all armed and ready for a fight, but Tummy 'Ducks' was hoping that violence would be avoided. The day after Fennel's wife had suggested he considered going into the narcotics business, an associate of Cedric Tanner had telephoned to inform them that Tanner wanted a 'sit down' and that he would be coming to the Neptune that night for a meeting. Fennel knew that his wife was eager to become richer and that she was in favour of entering the drugs game, but he still was not convinced. *It didn't feel right, but maybe he had no choice? He didn't have the muscle to be able to stand up to the likes of Cedric Tanner and sooner or later he would come under his thumb. It had been a miracle that he had survived for nearly ten years on his own without the protection of Billy Mucklow.*

"Mr Fennel." Tanner entered the back room of the Neptune with 5 huge men who Fennel was pretty sure were all heavily armed. Tanner stood in the middle, he was all of 5 foot 9 with wiry hair and intense staring eyes that were totally black.

"Hello Cedric. What can ar do for yer?" Fennel smiled and beckoned for the men to come into the room. "Tum, gew and fetch these boys a drink."

"No thank you Eddie, we won't be staying long. I would just like to have a little chat with you."

"Sit daahn." Fennel gestured to a stool that stood opposite the bench he was sat on and Tanner smiled and showed a mild annoyance. *He was Cedric Tanner, he sat wherever he wanted, whenever he wanted and he did not need this fucking soldier to tell him what to do!* Fennel knew that he had caused annoyance and he loved it. "Yow can stand up if yer want mate, makes no fuckin' difference to me." Fennel laughed and the three men sat alongside him did the same.

"I'd be careful if I was you Edward. Ar dow see Billy Mucklow and his band of merry men around to help you anymore." Tanner pulled another chair from an adjacent table and sat down on it. "Lets start again shall we?" Fennel shrugged and took a drink of his beer as Tanner's 5 thugs stood back from the table and looked on. Eddie Fennel hated Cedric Tanner with a passion and if he was deciding to go into the drug business then he would put a bullet in Tanner's head there and then. The Lugar was in his pocket and was loaded and ready to go. *If he wanted to be a drug dealer then this would be the perfect opportunity. He could wipe out the major player in the drugs market (Tanner) and then simply pay the 5 thugs to work for him. That would be a takeover!* As he sipped his ale and listened to Tanner whine on about his own importance he seriously considered blowing the fat little bastard's head off. *He had killed so many people in the war, many of them were probably decent men who were simply fighting because like him they had no choice. Cedric Tanner was a known paedophile and a drug dealer, he did not deserve to live whilst Fennel's war comrades had fallen. But then did he want to take over? Did he want to be a drug kingpin? The money and lifestyle would please Teresa, but was it right?*

"Are you fucking listening to me?" Tanner sensed that Fennel was not giving him his full attention.

"Not really Cedric, yow'm gerrin' on mar fuckin' nerves mate. Please get to the point or piss off back to Wolverhampton." Fennel sighed and gave Tanner his best 'Billy Mucklow' stare. Tanner seemed to find it somewhat amusing and started to laugh.

"Your lucky I'm even here Fennel, I could have had you shot in your bed alongside your Irish whore of a wife! But oh dear, what would happen to your poor little girl? I know people who really love poor little girls like that..." Fennel saw red and instantly lurched forwards and grabbed Tanner by the hair. He pulled the Lugar from his pocket and held it to Tanner's head as he used his other arm to hold him tightly.

"If yow lot move ar'm gunna blow this piece of shit's head off!" Fennel snarled at the 5 thugs who were poised and ready to strike.

"You stupid fucking idiot!" Tanner protested as Fennel grasped his hair and pushed the Luger further into the side of his face. "I've got a car outside your house in Furlong Lane. If anything happens to me then these boys behind me will get a message to the car to kill your family. A nice-looking family like yours would be great for those boys, I'm sure they'll have some fun with them first." Tanner began to laugh, a sick and twisted evil laugh and more than anything Fennel wanted to pull the trigger and watch Tanner die. "Lets say you let me go and we can sit back down again and talk business like adults." Fennel let go of Tanner's hair but he did not let go of the gun. "Look, I'm sorry for what I said about your wife Eddie, but I have every reason to be a bit pissed off." Tanner flattened his hair and composed himself.

"Why you pissed off?" Fennel sat back in his chair, the Lugar still in his right hand pointing firmly at Cedric Tanner. His eyes glowed with anger and hatred and he spoke through gritted teeth.

"A young lad that works for me, somebody wired up his bollocks and barbequed his balls! Ring any bells Eddie?"

"We dow have drug dealers in mar manor."

"Your fucking manor? You mean Billy Mucklow's manor, but Billy's inside and when he gets out he's gewin to Spain to see Harry Scriven... Everybody knows that Eddie. Yow'm on yer own kid."

"Yeah, and ar'm in charge now and we dow have drugs in mar pubs."

"I've gotta hand it to you Eddie, you've got some balls mate. They always said that you were Billy Mucklow's Rottweiler... But at heart I know that yow'm a businessman. Always looking for a scam, a fiddle, an angle. Well, there ay no fiddle in mar game Eddie, you just get fucking rich!" Tanner smiled and shrugged. "Now the way I see it Eddie, is you've got two choices mate. You can come into business with me, I can always use extra tough guys on the payroll plus you will get a percentage of what I sell in your pubs. Just as long as you guarantee the safety of my dealers. Or, you can go to war with me Eddie… But I warn you now Eddie, I play rough and I dow play by any rules. If you decide to fight me then you better keep an eye on that family of yours mate." Tanner knew that his words would enrage Fennel, but he didn't care, he was in control of the situation and Fennel had no choice but to do as he was told. Fennel seriously considered pulling the trigger, but he could not afford to play Russian roulette with his wife and daughter's life. "I don't expect a decision tonight Eddie. I will be back in two days time. I will expect an answer then. I wanna get my dealers in your clubs by the weekend!" Tanner stood up and straightened his tie. "Have a nice evening gents." He turned to face his gorillas and nodded for them to leave. Swiftly they all filtered out of the pub, out to their cars and then roared off into the night.

Eddie Fennel remained in his seat, his eyes transfixed on an ashtray that stood in the middle of the table. He needed to smash something, he needed to hurt somebody, he needed an outlet for his rage. Cedric Tanner had left him with an impossible decision and more than anything he needed Billy Mucklow.

Chapter 10

The big cat prowled through the winding country lanes that led from Halesowen to the village of Clent. Usually the sound of the big straight 6 never failed to put a smile on Eddie Fennel's face, but today as he negotiated the twisting lanes in his Mk 2 Jaguar he had more pressing issues on his mind. *He had worked hard to build his empire since he had returned from Ireland nearly twenty years previously, the last thing he wanted was to simply hand it over into the filthy, perverted hands of Cedric Tanner. On the other hand, his wife and daughter meant more to him than anything and he could not jeopardise their safety.*

Willie Mucklow had moved to an old, secluded farmhouse not far from Clent when he retired in the late 1940s. He had retired relatively young but he had made more than enough money and he was happy to let his son Bill take over the family business. Willie Mucklow was now nearing 70 years of age and was still enjoying his retirement with his wife. He didn't get many visitors and he liked it that way. In his younger days he had made many enemies and the elder Mucklow was eager to keep his new location a closely guarded secret. He still slept with a shotgun under his bed and he shared his home with several fierce Staffordshire Bull Terriers whom he loved with all of his heart.

The Staffordshire Bull Terrier or 'Staffie' as they are more affectionately known originated in the Black Country and Birmingham areas of Britain and had originally been used extensively for dog fighting. Willie Mucklow had grown up amongst dog fights which had been very common in Britain in the early twentieth century, and even though a lot of Mucklow's wealth had come from illegal gambling and unlicensed boxing, dog fighting was a 'sport' he utterly detested. He would quite happily make money from watching two men beat each other half to death, but with dogs it was different!

Mucklow recognised the red Jag immediately as it passed through the gates and made its ascent up the long driveway that led to

Mucklow's country home. The car rose in and out of muddy puddles and usually Eddie Fennel would be cursing the mud that was spraying his luxury car, but today he had more pressing issues on his mind. He pulled up outside the house and Willie Mucklow was already on the drive with three highly animated Staffies. Mucklow barked a command and the three dogs immediately settled at his feet obediently. Fennel got out of the Jag and approached his one-time boss and the cousin of his own father. Fennel had grown up amongst Staffies himself and he had one of his own at home that he had affectionately named Alan after the Aston Villa Captain Alan Deakin. He was certainly not fazed by the aggressive looking canines.

"Uncle Willie, good ter see yer." Fennel handed Mucklow a bottle of Scotch whisky and the old man accepted it approvingly.

"Yow wore followed were yer?" Mucklow cast his eyes down the long driveway and looked for signs of other vehicles.

"Dow be saft Willie, there ay many motors than can keep up with one of these!" Fennel nodded towards his Jaguar and waited for Mucklow to invite him inside.

"What do yer want then?" Mucklow wasn't quite gruff and he was pleased to see Fennel, but he did not like visitors and the potential safety risks they brought. There was a time in his life when Willie Mucklow was utterly fearless, but as he grew older and frailer he had become more conscious about such matters.

"Ar need yower advice Uncle Willie. Ar'm in a tricky situation." What Fennel really needed was Willie's son Bill Mucklow, but seeing as he was serving time in her majesty's prison, he would have to settle for the next best thing, Bill's dad.

"Yow better come in then aer kid." Mucklow lead Fennel into the house and into an old farm kitchen that looked like it hadn't changed much since the Victorian era. Mucklow had previously lived in a grand, elaborate art deco house in Halesowen but in his old age he had obviously developed simpler tastes. He gestured for Fennel to take a seat at the table and he pulled down two teacups from a cupboard and then placed them on the table next to the Scotch. He looked at his watch.

"Ar know its only 10 o'clock in the morning but fuck it." Mucklow smiled and poured two enormous measures into the teacups. "Cheers." He clinked his cup against Fennel's and then sat down in the chair next to his cousin's son. "So… What's up Eddie?"

"Yow ever heard of a fella called Cedric Tanner?" Fennel took a sip of his Scotch and waited for a response. Willie Mucklow sighed deeply.

"Ar… Sick little bastard. Nasty piece of work. His ode mon wore much better, but me and him, we sort of tolerated one another… Ode Eli always reckoned we should have put a bullet in the bastard but sometimes it was easier to just leave folks to their own business."

"Well, he's putting pressure on me. He wants me to get mixed up with drugs." Mucklow sucked his teeth and shook his head disapprovingly.

"Nasty business drugs. Very nasty. One of the reasons ar got ahht when I did."

"Ar know Uncle Willie. That's why ar'm in this situation. Cedric Tanner is a vicious fuck, he's threatening to hurt mar Mrs and aer Tina." Mucklow shook his head again.

"Things have changed a lot Eddie. In mar day yer didn't mess with people's families. It was an unwritten law. Now it's a fuckin' free for all. Ar dow envy yer kid." Fennel was waiting for nuggets of wisdom, so far Mucklow had proven to be particularly unhelpful. *But what did he expect? What could the old man do? He had been retired for over 15 years.* Fennel had just about given up hope when the sly old man spoke again. "Before Billy left, he gave yow a number… Have yow phoned it?"

"Er no." Fennel had forgotten all about it. "I, er forgot about it… How did yow know abaaht that?" Fennel wondered how the old man could have possibly known about the number Billy Mucklow had handed him on the night that he had fled.

"Ar might be ode Eddie, but ar still know things and Bill is mar son." Mucklow stood up and went and rummaged in a draw in a far corner of his kitchen before returning with a crumpled piece of paper that he gave to Fennel. "Remember, Bill said any problems, give these boys a call."

"Who is it?" Now that he had remembered, Fennel recalled the conversation with Billy well, but it had been nearly 10 years ago!

"Friends. Bill has done them a favour by gewin to jail. The agreement was that they would guarantee the safety of his family… Give them a call." Fennel shrugged and thanked the old man. *It had to be worth a try?*

The next night, the allotted time period was over and Eddie Fennel, Tummy 'Ducks', Sid Homer and Frakie Tromans were back in their usual spot in the Neptune. Cedric Tanner's arrival was imminent and they were bracing themselves for their visitor. Homer and Tromans chatted nervously and played cards whilst Eddie Fennel relaxed and smoked a cigar.

"Here we gew boys. They'm here." As ever Tummy 'Ducks' was at the window and he alerted the rest of the gang to Tanner's arrival.

"Ok boys. Just stay cool." Fennel took a drag of his cigar and waited for his foe to appear.

"Mr Fennel. We meet again. I trust you have some good news for me." Tanner was his usual obnoxious self and the 5 thugs trailed into the room behind their master. Fennel smiled and gestured to a stool as he had done two nights previously.

"Sit down Cedric." Tanner ignored the comment and did not rise to the bait. *He had plans for the rest of the night and the less time spent in this pokey little pub with these common low life thugs the better!*

"My dealers move in this weekend. Make life easy for them and I might have a little something for you…" Tanner was patronising and assuming.

"How about fuck you Cedric... If ar catch any of your drug pushin' bastards in mar pubs then ar'll fry their fuckin balls off just like that other little shit last week." Fennel blew smoke into the air and took a drink of his beer.

"Oh Eddie, Eddie, Eddie... I don't think you understand the implications of your actions. Very, very disappointing and so sad for that beautiful wife of yours and your little girl."

"You touch a hair on that family's head and you will answer to me!" A Cockney voice sounded from the back of the room and it temporarily stunned Tanner and his men. Two men in black suits sat in a secluded corner near to the door and until now Tanner had not even been aware of their presence. He turned to face them and was particularly surprised by what he saw. The first twin casually smoked a cigarette and the second, the one who had spoken, glared at Tanner with intense staring eyes through a pair of half rim spectacles and even Cedric Tanner felt intimidated.

"Well, well, well. Ronnie and Reggie, this is a long way from Bethnal Green boys. With respect I don't see what this matter has to do with you." Cedric Tanner knew of the twin's fearsome reputation. In London they were celebrity gangsters, but here in the Black Country they were a long way from home.

"You're an ambitious man Mr Tanner." The first twin who did not wear spectacles began to speak. "You are trying to build a narcotics empire across the country, but for that you need friends. Me and my brother are not the sort of people you want to disappoint Mr Tanner." Tanner thought about Reggie's words. *A fall out with the biggest gangsters in the country would be bad for business and hardly worth it for half a dozen backstreet boozers in a run-down part of the Black Country.*

"Why the fuck are you two backing up Eddie fuckin' Fennel?" Tanner could not get his head around why the biggest criminals this side of the Atlantic Ocean were 'in bed' with Eddie Fennel and his band of

Cradley Heath beer guzzlers. The twin with the spectacles suddenly looked very angry.

"Why the fack should we have to justify ourselves to you? You pompous facking worm!" Ronnie looked like he was about to explode but his brother Reg put a calming hand on his shoulder.

"You must forgive my brother Mr Tanner, but we have an agreement with Mr Fennel's relative Billy Mucklow guaranteeing the safety of his family whilst he is in prison." Reg took another drag of his cigarette. "So I suggest you fack off then me old cocker Sparra!" Tanner breathed deeply and turned back to face Eddie Fennel.

"Ar dow give a fuck anyway. It's your loss Fennel. You could have made some real fuckin' money." Fennel shrugged and then stood up and walked over to Cedric Tanner so that his face was pushed firmly into that of the smaller man's.

"If you ever threaten mar family again, then ar'm gunna fuckin' have you… Only it woe be fast Cedric. It will be very fuckin' slow and you will be looking into my eyes as you draw your very last breath upon this earth…" Tanner grunted and smirked.

"If it wasn't for them pair over there Eddie, you'd be my little bitch by now." Tanner grunted again and then turned to leave the pub. He nodded his respect to the twins as he left and then he never returned to the Neptune on Powke Lane ever again. Eddie Fennel had lived to fight another day. He may not be about to amaze his wife with the lucrative gains of the drug trade, but he still had his little empire and he still had his own self-respect.

Chapter 11

May 1974

When a man loves a woman by Percy Sledge was recorded in 1966 at Norala Sound studio in Sheffield, Alabama. As Suzy Miller sat in the small kitchen of her mother's Beauty Bank, Haden Hill home, she smoked a cigarette and wondered if any men loved her? She had been living in Old Hill with her recent boyfriend Dick Hickman, but Hickman was a notorious, hot headed criminal and he had disappeared on the Costa del sol just before Christmas. She could not afford the rent on her own, so she had subsequently moved back in with her mother Irene.

Suzy Miller had not heard anything from Hickman in months and how little she actually cared about that did not surprise her. She had never loved Dick Hickman… He was a link to the 'good' old days, happier times. Now she was rapidly approaching 40 years of age and her curvaceous body was slowly beginning to sag with stretch marks and more than her fair share of cellulite. She still made an effort with her appearance and her makeup was always meticulously overdone. Her hair was still a stunning shade of red and her face was pretty and seductive. Suzy Miller had heard that Hickman's associate Micky Cole was back in England after the trip to Spain, but she lacked the motivation to speak to him and find out what had happened to her man. Her last encounter with Cole had been just before he and Hickman had headed off to Spain and it had been particularly embarrassing for Suzy. She did have questions about the Spanish trip, but her curiosity involved the fate of a different man, the man she had been in love with and had been trying to replace for many years… Suzy Miller figured that Hickman was either dead or in jail and she almost felt guilty for her lack of compassion.

"That cars parked up the road again bab." Suzy's mother Irene was close on 60 years of age but she still looked good for her age. At one time she had been in a serious relationship with Billy Mucklow's cousin Harry Scriven, but Scriven had abandoned her many years previously when he fled to Spain and married a considerably younger Spanish girl named Antonia.

"Which one?" Suzy turned the radio down and faced her mother who had just emerged into the kitchen.

"Fancy one. Looks like a Jag or summet. It's bin parked at the top of the road a fair bit lately. Ar tried to see who was in it but ar cor see ahht the bedroom winda." Irene Miller shook her head and started to make a cup of tea. "Want a cuppa tay bab?"

"No thanks Mom. I ay long had one."

"Yow seen it ay yer Tony?" Irene called through to her male companion whom she had met a couple of years after Harry Scriven had left her. She had originally considered returning to her Scottish husband who owned a pub in Tipton, but she fell in with Tony Mason who was a war veteran and just a little younger than herself and he had become rather smitten with her.

"What's that bab?" Tony heard his name being called and he came through into the kitchen.

"That car parked up the road. Keeps coming back and just sits there. Is it a Jaguar?" Irene turned to face her partner and shrugged.

"No bab. It's a Mercedes. Cor believe we keep having these bloody Kraut cars in this country after we beat um in the war!"

"I ay seen it." Suzy Miller went back to her cigarette and barely gave the car a second thought.

The car parked in Beauty Bank Road was a blue 1973 Mercedes 350 SE W116, a huge luxury saloon which was the first Mercedes to be officially given the S-Class moniker. Inside the cabin, the single male occupant hid behind a pair of aviator sun glasses and chain smoked cigars. He watched the Miller's house intently as he pondered his life to date and the choices he had made. He was nearly 56 years old and he had found himself totally and utterly heartbroken. He had returned to

England after a narrow brush with death to look for his sweetheart and true love, but his dreams had been denied when he discovered that she had passed away just a few years previously. Now he was fabulously wealthy from the sale of his business interests abroad, but he was completely alone and drifting through old haunts, aimlessly and without purpose or relevance. He did not know where else to go.

The house in Beauty Bank had relevance to his past and he had already sat inside the decaying shell of his childhood home in Talbot Street Colley Gate, floated like an unnoticed ghost through his old stomping ground at the Haden Cross and visited his elderly relatives. Eventually he intended to catch up with his newfound son and try and build a relationship, but until then he continued to gaze at Irene Miller's home with a lost intensity that had no other purpose. *Should he knock the door? Should he go inside?* He had watched Suzy and her mother come and go from the house several times, so he was confident that they still lived there, but he had also seen an unknown man and he had almost felt a pang of jealousy for the life he had so easily left behind.

"Hi Harry." A sudden knock on the window came out of nowhere and Scriven had not seen the woman sneak up on the car. He opened the window and looked into the eyes of a woman he had not seen in nearly 20 years. She seemed immensely pleased to see him and Scriven could have not even began to understand just how much this woman had missed him and how much she was still utterly in love with him.

"Hi Suzy. It's been a long time. Yow still look good bab." Scriven's smile was genuine. *It was nice to hear her voice after so many years and she still had the same lustful, magnetic effect on him that she had always held.* She wore a polo-neck sweater with a short mini skirt and knee-high boots.

"Yow gunna teck me for a ride Harry?" Scriven raised his eyebrows at the fully intended erotic pun and he flung open the passenger side door so that she could get in. He followed her legs as she made her way round to the side of the car and got in. She put on a pair of sunglasses and settled back into the soft leather of the luxury vehicle.

Scriven fired up the V8 and the pair roared off down the road towards Haden cross where he turned left twice and then back up the hill towards Halesowen and one of their old haunts.

In December 1954, Harry Scriven and Suzy Miller had gazed lovingly into each other's eyes inside the King Edward VII pub on Stourbridge Road Halesowen next to the football ground. Their affair had been short lived and illicit. Scriven had been in his middle 30s and she had been barely 20 years old and the daughter of Scriven's then lady friend Irene Miller. They had held strong feelings for each other, but Suzy had not been able to save her older lover from a life of crime and horrific violence. She knew that at heart, Harry Scriven was a good man, but he had spent too long exposed to the brutal tendencies of his cousin Billy Mucklow.

"So…" Suzy broke the silence and took her long sip of her gin and tonic.

"So…" Scriven returned the syllable and thought about the animal lust he still felt for her.

"What happened in Spain?" Scriven looked away and tried to avoid the question. He did not wish to talk about recent history. He was more interested in the past and rekindling a physical contact with the daughter of his one-time spouse.

"What happened to Dick Hickman Harry?"

"Ar dow know bab." Scriven lied. "Why yow care abaaht Hickman?"

"Because me and him were together before he went to Spain. I know exactly why he went to Spain…" Suzy gave Scriven an intense look and he still found it hard to think of anything other than how much he needed to have her.

"Why did he come to Spain?" Scriven pretended he did not know about Dick Hickman's exploits on the Costa del sol.

"He went there with Micky Cole to take care of some business…" She crossed her legs sexily. "Now I know that Mick came back and I know that you are sat right in front of me, but what happened to Dick?"

"You know Micky Cole?" Scriven's ears pricked up at the mention of his recently found son.

"Yes." Suzy lit a cigarette and gave him a sultry look. "Do you know who Micky really is?" Scriven nodded and gave her a knowing look.

"I am back in England to try and get to know him. I wasn't there for my son when he needed me as a kid and now ar wanna try and make up for it." Scriven took a drink of his beer and continued to ogle her legs. Micky Cole was Scriven's son from an old relationship with his 'sweetheart' Lily Cole. He had not known anything about the existence of a son until a few months ago when Micky Cole and Dick Hickman had attempted to murder him and his cousin Bill Mucklow in Spain.

"Harry, truth be told ar dow give a fuck abaaht Hickman. He was a flash bastard and I don't know how I got mixed up with him, but ar just need to know what happened to him so I can move on with my life." Suzy's eyes pleaded with him for the truth and he had no reason to withhold it from her any longer.

"He's dead." Scriven was blunt and to the point.

"How?"

"Does that matter bab? He was a bad man and he did bad things."

"Did yow kill him?"

"No." Scriven did not lie.

"Who did?"

"That dow matter bab. He's gone. It's sad… He was one of the lads from the old days, but he fucked up." In reality Scriven did not give a shit about Dickie Hickman. Suzy stared thoughtlessly at her drink for an uninterrupted minute. All she could feel was numb. She hoped that Dick Hickman no longer suffered, that he no longer tortured himself and struggled to come to terms with the way his life had turned out. She hoped that he had finally found peace.

"What about Bill Mucklow?" She suddenly snapped out of her silence and turned to face Scriven again. The pub hadn't changed that much since they had been there as a couple in the 50s and Harry Scriven liked the traditional vibe that reminded him of his younger days. The bars in Spain were very different.

"Bill's still in Spain. Ar sold him my half of our business and he wants to stay out in the sun with his family."

"Wow! Can the great Harry Scriven survive without Billy Mucklow?" Now was not a time for her sarcasm and Scriven felt slightly offended.

"Well considering ar set up everything in Spain whilst Bill did 13 years in prison ar think I will manage fine!"

"Sorry Harry, ar day mean it like that." Suzy took another drag of her cigarette and blew smoke seductively into the air. She couldn't help it. "Ar remember when ar said that one day yow would hang for Billy Mucklow... Ar was wrong... Dick Hickman hung for both of you." Scriven frowned.

"What yow mean?"

"Dick rotted in jail whilst yow and Bill built an empire in Spain. When he finally came aaht he was so fucked up by what yow pair had done to him that he self-destructed and paid the ultimate price..." Scriven thought about what she had said for a minute and then sniggered. He could lose no sleep over Dickie Hickman. The man had abducted his former wife, tried to hold her for ransom and attempted to kill him, his son and his cousin.

"So what yow gunna do now?" Scriven took another drink of his beer and sat back in his chair. Suzy shrugged and looked totally helpless.

"Find another middle-aged gangster to please? Problem is I ay 25 anymore." She laughed subtly and pondered her situation.

"Yow'm better than that bab. Do yer still work behind the bar?" Suzy laughed again.

"I ay worked since that day in here when yow told me ar couldn't work at the Regis club anymore. It's easier to just be a slut and let bad men buy me champagne and new clothes." The outcome of Suzy's life did not surprise Scriven, but it disappointed him. He still lusted for her as he had in the 1950s. "What are yow gunna do now Harry?" She gave him a serious look and her hypnotic brown eyes met his with an intensity he had forgotten.

"Like ar said. Ar'm back in England to try and build a relationship with a son I never knew I had."

"Micky Cole… A chip off the ode block… Yow pair have a lot in common." Scriven detected a hidden meaning in Suzy's comment.

"Nothing happened between yow and Mick did it? How well do yow know him?" Scriven hated the thought of 'his' Suzy copulating with his son, it seemed immoral and incestuous.

"Fuck no." Suzy had tried to seduce Cole in an attempt to stop him from going after Scriven in Spain, *but Scriven did not need to know about that!* "Micky's loved up with a nice girl called Cathy. Her dad is some kind of gangster I think." Scriven was intrigued by the revelation about his son. He knew literally nothing about the man and was eager to catch up.

"Who's that?"

"Black guy called Bobby Murray." Scriven recognised the name instantly and if it was the same Bobby Murray he was thinking of he recalled fond memories of the man.

"Jamaican guy? Flash?"

"Yes, that's him. I only know from what Dick told me. Dick knew him too." Scriven nodded.

"Bobby used to work with Bill in the early 50s. He sells dope. Bit of a ladies man and ar bay a fan of drugs but I always liked the guy… Does Mick work for Bobby?" Scriven hated the thought of his son being mixed up in the same gangland he had grown up with, but he had not been there to make a difference and Micky Cole had very much taken the same career path as his father. Suzy put her drink on the table and held her hands in the air.

"Look Harry, ar dow know. I ay seen Mick or Cathy since he come back from Spain. Mick was working for Hickman before they went abroad but what has happened since ar dow know." Scriven nodded and returned to his drink. "So are we gunna sit around here all day and talk abaaht the past?" Suzy stubbed out her cigarette in the ashtray and pushed herself closer to Scriven. Her cheap perfume stirred him as it had done so many times and her bulging thighs that were generously displayed below her tiny skirt caused him to grit his teeth with pure need. She winked and placed her hand on his leg. "Or am yow gunna teck me somewhere a bit more private?"

Chapter 12

The sickly sweet aroma of marijuana trickled and teased his nostrils before he even got out of the car. Michael Cole, or Micky Cole as he was more frequently known was no stranger to drugs. He smoked his first joint at 13 and was experimenting with all manner of pills before he hit 15 years of age. His personal favourite pill were quaaludes, washed down with copious amounts of Scotch Whisky or cheap brandy. *Vodka and gin were for girls* and through his future father-in-law, he had also began to develop quite a taste for rum, the stronger the better. Before he reached the age of 20, Micky Cole had also gained a cocaine habit but had drawn the line at heroin and anything that involved needles. His childhood had been plagued by all sorts of sickening horrors and it was no surprise that Cole had turned to substance abuse. Unlike many addicts, Micky Cole was clear thinking and full of purpose. Narcotics and alcohol supplemented his life and gave him an edge that helped to mask his sensitivity and compassion. He was totally focused and after achieving his brutal and murderous life agendas, he was now in a position where he could build a successful and wealthy life for himself and his beloved fiancé Cathy Richardson.

Micky Cole was 25 years old, about 6 foot tall with broad shoulders and intense staring blue eyes. His dark hair was short and combed into an immaculate side parting with a good quantity of stubble that gave his face a somewhat dark appearance. He wore a smart black leather blazer with a white shirt that had oversized collars and almost always with a pair of dark aviator sun glasses.

Cole parked his aged Vauxhall Cresta outside of the Yorkshire Grey Pub on Dudley Road, Winson Green and got out. Upon exiting the car the smell of marijuana grew even stronger and Cole took a deep breath to savour it's relaxing odour.

"Can I watch the car for you man?" A young Caribbean boy of about 12 years of age approached Micky Cole. He had a huge afro and a beaming smile and Cole wondered why the boy was not in school.

"Sure kid... How much?" Cole smiled back and gave the child a high five. He knew that if he didn't pay his car would be vandalised and he could not be doing with the hassle.

"To you man, one pound!"

"A paahnd! Yow'm jokin' ay yer?" Cole laughed, the kid was trying and Cole couldn't help but respect the boys enterprise.

"No sir, I'm gunna give you a tip top service." The beaming smile was infectious.

"Here." Cole flung a 50 pence piece into the boys hand and the kid looked satisfied. "If it's still in one piece when ar come aaht yow get the rest then."

"Yes sir!" The lad saluted him in a mock gesture and stood watch as Micky Cole approached the front door of the pub. As he opened the heavy door a rich mixture of marijuana, beer, body odour and rum hit his nostrils and it seemed as if every face in the dark smoky bar was staring at him. It was extremely rare for a whiteman to enter the popular West Indian pub and Cole should have felt scared and intimidated, but he did not. In fact, he loved the atmosphere and as Across 110th Street by Bobby Womack blasted out of the jukebox, Micky Cole strutted confidently to the old wooden bar and ordered himself a large rum. His fiancé was half black and his association with the man he had come to meet would guarantee his safety in any of the 'Yardie' pubs and clubs in the midlands.

The barmaid had sumptuously tanned skin and her eyes were big, brown and tantalisingly enticing. She passed Cole his drink and then turned around to put the money in the cash register. Micky Cole could not help but notice her large, curvaceous rear end and it held his attention for several seconds.

"What is you lookin' at honky!" An angry voice beside him interrupted Cole's lascivious moment and he turned to face an irate man who had clearly been offended by the attention Cole had been giving the bar maid.

"Sorry mate... Is she yower lady?" Cole smiled apologetically and took a drink of his rum.

"No, she ain't my fuckin' lady, but she ain't for the likes of you mother fucker!" The man sucked his teeth and looked agitated.

"Sorry, is she your sister or something? Maybe she's your mother? I'm sure I ay the first bloke to look at your mother's ass?" Cole's temper got the better of him and he slammed his glass down hard on the table and waited for the first punch to be thrown.

"Gentlemen, gentlemen. What da fuck is going on here?" A voice Cole knew well approached at just the right time from out of the dark smoky bar room and the irate male suddenly backed off.

"This mother fucker is talkin' trash bout mar mamma!"

"I'm sure Mick didn't mean no offense. He's a good friend of mine." The man looked completely shocked and was surprised that Cole would have such a friend and he instantly backed off further.

"Ar'm sorry if I upset you mate." Cole extended his right hand and the man shook it sheepishly.

"Come over to my table Mick. We got business to discuss." Bobby Murray was a respected and feared man who had come to Britain in June 1948 as part of the original Windrush generation. He was also the father of Micky Cole's fiancé Cathy and Cole liked him. "You gotta be careful Mick. You cannot go around picking fights with people man. In our business it's best to stay low key, we wanna make money, not war... I don't need no Dickie Hickman wannabe working with me man." Cole wondered what was 'low key' about Bobby Murray. He was covered in brash yellow gold and his clothes were loud and expensive.

"I know Bobby sorry. That guy started it. I tried to apologise and make things right but he wouldn't have it." Cole was genuine and Murray could tell.

"Don't worry about it man. That guy is a stupid mother fucker. He won't give you no more trouble now he knows your working with me." Murray shot Cole a big wide smile and relaxed into his chair as the two men sat down at a small circular table in a discrete corner of the bar. "How is my daughter?"

"She's just fine Bobby. We are gunna get hitched next year and ar know she would love to have yow walk her down the aisle?"

"I would be honoured." Murray smiled again and clinked his rum glass against Cole's. "Now let's talk business man." Cole nodded and suddenly Murray became more serious and professional looking.

"My stepfather." Cole took a deep breath and contemplated the mental image of the man who had abused him throughout his childhood and murdered his maternal grandfather. "Cedric Tanner… He's dead."

"I know… It was in the papers… Nasty business." Murray took a drink of his rum and Cole suddenly had flashbacks to the horrific and harrowingly brutal night Cedric Tanner died. It made him smile.

"My stepfather, Cedric Tanner had a distribution network that stretched the length of the country. Now I wouldn't be able to take over the whole lot initially, but I have connections in the Wolverhampton and Dudley area and ar think that I could slide into the gap in the market…" Cole gave Murray a serious look. "I just need your product Mr Murray." Murray stroked his chin in thought.

"Ain't there no others from Tanner's organization who fancy taking over? Who could contest your position now that Tanner is dead?" Murray was very interested and offered his thoughts.

"There's one guy who has been pushin' dope raahnd the Lost City." Cole drained his rum and shrugged. "This chap reckons he's the new Mr Big or something, but he's small time. Ar thought me and yow could teck a ride over there now and you can see how serious I am?"

The Lost City was one of the first council estates built in Tipton in the 1920s. The real name of the estate was actually Moat Farm but became known as the Lost City as it was isolated from the rest of Tipton with only one road in and one road out. The estate would later become integrated with the rest of the town when the Glebefields and Gospal

Oak Estate's were completed. Between the Lost City and the Tibbington Estates, stood a patch of vast wasteland that had become a hub for teenagers, drug abuse and the occasional horse. This area was known locally as the 'Cracker' and it was here that Micky Cole expected to find his rival.

The Vauxhall Cresta pulled up at the edge of the Cracker and Cole and Murray were instantly greeted with hostile stares on account of the colour of Bobby Murray's skin. The area was a slum and home of some of the most deprived people in Britain, a white ghetto. Murray didn't really care. He had put up with it his entire life and he was not afraid of anyone. He was as familiar with the locality as his associate and future son in law Micky Cole and the area was known for its racist attitudes.

"Hey kid, where's Colin Perry?" Cole spoke out to a young lad who was fiddling around with an old motorbike that Cole assumed was probably stolen.

"Who want's ter fuckin' know?" The young lad spat on the floor and did not look Cole in the eye.

"I want ter fuckin' know!" Cole took out his wallet and puled out a pound note. "Ar can meck it worth yower while." The lad moved to grab the money but Cole pulled it back. "If he ay where yow tell me ar'll come back and give yow a damn good lampin!" Cole lied; he would never hurt a child, but he needed to make sure he was getting the right information.

"Yer see that oss over theyur?" The youth pointed to a brown horse that grazed freely about 50 yards away.

"Ar." Cole nodded and looked at the horse.

"Yer see that fence behind it and them trees?" Cole nodded again. "Colin Perry's behind them with a load of wenches. Sometimes he gives um free spliffs for blow jobs." Cole felt instantly sickened and shook his head. He gave the lad the money and he and Murray headed up towards where they hoped to find Perry.

Colin Perry was a rough, skinny man in his late 20s. He had worked for Cedric Tanner as a street dealer since he was a teenager and since the demise of his former employer, he had become obsessed with trying to take over his empire. In reality, he was a long way from achieving such success. He worked around the estates of Tipton and his supply of product was quickly running out, but in the absence of Cedric Tanner and his right hand man Davey Price, Perry was roaming the streets unchallenged and making out he was the new 'king.'

"Hello Colin." Micky Cole found the skinny drug dealer in exactly the spot the young lad had directed him to. He was surrounded by young girls, some of whom looked like they were probably still of school age.

"Mick... What can ar do for yer aer kid?" Perry strutted over and pushed his chest out and tried to make himself look as tall as he could.

"I'm taking over Colin. Cedric's old network belongs to me now. I've made arrangements with everyone from here to Cannock. You're the only one who's holding out on me Colin." Perry began to laugh obnoxiously.

"Hey Mick, gew Fuck yourself, this is mar turf."

"Ar'm gunna pretend ar didn't hear that Colin." Cole took off his aviators so that Perry could see into his intense eyes. "Yow work for me now."

"Go fuck yourself and fuck yower dead fuckin' mother too!" Perry was trying to play the 'tough guy' in front of his teenage fan club and in mentioning Micky Cole's deceased mother Lily, he had made a terrible mistake.

"Hey girls can yow leave us alone for a few minutes please?" Cole turned to face the young girls who continued to look on and stare. A couple of them turned and made off back towards the Lost City but a handful chose to stay. Cole took a deep breath in frustration and then pulled out a small handgun. "I said get the fuck aaht of here!" He screamed at the audience and pointed his gun in their direction. The girls got the message and quickly turned and fled.

"Make yow feel big does it? Scaring little girls?" Perry spoke again but Cole did not listen. He swiftly smashed Perry in the face with the butt of the gun and a tooth flew out as he fell back onto the floor with blood splattering his shirt. Micky Cole lunged forwards and placed his right foot down hard on Perry's windpipe, pinning him to the floor. He placed the gun back into his pocket and then pulled out a glass Lucozade bottle. Cole unscrewed the top and suddenly the stench of four-star petrol filled the air. The bottle was filled with the stuff and Cole proceeded to pour the entire contents onto Perry's head, dousing his face and greasy hair. Colin Perry spat and cursed and his eyes immediately began to sting like hell as the highly flammable liquid pierced through his eye lids. He screamed with the pain and flapped about with his arms but it was useless; he was pinned to the floor and he could not move. Cole pulled a cigarette from his pocket and placed it in his mouth.

"Ar think ar fancy a fake. Would yow like one Mr Murray?" Cole turned to face the older man and offered him his packet of Embassy Gold cigarettes.

"Yeah man, I could use a smoke right now." Murray grinned and took a cigarette from the packet. Cole then pulled out his gold plated lighter and lit Murray's cigarette before lighting his own. He breathed in deeply, filled his lungs with tobacco and then slowly exhaled as Perry was still pinned to the ground.

"Would yow like a light down there Colin?" Micky Cole then lowered the lighter to Perry's petrol doused face and held it close, both men fully aware that one flick of the flame would incinerate Perry's face and cause him immense suffering and almost certain death.

"No Mick, please, no, Mick, ar'm begging you!" The once arrogant and cocky drug dealer was now a jabbering wreck and he begged for his life.

"Who do you work for now Colin?"

"Yow Mick, ar'm sorry." Cole eased his grip from Perry's throat slightly and pulled a little pressure away from his foot.

"Good… If ar catch yow selling shit to kids or getting blow jobs from young girls again ar'll cut yower fuckin' fingers off!" Cole was not lying; he had done it before!

It was quite a drive back to the Yorkshire Grey pub in Winson Green and the two men laughed and joked as Cole's Cresta passed through Great Bridge, West Bromwich and Smethwick. Micky Cole had proven himself to the Jamaican father of his fiancé and now he would have the 'supplies' he needed to be able to take over his much-hated stepfather Cedric Tanner's drug distribution network in the Black Country. *He was going to be very rich!*

"There is just one question Mick." Murray's voice suddenly became serious.

"What's that Bobby?" Cole kept his eyes on the road ahead of them as they passed through the streets of West Brom.

"Where are you going to get finance for your first shipment man? Now I know you is as good as family, but we are talking about a lot of fuckin' dope. I is gunna need some security for my investment man."

"Dow worry abaaht finance Bobby. I know a fella who owes me big time and he is as rich as fuck… Leave it to me."

Chapter 13

At 5:30 on Friday the 17th May 1974, three car bombs exploded without warning in Dublin city centre. It happened in the middle of the evening rush hour and 33 innocent civilians and one unborn child lost their lives. This was the deadliest terror attack to occur in Ireland and had been carried out by the Ulster Volunteer Force, a loyalist paramilitary group from Northern Ireland.

Upon first hearing the news of the bombings, both Eddie Fennel and his wife Teresa had become incredibly concerned about the welfare of their family in Dublin. A discrete phone call between Teresa and her elder sister, whom she had secretly remained in touch with, eased their worries and none of their relatives had been caught up in the attacks. Fennel was now free to go to the pub!

Eddie Fennel's life had changed a lot since the mid-60s when he had used his cousin Billy Mucklow's allegiance with the Kray twins in London to prevent himself from coming under the thumb of Cedric Tanner. Tanner had been brutally murdered in obscene circumstances just a few months earlier at the end of 1973 and Eddie Fennel had certainly not lost any sleep over it. Fennel had used his tough guy persona to build a legitimate security business and alongside owning several pubs and businesses in the Cradley Heath area he also provided security and door staff to pubs and clubs throughout the midlands. He was making more money now from legitimate businesses than he was from crime. Of course, he still kept a hand in with the local underworld and since Bill Mucklow's release from prison in 1968 he had kept in contact with his old army commander and business associate. Just a few months previously he had been 'sent for' and had had to travel to Spain with his family to meet with Bill Mucklow and Harry Scriven where he was quizzed about the murder of the former family associate Eli Davis.

"Ar dunno why yow still drive that ode Jag Eddie." Tummy 'Ducks' sat in the back room of the Neptune on Powke lane with his boss Eddie Fennel. Fennel had been relieved to get to the pub. The drama in Dublin had understandably caused some upset for Fennel's wife Teresa but now he was finally getting his Friday night quota of beer. Fennel's concern had been more for the sake of his wife. Fennel was in his 50s now and his grandmother had died long ago. He had no contact with his family in Ireland, not even with his cousin Johnny O'Connor who had saved his life back in the 40s.

"There ay nothing wrong with that Jag Tum!" Fennel still drove the same bright red Jaguar mk2 he had owned since the 1960s, but he liked it.

"With all the money we got coming in now Eddie, yow should treat yourself mate." Tummy 'Ducks' had just purchased a brand-new Rover P6 and he could not understand why his employer did not update his own vehicle. Fennel shook his head.

"Sometimes, flash ay always the best Tum... Last thing ar need is to attract attention from the law or rival firms who want a piece of the action... Look what happened with ode Cedric Tanner back in the 60s! Ron and Reg went inside 5 years agew and Billy Mucklow ay showin no signs of coming back from Spain so we'm on our own mate..."

"Ar thought yow was a legitimate businessman now?" Tummy 'Ducks' smirked sarcastically.

"Kind of, but the Inland fuckin' Revenue dow know that!" The last thing Fennel needed was a stretch in prison on tax evasion charges. Eddie Fennel suddenly remembered that it was his turn to get a round of drinks in. He felt in his pocket for his wallet and a familiar face appeared in the doorway.

"Hello Eddie... Aer bin yer?" Harry Scriven was dressed in a dark blue three-piece suit with a white shirt and red tie. His thick neck was threatening to burst out of his tight collar and the expression on his face was genuinely happy to see an old friend.

"Fuckin hell! Harry Scriven! Where's yower fuckin' hair gone aer kid?" Fennel burst out in laughter and rose to embrace his friend and distant cousin.

"What yow mean? Ar bay had no hair since 1951!" The two men laughed.

"When did yow get back from Spain Mukka?"

"Bin back a couple of weeks now mate." Scriven looked happy and Fennel remembered that he was supposed to be fetching a round of drinks.

"What yow having Harry? Pint of mild?"

"It's alright Eddie, aer kid Micky's bringing a tray full of ale in for all of us." Fennel looked confused.

"Who's Micky?"

"He's mar son Eddie… Ar never knew nothing abaaht him then he turned up in Spain." Fennel was surprised at the revelation. "Do yow remember that wench are used to knock abaaht with when ar come ahht the air force after the war?" Fennel shrugged. "Her name was Lily Cole. Her ode mon had a scrap yard over the road from here." Scriven gestured towards the window. Norman Cole's scrapyard had been literally just over the road from the Neptune pub. Fennel nodded.

"Ar. I remember… Nice wench." Fennel could not have known just how much Harry Scriven really had loved Lily Cole, but it wasn't to be.

"Well Lily was pregnant with Micky when we split up… He's a chip off the ode block, yow might have heard of him? Micky Cole?" Fennel raised his eyebrows. How could he not have heard of Micky Cole? He was a borderline psychotic thug who had stirred up trouble locally the previous year when he had been working for Dickie Hickman.

"I know the name… Works for Dick Hickman… Drugs…" Fennel shook his head. Narcotics did not impress him. Scriven lent closer so that he could whisper.

"No mate… Hickman ay around no more… We woe be seeing him again." Scriven had said enough and Eddie Fennel understood. He did not need to ask any more questions. "Micky works with me now… We can all be a family business again and meck a fuck load of cash! Like the ode days." Scriven spoke enthusiastically about the prospect of working with his son Micky Cole and Fennel wondered what he was referring to.

"What yow mean we can all be a family business again? Yow saahnd like Billy fuckin' Mucklow mate. Yow the new gaffer or summet?"

"Billy ay around no more Eddie. Ar want yow on board with me and Mick. Yow'm family and we've got something up our sleeves that with yower help will meck us all rich." A lorry thundered past the window and Fennel was temporarily distracted by how close it had passed to the side of the building.

"Ar thought yow'd med enough cash selling yower share of the hotel in Spain to Bill?" Scriven was surprised that Fennel knew about his business but then he remembered that Fennel spoke regularly on the telephone to Billy Mucklow on the Costa del sol. Scriven nodded and the two men sat down as they waited for Micky Cole to arrive with the drinks.

"It ay about me Eddie… Ar missed enough of mar lad's life and ar wanna meck it up to him now by helping him to earn his own cash." Scriven had always strived to try and do the right thing, but what he was about to tell Eddie Fennel would be deeply out of character.

"Look Harry, I will listen to what yow and yower lad have got to say but ar'm a legitimate businessman now." Scriven smirked and then burst into laughter.

"Legitimate businessman, yow? Yow got more scams up yer sleave than ode Willie Mucklow and Eli Davis had back in the 20s and 30s, and that's bloody sayin' summet!" Before Fennel could answer, Micky Cole appeared with a tray full of beer for all of them. The men thanked him and Cole sat down next to his father so that he was facing Eddie Fennel and Tummy 'Ducks.'

"Hello Mr Fennel. Nice to meet you." Cole was polite and respectful and he extended his right arm to shake Eddie Fennel's hand.

"Hi kid… Aer bin yer?" Fennel returned the gesture and Scriven was pleased that the meeting had got off to a good start. "This is mar associate Tum." Fennel introduced the man to his right and Cole reached out to shake his hand as well.

"Me and Harry have got a business venture we would like you to be involved in Mr Fennel." Scriven listened to the words of his son and felt a tinge of disappointment when he was referred to as Harry. *But what could he expect? How could he expect the man to call him 'dad' after such a short period of time.*

"Please, call me Eddie." Fennel lit a cigar and sat back in his seat in anticipation.

"Just listen to what he has to say Eddie." Harry Scriven interrupted the exchange, fearful of Fennel's reaction. Fennel nodded and took a drag of his silky-smooth cigar and Cole continued to speak.

"I understand that yow own a security firm that provides the muscle that manages the doors of pubs and clubs around the midlands?"

"Yes… All except the Fewtrell's places in Brum, they manage their own security."

"Have yow ever heard of a fella called Cedric Tanner?" Cole could hardly bring himself to say the name of his deceased stepfather and he could tell by Fennel's reaction that they both shared a hatred for the man.

"Yes… I'd like to shake the hand of the fella that set the bastard on fire and watched him burn!" Eddie Fennel had loathed Cedric Tanner and Cole smiled subtly.

"Cedric had an impressive drug distribution network that I now control on the streets. What I need now is access to the pubs and clubs… Everyone knows that whoever controls the doors controls what gets inside and you control the doors." Micky Cole spoke with his hands and Fennel closed his eyes and shook his head.

"You surprise me Harry." Fennel looked over at Scriven and gave him a look of utter disappointment and disgust.

"Mick, why dow yow and Tummy 'Ducks' gew into the bar for a bit." Scriven could tell by Fennel's reaction that things were not going well and he wanted to speak to his distant cousin alone. Micky Cole and Tummy 'Ducks' picked up their beer and made their way towards the exit.

"It's good business Mr Fennel, family should all look out for each other." Cole chose his parting words wisely in a bid to persuade both his new-found father and Eddie Fennel. Fennel waited for 'Ducks' and Cole to leave the room and then gave Scriven another look of disgust.

"What the fuck has happened to yow Harry?" Fennel sighed deeply and then looked away. "The Harry Scriven ar knew was against drugs... Ar remember back in the 50s when Bill went into business with that Jamaican fella and we all spoke out about it... Bill didn't do it for long."

"It ay 1951 anymore Eddie." Scriven banged his glass down on the table and adopted a more assertive tone. "All we are talking about is a bit of weed... Mick dow have nothing to do with the hard stuff... He's a good kid at heart and he woe have that heavy shit on his conscience." Fennel looked away. He was not interested.

"Look Eddie, we are gunna meck serious money on this aer kid.. The supplier is a close relative of Micky's Mrs and he's getting a bostin' deal." Fennel turned back to face Scriven and exhaled cigar smoke. *He understood what was going on fully.*

"Yow ay doing yower kid no favours Scriv... Ar can see what's happening here... Yow'm trying to meck up for lost time and the fact that yow've been a shit dad... But being a parent dow work like that mate. You dow just give yower kid everything they want just to get in their good books! Yow cor buy kids Harry." Fennel continued to look at Scriven and for a second he thought he saw a tear in the eye of one of the toughest men he had ever known.

"What am ar supposed to do Eddie? If yow knew what my son went through as a kid you would help us. I owe him big time and I've gotta do whatever it takes."

"Even if it means sacrificing your own morals Harry? What would Bill say?" Fennel could see Scriven's dilemma, but he did not agree with narcotics, even if it was just marijuana.

"I've spoken to Bill… He's all for it Eddie, he knows that times are changing and we have to move with the times. If we dow teck over Tanner's empire, somebody else will. And then they will come after us." Scriven was feeling weary of the situation already. He had not missed gangland politics and he wished that he had remained in Spain, but he had to do the 'right' thing and he could not make enough sacrifices for the sake of his son. "All you will have to do is let Micky's boys into the venues. If they ever start pushing pills or cocaine then yow have mar blessing to sling um aaht… Come on Eddie, do it for me, do it for the family and legacy of all that we had back in the day." Harry Scriven surprised himself with the spiel that was coming from out of his mouth. All he wanted was to make his son happy and try and make up for lost time. He also knew that in having Eddie Fennel onside they would be able to keep an eye on Cole and make sure that he was not going to be dealing in harder drugs which Harry Scriven would most certainly not approve of. He wanted to buy a relationship with his son and he wanted to keep him safe from the dangers and prison sentences associated with harder narcotics. *Of course, he hated drugs just as much as Eddie Fennel, but he needed to have some control over what Mick was doing and the only way he could do that was by having Fennel and his men on board to keep an eye on him.* Fennel shook his head yet again and sighed.

"Yow sure he's not selling cocaine or pills?"

"Yes… That's why I need yow involved so we can meck sure he ain't getting in too deep and we can meck a few quid too." Scriven gulped down a big swallow of his beer. He could see that Fennel was slowly starting to come around. "Ar dow want drugs on the street as much as yow dow Eddie. This way we get some control over it." Fennel thought again. His wife had been eager for him to enter the drugs trade because she knew how much money they stood to make. *If Scriven was right then he could make his wife happy. He had been doing well anyway with his security business but maybe now he would be able to buy a villa in Spain like Billy Mucklow? His wife had thoroughly enjoyed going to Spain the previous year when they stayed with Mucklow's family on the Costa del sol. Maybe he could make that villa dream a reality for his beloved Teresa? Even if he did have to sell his soul to the devil. Again...*

Chapter 14
June 1975

One year passed and Micky Cole's business venture went from strength to strength. Elsewhere in the midlands, Aston Villa football club won the football league cup whilst chasing promotion from the second division with a goal from Ray Graydon in a 1-0 win against Norwich City at Wembley. In Longbridge, British Layland released the famous 'wedge' shaped Austin 1800 that would later become known as the Austin Princess and Black Country rock stars John Bonham and Robert Plant performed with their band Led Zepplin at 5 sold out shows at London's Earls Court.

In just over 12 months, Micky Cole's life had changed considerably. He had married his sweetheart Cathy Richardson and Harry Scriven had been proud to be his son's best man with Bobby Murray walking his daughter down the aisle. The newlyweds had then moved into a plush detached house in the affluent and highly sought-after area of Pedmore in Stourbridge. Cole had also changed his beat-up old Vauxhall Cresta for a brand-new BMW E12 535i and he was every inch the dapper and successful businessman. The fact that his business happened to be the sale of highly illegal drugs was a matter for his conscience; but seeing as he was a high functioning addict himself, he saw himself as a champion of the people, giving the punters what they wanted in an era of prohibition. The situation presented more of a moral dilemma for Eddie Fennel, but his wife now travelled in style with her brand-new Lotus Europa and the family had enjoyed another luxurious holiday on the Costa del sol with the Mucklows. Eddie Fennel may have had his reservations about drugs, but he certainly was not complaining about the financial rewards. He had become close with Harry Scriven and Micky Cole and the trio regularly socialised. They would go drinking together often and their families had also become close. Harry Scriven was a happy man. He had built a relationship with his son and he had moved into a huge art deco house on Haden Hill Road near the crossroad with Coombs Road and Furnace Hill in Halesowen. He had also settled down with and got engaged to Suzy Miller which had been awkward on account of his previous relationship with Suzy's mother Irene, but love was love… Teresa Fennel, Suzy Miller and Cathy Cole had their friendship somewhat forced upon them as their other halves became increasingly isolated with each other. Drugs were a risky business and it made sense for them to remain low key and keep their social circle tight.

On Monday the 2nd of June 1975, something quite remarkable happened. As Eddie Fennel walked his Staffordshire Bull Terrier through Homer Hill Park, known locally as the 'rec' in Cradley, he looked up into the sky with amazement as snow began to fall! Snow in June was completely unheard of, but for some insane reason it was actually snowing!

Homer Hill Park was opened in October 1922. In February 1919, it had been suggested that a public memorial should be constructed in Cradley to remember those who had served and died during the First World War. On Monday the 1st of March 1920, a Mr R. Green of Halesowen Urban District Council suggested that a recreation ground or open space should be part of the plans for a memorial scheme. On the 11th of October 1922, Homer Hill Recreation Ground trust agreed that 'the council, its successor as assignees will forever hereafter support, maintain and improve the said hereditaments as and for the purposes of public recreation ground.' With this, Homer Hill Park was opened to the public and Eddie Fennel would later become a regular user of the space for the purpose of exercising his dogs.

After the formation of the park, it was decided to site a band stand within its grounds so that musicians could perform there for the entertainment of the local population. It took several years for the funds to be raised but on Saturday the 28th of January 1928, Viscount Cobham declared the bandstand officially open. In his opening speech he reminded everyone present of the sacrifices that had been made by many during the Great War:

"There are those who have suffered intensely, who have made the great sacrifice, not only men who were crippled with wounds and disease, but the women who gave their men into the struggle and whose men did not come back again, happy are they for they have earned the undying gratitude of their country."

As an old soldier himself and a veteran of the Second World War, Eddie Fennel found peace amongst the memorial gardens and would often reflect upon his friends and comrades who had not made it home.

As the freak snow shower intensified, Fennel called his dog, attached it's lead and proceeded to take shelter in the old band stand. Under it's cover also stood a man whom Fennel estimated to be about 10 years older than himself. Fennel thought he recognised him from somewhere, but the man's gaze was haunted and disturbed and he looked straight through the middle-aged gangster. Fennel could not help but feel pity for the man, whatever it was that was bothering him must have been pretty awful. Fennel's dog tried to jump up the man and lick him affectionately but the man did not flinch and had no interest in the canine. Fennel calmed his dog and the animal rested obediently at his feet.

"This is strange ay it mate? Bloody snow in June!" Fennel tried to engage the morbid man in conversation as he took out his cigarettes. He lit one for himself and then offered the packet to the lonesome figure who stood beside him. The man's eyes showed a hint of gratitude and he took a cigarette and said thank you, his voice quivering as he spoke. Fennel produced his lighter and lit the man's cigarette. "Yow alright Chap? Yow dow look too good." Tears began to roll across the man's face as he stared ceaselessly into the white snow that was beginning to settle on the park grounds.

"This weather ay a freak… It's a sign from her…" The man's voice was horse and frail, as if he had been crying for some time and

Fennel was beginning to think that maybe he should have kept his mouth shut. "Her always loved the snow…" There was an eerie silence and as the snow fell peacefully upon the grass it was as if the whole world had stopped and not a sound could be heard apart from the incessant beating heart of a heavy hammer that echoed hauntingly through the Black Country air. "When her was a kid, we used ter meck snowmen… Her always loved that." There was another long pause and the two men continued to watch the snow. "My daughter died on Saturday night." The announcement came suddenly and Fennel was lost for words.

"Ar'm so sorry to hear that mar mon." Fennel did not know what to say and he patted the stranger on the back.

"Her was 27 years ode… Have yow got kids?" Fennel nodded.

"Yes… One daughter."

"Her had 3 babees and now they've been took into orphanages… Her wore married yer see." Tears streamed freely from his eyes and the man broke down. "Ar could gew home, but mar Mrs is devastated an ar just dow know what to say to her. We have lost our beloved daughter and what life will our grand kids have now?" Fennel looked at the floor and breathed into his cigarette. "They have been split up from each other and we've been told we cor see um no more…"

"What happened to their mother?" Fennel was curious to know what had killed the poor man's daughter so suddenly.

"Her worked hard for them babees. Her never went aaht nowhere, but last Saturday ar told her to have a night aaht with her friends from work. Me and the Mrs had the kids… Anyway, she had too much to drink and some filthy bastard gave her a tablet… Some filthy drug he had bought in the club." The man put his head in his hands and sobbed. "She ay never took drugs before an it killed her…" Fennel froze and could not look the man in the eye. Despite his initial insistence on no pills and cocaine in their business, Fennel knew that Micky Cole had branched out into harder more lucrative narcotics, but they had all been so busy enjoying the financial rewards that Fennel had elected to turn a blind eye… *His wife had a new sports car, he had built an extension on his house, he was looking at properties in Spain, he had put his daughter through university, he smoked expensive cigars and his wife wore designer clothing- and this man's daughter was dead...* Fennel felt suddenly nauseous. *He did not know for a fact that it had been one of Micky Cole's men that had sold the tablet, but it was highly likely and what difference did it make? There must be hundreds if not thousands of other people up and down the country who were going through the same ordeal as this man.* Fennel thought about the three orphaned children and the lives that they would now lead and he likened them to the disrupted and disturbed childhood of Micky Cole. *How ironic,* he thought, *that the circle would remain unbroken.* Eddie Fennel reached into his wallet and pulled out a crisp £20 note.

"Here mate... Teck this..." The man looked at the money with utter disgust.

"What's this? Why? Ar dow need yower money?" The man was offended. "Do yow think that's gunna help? Do yow think that it will bring mar daughter back?" The man had no knowledge of Fennel's business but his words still rang true. He swiftly turned around and rushed off into the snow, his figure quickly becoming invisible as he disappeared into the snowy white abyss of his grief.

As Fennel stood holding the worthless money, he felt cold, shallow and alone with his total utter self-loathing. All that he had earned, all that he had achieved and all of the materialistic wealth that he had amassed were simply irrelevant...

Chapter 15

Roger de Montgomery was one of William the Conquerors chief aids and he came to Britain with the Norman invasion in 1066. He eventually became the first Earl of Shrewsbury and was responsible for the construction of many Norman buildings throughout England. One of these buildings was the original church of St John the Baptist in Halesowen which was mentioned in the Domesday survey of 1086. The modern-day structure was built in 1120 and its famous tower and spire would go on to become synonymous with the town. It was here that on Saturday the 12th of July 1975, Harry Scriven married Suzy Miller.

Harry Scriven and Suzy Miller's wedding was a small and elaborate occasion. The guests included a handful of Suzy's female friends and their husbands, Irene Miller and her partner Tony, Harry's parents Horace and Eliza, Willie Mucklow and his wife, Eddie Fennel, his wife Teresa and their daughter Tina, Barry O'Leary and his lady friend, Micky Cole and his wife Cathy, Bobby Murray and a female companion and Bill Mucklow and his family who had come over from Spain.

The couple said their vows and then gathered outside the historic church for photographs with their guests. Much to the disappointment of Billy Mucklow, Micky Cole had been chosen to be best man but his behaviour throughout the ceremony had been somewhat erratic. He was sweating heavily and he had been finding it hard to stand up straight. It was no secret that he was a drug addict and he had been an embarrassing talking point amongst the guests as he had almost fallen over in the church, dropped the ring and struggled to walk in a straight line. Suzy Miller, now Scriven, was feeling particularly disappointed with Cole's conduct, but Harry Scriven as usual could see no wrong in his treasured son.

As the newlyweds had been driven from the church to a plush wedding reception at the exclusive Plough and Harrow hotel on the

Hagley Road, Birmingham, Suzy had tried to speak to her husband about her concerns with Micky's behaviour, but Scriven would have none of it.

    The Plough and Harrow hotel was built in 1704 and was considered to be one of the finest hotels in Birmingham. It was popular with celebrities and sports stars and was a regular haunt of the England cricketers when they played test matches at the nearby Edgbaston cricket ground. Harry Scriven had paid a lot of money for the occasion and it had all been for Suzy's benefit. He would have been happy with a cob and a packet of scratchings in the Haden Cross, but Bobby Murray had paid a lot of money for Cathy and Micky's wedding and it was only right that he was seen to be 'keeping up appearances.'
    Suzy wore a beautiful ivory dress with a corset that accentuated her generous cleavage and Harry simply could not take his eyes of his gorgeous bride. *Sure, she had had her fair share of ex partners but so had he!* As she made her way around the elaborately decorated tables in the wedding reception, speaking to the guests and thanking them for their gifts, Scriven noticed that Micky Cole was alone at the bar. As he approached his son he noticed him take a pill from out of his pocket and then swiftly swallow it down with neat Brandy. Cole ordered another double and staggered as Scriven joined him at the bar.
    "Yow ok aer kid?" Scriven had promised Suzy that Micky would not let them down and they still had the best man's speech to come.
    "Ar saahnd." Cole could not look his father in the eyes and he almost fell over again. Scriven's initial reaction was to get angry and give the man a slap and if it had of been anyone else then that was exactly what he would have done.
    "Yer dow look it mate, yow got a speech to do!" Scriven was genuinely starting to get anxious but he could not let on to Suzy.
    "Can I ask yow something Harry?" Cole grasped the bar tightly and composed himself as he looked deep into Scriven's eyes.
    "Of course Mick… Yow can ask me anything." Scriven braced himself.

"Why day yow marry mar mother?" Cole was deadly serious and tears appeared in his eyes.

"It's hardly the time to bring it up Mick, but ar'll be honest with yer... Ar loved yower mother more than ar loved any other woman... But it day work ahht... Maybe one day I will gew into greater detail but now is not the time." Scriven suddenly felt immense guilt. The same guilt that he had been feeling constantly since finding out about the existence of his son. *If he had not abandoned Lily Cole, then they could have been one happy family and Cole would not have had to endure the horrendous childhood that he had suffered... But what could he do about it now?* Micky Cole looked unsatisfied with the response and he shook his head and went off in search of his wife Cathy who had the quaaludes.

"This place brings back some memories Eddie." Bill Mucklow and Eddie Fennel had disappeared into a side bar so that they could have a discrete chat before the wedding breakfast and speeches. "Back in the day ar used to drink champagne in here with ode Isiah Boswell... Do yow remember him Eddie? He was boss of The Brummie boys. Ar was good mates with him for a while." Fennel nodded. He remembered Isiah Boswell from the old days. Mucklow continued to reminisce about old times with Isiah Boswell and the 1950s in general and Fennel waited for the ideal opportunity to bring up the dilemma he was suffering with. Mucklow had consumed several drinks and he was in a particularly chatty mood and it was almost impossible to get a word in.

"What do you think of Micky Cole Bill?" Fennel finally found his opportunity.

"He's Harry's boy ay he. It dow matter what we think... He had a fucked-up upbringing by all accounts." Mucklow took a gulp of his beer and lit a fat cigar. "Hey wench." Mucklow caught the attention of an attractive barmaid who was dressed in a tight little hotel uniform that Mucklow found particularly alluring. "Can yow fetch us two large scotches please?" Mucklow handed her a £5 note and winked. "Keep the change bab." The barmaid smiled flirtatiously and went to fetch the drinks. "Hers on the game." Mucklow looked at Fennel and smiled lasciviously.

"How'd yow know that Bill?" Fennel laughed.

"Ar can just tell." Mucklow sucked on his cigar and Fennel thought he looked just like Winston Churchill as he sat back and exhaled.

"What do yow think of this drugs business Bill?" Fennel finally spat out the question he had been meaning to ask for a while. Mucklow grunted.

"It's a dirty business and it ay for me, but it's the future… Ar'v med mar money and ar'm happy in the sun, but young Mick wants to prove himself and Harry's doing all he can to meck sure that Micky gets what he wants."

"But that's the problem Bill, Harry is blind when it comes to Mick. He throws money at him and lets him do whatever he wants." Mucklow agreed with Fennel but he just shrugged. "The problem I have got is Micky was only supposed to be selling weed, but he is into the harder stuff now Bill and ar dow like it. Me and Harry could end up in prison for the rest of our lives at this rate, yow know they come down harsh on hard drugs… Besides, it dow sit right with mar conscience. Ar'v tried talking to Harry but he just woe listen where Micky's concerned." Mucklow looked deep in thought and then he finally spoke.

"If Harry cor keep Micky in check then ar may have to hang abaaht for a bit… Ar'll come and see yer in the week and perhaps we can gew and have a word with Micky." Mucklow's words pleased Eddie Fennel. Ever since his encounter in Homer Hill Park with the bereaved father he had wanted out of the drugs business and he had tried everything to try and get through to Harry Scriven. He felt relieved knowing that the mighty Billy Mucklow was back around and would help him to try and straighten things out.

The grand wedding meal passed by without drama and finally it was time for the speeches. Harry Scriven hated public speaking and he was relieved that he would not be called upon to make a speech. First up was Billy Mucklow. He had not been chosen to be the best man, but he had still insisted on an obligatory speech. Mucklow had a talent for it and he spoke at length about his and Scriven's childhood growing up together and how Scriven had been more like a brother to him than a cousin. He had also shared the odd joke and humorous memory and he had left the guests clapping and feeling highly entertained. Next up was the official best man, Micky Cole and the applause died away as the guests sat in anticipation. He had not prepared anything and he had hoped to improvise a speech on the day but by now he was so messed up on alcohol and narcotics that he was struggling to function. A few people whispered amongst themselves as Cole was visibly in no state to be public speaking. The guests were wondering what was about to happen.

Micky Cole rose to his feet slowly and he instantly stumbled slightly and had to steady himself by grasping the table tightly. Beads of sweat ran down his forehead and before he spoke he belched and his eyes rolled in his head.

"Good evening ladies and gentlemen… Please excuse me cus I am a little bit pissed…" Cole belched again and started to laugh but the room remained silent.

"So… If yow dow know me ar'm Micky Cole and mar father abandoned mar mother before I was born…" The guests held their breaths and Scriven was lost as to what to do as his new wife held her head in her hands. "Ar watched my grandfather get murdered when I was four years old and I was abused pretty much everyday throughout mar childhood… Maybe if Harry had of married mar mother in 1949 that would not have happened but it fuckin' did… As you will all know, mar father Harry Scriven used to hurt people for a living on the orders of that man over there." Cole stumbled yet again and pointed coarsely at Billy Mucklow who remained unphased. "They were gangsters, thugs, criminals, hoodlums, fraudsters, all raahnd nasty bastards… But ladies and gentlemen, I ay much better… I sell drugs to kids in nightclubs and I pay blokes to hang around on council estate looking for junkies." Cole looked at the floor and almost broke into tears. He was clearly not proud of what he did for a living and as the cocktail of alcohol and drugs played tricks on his brain, he felt sick with the responsibility and realisation of that what he was doing to young minds, was the same as what had happened to him. "Yow probably think that ar'm a bastard, but ar dow give a fuck what yow think of me... Harry should have been marrying mar mother... And guess what? She's fuckin dead... Maybe if good old Harry had of done the right thing she would still be alive... Instead, my father chose to marry Suzy Miller." Cole spat across the top table as he erupted into laughter at the mention of Suzy's name. "The biggest fuckin' slag gewin... Ar reckon her must have fucked every gangster wannabe this side of fuckin' London... What a nasty slut... Her even tried it on with me!" Suzy had heard enough, she suddenly stood up and slapped her new husband hard across the face.

"Why do you let him say these things Harry? You would not allow anyone else in this world to speak about me like that." With that, Suzy ran out of the room in floods of tears and Scriven sat red faced and embarrassed looking at the table.

"Wow, look at that bitch gew!" Micky Cole could not help himself and continued to speak, but by now his wife Cathy had come to his side and tried to get him to sit down. She was also ashamed and embarrassed of her husband's behaviour and she was at her wits end with his constant abuse of alcohol and drugs. As the circus unfolded, Eddie Fennel and Billy Mucklow looked at each other from across their tables and nodded. Something needed to be done...

Chapter 16

The Sweeney starring John Thaw and Dennis Waterman was an ITV television series that was originally broadcast between January 1975 and December 1978. The gritty drama was based around the activities of the London Police unit the flying squad and the show's title was derived from the cockney rhyming slang Sweeney Todd – flying squad. The show was hugely popular and was particularly known for its cars. The lead character was driven around in a Ford Consul 3.0 GT which was a lower spec variant of the Ford Granada. When Billy Mucklow came back to England for Harry Scriven's wedding in the summer of 1975, he decided to remain in the country for a few weeks and he rented a Consul 3.0 GT as a hire car for use whilst he was in the country.

"Its always bin like the wild fuckin' west raahnd here." Bill Mucklow negotiated the streets of Tipton and pulled up the Ford on a stretch of road next to the 'Cracker' between the Lost City and Tibbington estates.
"Ar thought we were looking for drug dealers not osses?" Eddie Fennel got out of the passenger side and the two walked onto the wasteland that was littered with several horses. A group of teenagers sat in a circle smoking weed nearby and Mucklow and Fennel approached them.
"Hey… Can any of yow lot tell me where ar can get my hands on some mandies?" Mucklow felt awkward asking the youngsters about drugs. Mandies was the street name given to methaqualone. A sedative and hypnotic medication that was also known as a quaalude.
"Fuck off coppers!" The teenagers wrongfully assumed that Mucklow and Fennel were police detectives based on the fact that they were wearing suits.

"We ay bloody coppers. Do yow know how much these Italian shoes cost? Cor buy these on a coppers wage." The teenagers were still not interested so Mucklow pulled out a pound note. "Who wants this? Just tell me where ar can get me some mandies." One of the teens went to grab the money and Mucklow pulled it away. "Where kid?"

"Raahnd the back of that fence over there. Ask for Colin." The teen went to accept the money but Mucklow put it back into his pocket.

"Fuck off kid... Ar bay giving yow money so yow can gew and smoke more of that shit." Mucklow felt a little hypercritical as he had dabbled with marijuana himself over the years, but he did not want to fund any bad habits of the younger generation.

Colin Perry was sat on top of an old wooden cabinet that had been abandoned in the wasteland and was smoking a spliff. Next to him was a 14-year-old girl who was performing an inappropriate act on him and Mucklow and Fennel were instantly sickened. As the two suited, middle aged men approached him he was glad that he wasn't carrying any drugs as he also assumed that they were Police officers. He had his gear stashed in a local flat with a teenage lady friend. It was not safe to keep all of his supply on him over the 'Cracker' in case he was robbed and then he would be in debt to Micky Cole and that was not a good place to be.

"Ar'm looking for a fella called Colin." Mucklow strolled over casually. He instantly took a dislike to the tall skinny man and Mucklow thought that he had a face like a ferret. The young girl pulled away from the drug dealer and Perry pulled up his flies.

"Who wants ter know? We dow have coppers raahnd here." Perry spat aggressively and it landed on Mucklow's Italian shoes. Bill Mucklow starred at his shoes for about ten seconds and then he slapped Perry hard with the back of his hand, knocking him off the cabinet and onto the floor.

"Fuck off copper!" Perry screamed defiantly and Mucklow responded by giving him a hard kick in the rib cage that winded him badly.

"Yow really dow know who I am do yer mate?" Mucklow lit a cigar and stood over the dealer. "When ar'm finished with yow, yow'm gunna wish ar was a fuckin' copper! Now am yow Colin?" Mucklow went to kick him again but Perry raised his hands up and protested.

"Yes ar'm Colin, leave off." Mucklow restrained his foot and took a drag of his cigar.

"See, it wore that hard was it? Ar was told yow could get me some mandies?" Perry struggled back to his feet.

"Yow dow seem the type to be after mandies?"

"They ay for me… Now can yow get them or not?" Perry smiled.

"How do ar know yow ay a copper?" Mucklow thought for a minute and then punched Perry full on in the face with a straight right hand that sent him back down to the floor and almost knocked him unconscious.

"Grab him." Mucklow barked the order and both him and Fennel sprung into action. They tied Perry's hands firmly behind his back and then stood either side of him so that they could frog march him back to the Ford Consul. Once at the car, Mucklow hit him hard again and then the two men bundled him into the boot before slamming down the lid and locking him in. Mucklow and Fennel then got back into the car and drove towards Rowley Regis where Fennel had a lock up garage. *It was good to have the old Billy Mucklow back.* Fennel thought to himself as he lit a cigarette and felt relieved that Mucklow had not turned soft in the Mediterranean sun.

The black Ford Consul pulled up outside Fennel's lock up on the Brickhouse Estate Rowley Regis and Mucklow opened the boot. Perry had been hammering and banging on the inner lid throughout the journey and Mucklow had simply turned up the radio and drowned out the noise with a mixture of disco, soul and funk. Fennel and Mucklow pulled him out of the boot and frog marched him into the garage where they secured him to a wooden chair in the middle of the room. Fennel pulled the door shut and the room descended into absolute darkness. He went for the light switch but Mucklow stopped him.

"Leave it a minute Eddie. Ar want this drug pushing piece of shit to sit in the dark for a bit cus ar'm gunna hurt him real bad… Only in the dark he woe see me… He will know that ar'm there and he will know that ar could strike at any moment, but he woe know where." Mucklow then lent back against the wall and waited for a full hour so that the fear and tension could rise. Perry went from shouting and swearing insults to crying and begging and Mucklow had not even lifted a finger yet. He had simply stood breathing in the dark and said nothing. Billy Mucklow was playing mind games with the drug dealer and he was a master of it, as was his father before him. He finally lit a cigar and then moved his face so close to Perry that the drug dealer could feel his breath upon his skin. Perry could not see him, but he knew that he was there. Mucklow then used his lighter to reveal a carving knife and a honing steel that had been conveniently positioned on a nearby cabinet. He then pulled them together and began to sharpen the knife by rubbing the steel up and down the blade. He remained deadly silent and the room was in absolute darkness as the sound of Perry's fearful and laboured breathing grew louder as he listened to the forbidding sound of the blade being sharpened.

"What do you want? Who are you? Ar can get mandies?" Perry called out helplessly into the darkness but still all that could be heard was the chilling sound of the sharpening steel. After another significant period of time Mucklow finally broke the silence.

"Put the light on Eddie." The light suddenly flickered on and as Perry's eyes took a few seconds to adjust, he suddenly noticed that Billy Mucklow and the blade were inches away from the side of his face. Mucklow lowered the blade slowly so that it was level with Perry's ear and then he made a slow, deep and precise cut from his ear to the bottom of his jaw. Perry gritted his teeth and groaned with the pain and

Mucklow withdrew the blade and wiped it clean on Perry's urine stained trousers. He then walked around to the other side and cut an identical mark on the other side of the drug dealer's face.

"Do you like history Colin?" The randomness of Mucklow's sudden question surprised Perry and he was too traumatised to speak. "In 1303, Westminster Abbey was robbed of a large sum of money that belonged to King Edward the first." Perry was confused and wondering what Mucklow was talking about. "When they eventually found the culprits, they were flayed... Do you know what that means Colin?" Mucklow spoke slowly and deliberately for dramatic emphasis and Perry shook his head. "They were skinned alive. Then their skin was attached to the church doors as a warning against robbers of the state." Perry tensed and began to cry. "Would yow like to be skinned alive Colin?" Bill Mucklow was ruthless but he was not that sick. It was for dramatic effect and he needed to make sure that the answers to his questions would be accurate. Perry shook his head wildly.

"What do you want?"

"So you do sell mandies Colin?"

"Yes, ar can get yow mandies."

"What else do you sell Colin?" Mucklow teased the blade around Perry's face wiping fresh blood over his skin from the vicious wounds he had already inflicted.

"Ar can get yow mandies, or weed?"

"Anything else Colin?"

"Ar can get yow coke or acid too!" Mucklow took a deep breath. Whoever Perry was working for was supplying the Black Country streets with quaaludes, cocaine and LSD and that was not acceptable.

"Who do you work for Colin?"

"Ar cor tell yow that, mar life woe be worth living!"

"Oh dear... Eddie, pull his shoes and socks off." Mucklow gave the order and Fennel obediently pulled off Perry's shoes and socks.

"What am yow doing? Please?" Perry tried to protest but Mucklow picked up a pair of bolt cutters and brought them over to Perry's feet and the drug dealer began to cry again.

"Do you like nursery rhymes Colin?" Mucklow clasped Perry's toes one by one, gently in between the cutters, applying just enough pressure so that Perry knew that they were there. "This little piggy went to market, this little piggy stayed at home. This little piggy had roast beef and this little piggy had none… But this little piggy?" Mucklow rested the cutters on the little toe of Perry's left foot and the drug dealer began to beg and protest before Mucklow squeezed the cruel levers together and the sound of snapping bone and Perry's blood curdling scream filled the room. Perry lost control of his bladder again and almost passed out with the pain.

"Who do you work for Colin?" Mucklow repeated the question and Perry whimpered and nodded as snot and salty tears covered his anguished face.

"Ok… Ar'll tell you, but it day come from me ar'm begging you." Perry's breathing and speech was laboured and all he wanted was for the suffering to end.

"Spit it out aer kid." Mucklow was still unsympathetic.

"Micky Cole…" Perry said the name quietly but Mucklow could not hear.

"Yow'm gunna have to speak louder than that!"

"Micky Cole." Perry spoke the name louder and Mucklow and Fennel's fears were confirmed. Harry Scriven's son had been dealing in harder narcotics and that was not acceptable.

"Good… Eddie, put his shoes and socks back on." There was a lot of blood and Fennel did not relish the prospect of sliding Perry's shoes and socks back on, but who was he to argue with his commanding officer? Orders were orders.

Once his shoes were back on, Perry was led back out to the Consul and then bundled back into the boot. Fennel locked the garage door and then climbed into the passenger seat alongside Billy Mucklow.

It was now nearly 9 o'clock on a late summer's evening and the sun had started to descend. Mucklow started the engine and then drove a relatively short distance to Netherton. As he drove through the Black Country streets, he thought that he did not miss this life. He was happy in Spain with his family. Sipping chilled lager whilst lounging by his grand swimming pool whilst the Mediterranean sun warmed his bones and he listened to Frank Sinatra records. Billy Mucklow could not wait to get back to the Costa del sol, but right now his best friend and brother Harry Scriven needed him.

The black Ford Consul puled up near to the side of the canal and Mucklow and Fennel got out. It was getting darker by the minute and Mucklow was grateful for the cover of night. They opened the boot and helped Perry to get out as he found it difficult to move on account of his recently amputated little toe. Perry's hands were still tied behind his back and Mucklow placed a paper bag over his head so that he could not see where he was being led. They took him down to the side of the canal and then along the towpath until they reached the opening of Netherton tunnel.

Netherton tunnel was the last canal tunnel to be built in England. Construction began on the 31st of December 1855 and the tunnel was officially opened on the 20th of August 1858. It stretched for 1.7 miles and was built entirely by men using picks and shovels. This was extremely dangerous work and 9 men had lost their lives during the tunnel's construction.

As Mucklow, Perry and Fennel reached the tunnel opening, an eerie wind blew from deep within the long forbidding abyss and Fennel wished that he was in the Nep drinking several pints. The slow walk went on and when Mucklow reached a point that he deemed to be satisfactory he instructed Perry to kneel down upon the floor next to the cut. He then removed the bag from his head and pulled out a pistol from his pocket.

"Goodbye Colin." Without further ado, Mucklow placed the gun firmly into the back of Perry's head and blew his brains out into the canal. He stood up confidently and then rolled the lifeless drug dealer's body into the dark murky water with the soles of his Italian shoes. "Well… At least that's one less filthy drug pusher in this world to pollute our children's minds." The two middle aged thugs then strolled purposefully back along the towpath and back towards the Ford… Their work was not yet complete…

Chapter 17

The sun rose slowly over the affluent Stourbridge suburb of Pedmore and Bill Mucklow thought about his home and bed in Spain. He had spent the entire night inside the Ford Consul and Eddie Fennel lay asleep against the passenger window.

Micky Cole had a detached house on Ham Lane, Pedmore and Mucklow and Fennel had parked slightly down the road where they could keep a constant surveillance on the property. It was their intention to abduct Harry Scriven's wild and out of control son, but they did not want to alert his wife as to who was responsible for the abduction, so they sat and waited for him to leave the house. After dumping Perry in the canal the previous night, they had driven straight to Cole's house where they had started their vigil. Eddie Fennel had slept and snored loudly for most of the night but Mucklow had remained focused and unable to sleep in the discomfort of the car. He glanced at his watch and saw that it was nearly 6AM. *When would Cole leave the house? Would he even leave the house that day? Where would he go?* Mucklow thought a little longer and then came to the conclusion that if all else failed Eddie Fennel could phone Cole off a pay phone and arrange a meeting.

"Anything happened Bill?" Fennel awakened, yawned and stretched in the seat. Mucklow shook his head and took out a cigarette. He had smoked all of his cigars and that annoyed him further.

"If ar was at home in Spain ar would just be having a cup of tay in the sun before tecking a quick dip in the pool." Mucklow wished more than anything that he was there, but he had a responsibility to sort things out in his old manor.

"Saahnds bostin' mate." Fennel was envious. With the money he had been making from the drugs trade, a Spanish villa had been 'on the cards' but now that they were clamping down on Cole's activities the window of opportunity was closing. Mucklow put his head back in the chair and yawned loudly. He had had enough of this gangster life years ago and he hoped that things would be sorted quickly so that he could return to the Costa del sol before the law caught up with him again. He could not face another long stretch in prison.

Eddie Fennel had also served a short prison sentence in the late 60s for fraud. He had been sentenced to 14 months but had ended up serving just 8 and he did not relish the prospect of going to jail again either. He thought about the drug dealer they had dumped in the canal earlier and he hoped that the killing would not get linked back to them.

The two men sat and waited for another two and a half hours and then Cole's front door finally opened and he emerged into the bright summer's morning. He got into his prized BMW and reversed carefully off the drive before heading down the road towards the Ford Consul. Fennel ducked down and Mucklow looked at the floor so as to try and hide his face before starting the engine, turning the car around and then following Cole's BMW at a safe distance so as not to get noticed.

Micky Cole drove along Ham Lane towards the island where he turned right onto Wollescote Road towards Oldnall Road. As he drove he had only two things on his mind. On a normal day he may have noticed the Ford Consul on his tail, but today he was meeting up with a prostitute friend who stashed cocaine for him in her council house. He had promised Cathy that he no longer dabbled in the white powder so he was no longer able to keep it in his own house. It also made more sense to keep it at a separate location in case he was raided by the police. As he drove along Oldnall Road towards the Halesowen suburb of Colley Gate he looked left at the three imposing council tower blocks that made up part of the Tanhouse estate. He recalled a not-so-distant memory of when he had been there with Dick Hickman and he wondered what had become of the lonesome junkie he had amputated the finger of on the orders of Hickman. His life had changed so much since then and sometimes he felt that in achieving his life's ambition of destroying Cedric Tanner and his second in command Davey Price, he had peaked and now there was nothing left for him other than the constant vicious cycle of alcohol, drugs and hookers. Other men found pleasure in mundane everyday activities such as football, playing cards, DIY, even just watching television, but at this point in his life, Micky Cole could focus on nothing other than his drug dealing empire and where his next 'fix' was coming from.

He sweated with anticipation as he travelled along Furlong Lane, Colley Gate, past Eddie Fennel's house and then right onto Overend road before turning right again up Barrs Road towards Haden Cross. There he carried straight on Beauty Bank Road and then up Waterfall Lane towards Blackheath. Once at the top of the hill he turned left onto Holly Road where he followed it straight through Ross until he arrived in Rowley Regis. He then cut through the rows of council houses until he came out on the Lion Farm Estate in Oldbury.

The Lion Farm Estate stood between the Black Country towns of Oldbury and Blackheath and was built in the early 1960s to house a growing population; many of whom had been living in prefabs in nearby Whiteheath. Prefabs were a type of temporary home that were erected after the Second World War for those that had lost their houses during the Blitz and for returning servicemen and their young families. Lion Farm quickly became an extremely deprived hive of crime and poverty was rife.

Micky Cole eventually pulled up his BMW outside a house on Hartlebury Road opposite the tower blocks and got out. Usually it would be unheard of to leave such an expensive car outside such an unsavoury address, however, Micky Cole was known and he was not somebody who's car local kids would dare to vandalise. He locked the vehicle and hammered enthusiastically on the front door of the house, still completely unaware of the tail that had pulled up just down the road and was watching him intently. A young blonde woman opened the door in a skimpy night dress. She had pretty eyes and hair but her teeth were rotten and she smelt strongly of cannabis and the body odour of the many men who had paid for her affections. She led him through the filth ridden house that smelt as if it had not been cleaned in years and into her bedroom where she slept and earned her living in sticky, stained foul smelling sheets. She handed him a sealed packet of cocaine and he used a pocket knife to cut an opening so that he could enter his eager fingers and then rub the precious white powder into his gums. The whore then giggled cheekily before lying face down on the bed and exposing her naked buttocks by pulling up her stained and dirty nightdress. Micky Cole then meticulously formed a line of cocaine on her milky white bottom before taking a £10 note from out of his wallet and using it to snort the prized powder into his nostrils. He pulled his head back in ecstasy and felt the mighty rush sweep through his body like an orgasmic tremor. The woman giggled again as he parted her legs slightly and began to undo his flies.

"Get yower hands behind yower fuckin' head right now Micky!" Bill Mucklow suddenly kicked the door open and burst into the rancid room, closely followed by Eddie Fennel. He had a gun in his right hand and he pointed it intimidatingly at Micky Cole.

"Bill, what the fuck am yow doing here?" Cole was confused and had no idea what was going on. Mucklow took the barrel of the gun and struck Cole across the back of the head with it. Not hard enough to knock him out but just enough to subdue him slightly. He then placed the gun back into his pocket and grabbed Cole by the hair.

"Yow'm coming with us sunshine!" Cole quickly turned around and tried to land a punch on Bill Mucklow, but the older man grabbed his arm with force and then pushed him back down onto the bed with a rear wrist lock. Cole tried to struggle but Mucklow twisted his wrist tighter and he was in agony. "Do yow know how easily ar could break yower arm?" Mucklow was not exaggerating and Cole was surprised at how quickly Billy Mucklow had over powered him. *He was Micky Cole, he did not loose fights and he was not scared of anyone, but he had met his match. It looked as if the great Bill Mucklow was exactly as tough as his legend had portrayed him to be.* He relaxed and accepted he was beat.

"Ok Bill, ar bay moving… What's gewin on?" Mucklow raised him off the bed and slowly started to walk him towards the door as he held Cole's arm tightly behind his back.

"Me and Eddie want to have a word with yow aer kid." Mucklow and Cole moved back through the house when Fennel suddenly stopped.

"But Bill, what about the whore? What if she lets it out that we've got Mick?" Mucklow paused and then looked at the rough prostitute who was watching closely.

"If yow breathe a word of this to anyone then ar'll let it be known that yow am a police informant… Yow woe last 5 minutes on the Estate with that hanging over you." The woman was not a police informant but it did not matter, she protested and shook her head wildly.

"Ar woe say nothing ar swear!" Mucklow believed her and Fennel handed her a £5 note before the two men led Cole out to the Ford Consul where they securely tied his feet and hands together and bundled him into the boot…

The Consul boot was dark, claustrophobic and smelt of Colin Perry's sweat and urine. *Was this the end? Had the awful wedding speech cost him his life? Why were members of his own family abducting him? Did Mucklow intent to return from Spain permanently and take over?* Despite his awful and drunkard wedding speech, Micky Cole had actually started to like having a family around him. Apart from his mother, it was something he had never really experienced and he was beginning to cherish building a relationship with his natural father. He had grown fond of Eddie Fennel too and had come to regard the man as a kind of uncle. It disappointed him and made him angry that Billy Mucklow had simply walked back in and wanted him gone… He could think of no other explanation for it. He had gotten away with the brutal murders of Cedric Tanner and Davey Price, married his sweetheart and finally began to find happiness and now it was being cruelly taken away way from him… *It wasn't fair, but what did he expect? Maybe it was no more than he deserved…*

The car journey seemed to go on for an eternity and Cole could not stop thinking about where they were going and his final destination. At first, the journey had been 'stop start' as they travelled through town traffic but now he assumed that they must have reached the open road as the drive was continuous with fewer stops.

Eventually the Ford stopped and Cole could hear muffled voices as Mucklow and Fennel got out of the front doors. The boot lid suddenly rose and the intensity and brightness of the summer sun penetrated his eyes that had become accustomed to the darkness of the boot.

"Let's have yer then aer kid." Cole was surprised that Mucklow's voice was suddenly less intimidating and actually carried a hint of compassion. The two men lifted him out of the boot and undid the rope that was around his legs so that he could walk at least. Micky Cole's eyes adjusted to the light and he looked around at his surroundings. He appeared to be in some kind of farmyard and he could smell the manure and hear the sound of cows mooing relatively close by.

"What the fucks gewin on? Where the fuck am I?" Cole considered trying to make a run for it but he was curious as to what was happening. Mucklow and Fennel led him towards the farmhouse that was tucked around the corner from the yard. Mucklow knocked loudly on the door and eventually a plump woman who Cole assumed must have been about 45 years of age opened the door. She had kind eyes and looked oddly familiar as she held the door open and invited the three men in. The farmhouse was dirty and dated, but dirty in a natural farm-like way; nothing like the sleazy filth pit Cole had been abducted from. The woman led them into a large kitchen that had a worn wooden table in the centre. Placed in the middle of the table was a fruit bowl and a pot of fresh tea. Sat at the table was a grumpy looking man who wore a flat cap and starred morbidly at the tea pot. He did not acknowledge the visitors and he maintained his mundane gaze.

"Micky, ar'd like yow to meet mar sister Susanah who was named after mar grandmother- yower great grandmother." Bill Mucklow pulled back a chair for Cole to sit down on, but he still did not remove the rope that bound his hands together. "This is her husband Bernard... He dow say much do yer Bernard?" The farmer grunted and then managed a half smile for his brother-in-law. "Nobody can get a bloody word in with you about Bill!" Cole noticed that Mucklow's brother-in-law had a strong country accent and was clearly not from the Black Country. *Just how far had they come and where the hell were they?*

"Micky's gunna be helping you on the farm for a couple of weeks Bernard... If he tries to run away, shoot him... It's for his own bloody good!" Mucklow smiled but Cole was unsure if he was joking or not. Mucklow's sister poured them all a cup of tea and Mucklow cautiously removed the rope from Cole's hands. "Yow'm amongst family Mick and we only want what's best for yow and Harry aer kid... Ar think aer Eddie would like a word with yow." Bill Mucklow took a sip of his tea and looked over to Eddie Fennel who was sat opposite.

"Look at yowerself Mick... Yow'm so fucked up on drugs that yer dow know what yam doing mate..." Fennel looked apologetically at Susanah for swearing in her kitchen. "Our agreement Mick was for the sale of weed, but things have progressed. Yow, me and Harry am gunna end up in jail for a long time if yow dow sort yer life aaht mate." Cole looked shamefully at the floor and a tear formed in his eyes. *He was not getting whacked, he was getting saved...* He knew deep down that what he had been doing was wrong and he had not been a good husband to Cathy. "Bill has arranged for yow to come and live here on the farm for a couple of weeks."

"Yow will be up at the crack of dawn every day and yow will work like a mother fucker. Yer woe have time to think abaaht that junk yow been tecking... It ay gunna be easy kid but Bernard WILL shoot yow if yow try to escape." Mucklow used his index finger to accentuate his point and Cole did not doubt that what he was saying was true. "We will get a message to Cathy and Harry and when we think that the time is right we will come and pick yow up... It's up to yow now kid... Do yow wanna get clean for yower family?" Cole nodded and Mucklow sensed that it was genuine. "But listen to this kid and be warned. Ar will only ever give yow one chance… Do not fuck this up…" Cole looked deep into Mucklow's eyes and he had absolutely no hesitation in believing him. It was in his hands now. He had been handed another chance and if he wanted to enjoy a happy and positive future with Cathy and his newfound family then he knew what he had to do…

Chapter 18

The Haden Cross public house dates from as far back as at least the 19th century. It was advertised for sale in 1890 with its own Butchers shop, slaughterhouse and 10 quarter malthouse. The pub was originally owned by J Rolinson and Son who owned the Five Ways brewery in Netherton but in 1912 the pub was sold to Wolverhampton and Dudley Breweries. At this time a Mr Harry Pearson took over as the licensee and his official documented profession was beer retailer. The pub changed hands again in 1919 when a Mr Michael Cockin became the licensee followed by Rachel Cockin in 1924, William George Matthews in 1925, James Bally in 1926 and then David C Priest in 1927. After a succession of other licensees, Mrs Myra Downing took on the pub from 1938 – 1955 and as Harry Scriven sat and relaxed in the side bar he looked back on that period with fond memories and enjoyed how the décor and atmosphere had not changed that much since then.

The sun was high in the sky and Scriven looked at the brilliant sunlight as it reflected off the windows of the mock Tudor house opposite. Scriven could remember the house being built in 1931 when it was originally a three-bedroom detached house built by a Cradley Heath school master called Wilfred Parsons. Scriven remembered how during the Second World War the house had been used as a fire station and then he looked down the road and thought about how much things had changed since he was a child. He looked around the room in which he sat on his own and recalled how it had once been filled with all the old faces. Willie Mucklow, Eli Davis, Bill Mucklow, Dickie Hickman, Barry O'Leary. Willie's health was rapidly deteriorating and he was in his final days and Davis and Hickman were already dead. Scriven pondered his own life. *He was 56 years of age, how much longer did he have left? Would he be spending it in prison on account of his out-of-control son?* And then the age-old question that had troubled him for the last 20 years returned to haunt him. *Would he be heading straight to hell to pay for the horrendous crimes he had committed?*

"They've run aaht of scratchun's Harry." Barry O'Leary returned to the room with two pints of beer and a packet of KP salted peanuts.

"No bloody scratchun's?" Scriven was disappointed. He watched as O'Leary placed the beer on the table and he nodded a thank you.

"We ay sid yower Mick abaaht for a while Harry?" O'Leary sipped his drink and remarked on the notable absence of Scriven's son Micky Cole. It had been over a week since Bill Mucklow had put him to work on his sister's farm and upon receiving the news from Mucklow several days ago, Harry Scriven had agreed that it was a good idea. Scriven had disliked the drug business as much as anyone, but after the way he had let his son down as a child he found it very hard to disagree with him and not give him exactly what he wanted... Harry Scriven was new to parenthood and he felt as if he had failed yet again. *As usual it was his cousin Bill wading in to pick up the pieces. He was 56 years old and still relying on his cousin. Nothing ever seemed to change...*

"He's gone away for a bit Barry. He's got to try and sort this drugs shit aaht." Scriven eventually answered O'Leary as he continued to gaze out of the window.

"Definitely for the best Harry. He was pretty fucked up at yower wedding mate." O'Leary gave a cheeky smirk and resisted the temptation to laugh. Scriven chose to ignore it. The wedding had been turned into a total farce and Suzy had only recently begun speaking to him again.

The door swung abruptly open and in walked a sly and cocky looking man with immaculately bryl-creamed hair and a cheap shiny suit. Scriven caught sight of him and groaned inwardly. *The damage had been done, his time was up.*

Detective Chief Inspector 'Clubber' Clark was a nasty piece of work. He was more crooked than the worst criminals and he had less morals than a sewer rat. He did not care about the public and the people he was paid to protect and the only thing that motivated him was a greed for the ill-gotten gains of the criminals he feasted upon like a leech.

"Hello Harry… Ar wanna word with you." Clark had a nasal high-pitched voice and the most annoying of squeaky laughs coupled with a face that just about everyone wanted to punch. He was hated by crooks and fellow officers alike, but he always found a way to come up smelling of roses and with pockets full of dirty money. Clark turned to face O'Leary and gave him a look of disgust. "Not you sunshine… Fuck off." Clark pointed to the door with his thumb and Barry O'Leary obediently stood up and walked out. Scriven continued to stare out of the window and waited for the detective to speak. He stunk of Old Spice and Brylcreem and Harry Scriven absolutely detested the man.

"Your lad Micky's been a busy little bee hasn't he Harry?" Scriven said nothing. "He's been making you lot a nice bit of money with his mandies business. I bet the Mucklow's are proud…" Clark's face was inches from Scriven and he spoke with an intimidating whine that was attempting to anger Scriven.

"My son has gone away for a while. Ar can assure you that there is no dealing going on." Scriven spoke the truth. Since he had been trying to get rehabilitated, Micky Cole had cut all links to the drugs trade and had vowed to himself that he would not be going down that road again, besides, Billy Mucklow would more than certainly kill him if he did.

"I know that as well Harry… That's the problem." Scriven turned and looked at Clark with confusion.

"Problem?"

"Yes Harry… You see Michael was paying me 5 percent of the gross… How do you think he was getting away with it? The problem is, now that Michael is being?" Clark paused and searched for the word, "Rehabilitated, that is loosing me a lot of fucking money Harry and I cannot have that… I need Michael's business back up and running as quickly as possible or I will not be happy…" Scriven could not believe what the police officer was saying, but the more he thought about it the more he realised that he should not be surprised with anything when it came to 'Clubber' Clark.

"So yow'm telling me that yow want drugs back on the street?"

"I think that it is in yours and Michael's interest Harry, and Mr Fennel's..." Clark shot Scriven a twisted smile.

"Why's that?"

"About a year and a half a go we found a dead gangster over Kinver way. He had been burnt alive and some fucker had cut his cock off before they set him on fire... That man was called Cedric Tanner and his second in command Davey Price has been missing ever since... Does it ring any bells with you Harry?" Scriven said nothing again, he knew exactly what Clark was getting at and his heart sank. "I know exactly who killed Cedric Tanner Harry and I reckon I can make it stick too... So unless you want your precious son doing life for murder then I suggest you boys get dealing again." Clark gave one of his trademark sniggers. "Only this time Harry, I want 10 percent." Clark sniggered again and he gave Scriven a patronising tap on the cheek as he stood up, buttoned his suit jacket and left the room smelling of his aftershave.

As Harry Scriven sat and came to terms with the consequences of what was about to happen, he sighed and stared sadly at his beer. He had planned for this eventuality and had truly hoped that this day would never come. He reflected back on his thoughts from just a few minutes before Clark had arrived and now they seemed distant, meaningless and irrelevant. He trudged into the bar, ordered a large Scotch and a cigar and then went back into the small room where he stood in front of an oval mirror that hung over a drab 1930s fireplace. He lit his cigar and toasted himself with his whiskey before closing his eyes and reflecting upon his life. He recalled playing with Bill at Haden Hill Park as a child, fighting, playing football and cricket. He thought about his RAF days, he thought about Irene and Suzy Miller, but most of all he thought about Lily Cole and their son. He thought of the words of Micky's wedding speech and he wished more than anything that he could turn the clock back. But he could not… He sipped and savoured the whiskey, which was the finest in the pub and he wondered if and when he would ever drink another one. Where he was going, he would have a lot of time to ponder the past and torture himself with regrets and thoughts of what might have been. In that moment he wished that the punishment for murder was still hanging, it would be a quicker and less painful way of going straight to hell…

Scriven parked his Mercedes outside Old Hill Police station and walked straight inside and up to the front counter. A sergeant on the front desk was busy on the phone and Scriven's humiliation was prolonged.

"How can I help you sir?" The sergeant finished his phone conversation and turned his attention to Harry Scriven.

"I want to confess to something…" Scriven stammered slightly with nerves. "I want to confess to the murder of Cedric Tanner." Scriven had decided months ago that if Micky ever got fingered for the brutal murder of his stepfather, he would take the rap for it in his son's place. It was the least he could do after he had deserted Cole's mother before he was born. The sergeant looked lost for words and he instantly led Scriven through to an interview room where he was locked inside as the officer went to speak to his superiors. It took a while and Scriven sat back and lit a cigarette. He would have lots of time on his hands so it didn't matter how long he was there.

After about half an hour of waiting, the familiar smirk of DCI 'Clubber' Clark appeared looking highly amused.

"Hello Harry… Fancy seeing you again." Scriven looked at the floor and waited for the formalities of his arrest. "I've just heard the funniest story mate. You won't believe this." Clark's voice was soaked in sarcasm. "All about this old school villain… You might know him Harry? Anyway, he isn't an ordinary villain, no… He has special superpowers." Clark's voice was patronising and Scriven wanted to grab his head and ram it repeatedly into the table. "You see this villain, he has special fucking arms... Arms that can stretch all the way from the Costa del fucking dol to Kinver to cut a fella's dick off and then set him on fire!" Clark's expression changed and he did not look impressed. Scriven's heart sank, he would not be able to save his son. "I ought to charge you for wasting police time you stupid bastard!" Clark lent in close across the table so that he could whisper. "Remember, 10%... You've got 2 weeks to make the first payment, or I get a warrant for your son's arrest." Clark stood up and walked over to the door. "Now... Fuck off!"

Chapter 19

Micky Cole had been to hell and back. He had gone 'cold turkey' whilst working non-stop 16-hour days on the farm of Billy Mucklow's sister. At first, he had thrown himself into it with enthusiasm, but then after a couple of days the withdrawal symptoms had started to kick in. He had hallucinated, vomited frequently, had constant headaches and aggressive tremors that rendered him almost paralysed. All he had used to try and help him through was a daily allowance of Bernard's roll up cigarettes and two cups of homemade scrumpy cider before he went to bed. Halfway through his two week stay, he felt as if his body was about to explode out of his skin and he considered trying to escape, but a determination to do the right thing by his wife and newfound family had seen him through and when Fennel and Scriven returned to collect him he felt like a new man. On his darkest nights he had hallucinated and seen the spectres of Davey Price and Cedric Tanner who had taunted him from beyond the grave. Those two would have a hold over him for the rest of his life and he knew that he would never escape.

Upon Micky Cole's arrival back at home, he had maintained his resolute abstinence from drugs and had made it clear that he no longer wanted to be a drug dealer. Harry scriven did not have the heart to tell him about the actions of DCI 'Clubber' Clark and the potential implications it could have for them. The clock was ticking and Scriven had less than a week left to come up with the first payment. Of course, he could have funded it out of his own pocket, but that would only last for so long and what would become of him and his new wife? Scriven had also elected not to let Bill Mucklow know of the situation either. It was time he stood on his own two feet, he was 56 years old and he needed to sort things for himself... Mucklow had happily said his goodbyes and returned to Spain and Scriven had been almost relieved to see him go. *But what would he do now?*

The late summer sun penetrated the windows of Micky Cole's BMW and the black leather interior was sticky and hot to the touch. His throat was dry and as he approached the entrance to the Crooked House pub near Himley he was tempted to turn in for a drink. He had not touched a drop of alcohol since the first week at the farm where he had been given limited amounts of cider and since arriving home he had been strict on himself and with the support of his wife managed to avoid alcohol.

Micky Cole had been out that day in his car to put flowers on his mother's grave and as he neared the pub's entrance, he quickly turned into it at the last minute. The driveway to the Crooked House was long and as Cole drove slowly down, he kept telling himself that in a minute he would turn back; but he did not.

The Crooked House was originally a farmhouse and was built in 1765. Like much of the Black Country, the land on which it stood had been used extensively for mining and in the 19th century, one side of the building began to slowly sink due to the unstable mine shafts below. This gave the structure a lopsided appearance. In 1830 the building became a pub and was christened the 'Siden House' as 'Siden' means crooked in the Black Country dialect. It was later renamed the Glynne Arms after the local landowner Sir Stephen Glynne who owned the land on which the pub stood. In the 1940s, the building was condemned as unsafe due to the deteriorated subsidence and the pub was set to be demolished. However, at the last minute, Wolverhampton and Dudley Breweries purchased the property and made the structure safe by installing buttresses and girders so that the building could retain its lopsided character. It was at this point that the pub became The Crooked House and customers would come from miles around to see the famous optical illusions where marbles would amazingly appear to roll uphill.

As Micky Cole pulled up on the car park, he watched with envy as men and women sat at wooden benches at the front of the pub with ice cold beers to quench their thirsts in the hot summer sun. What he wouldn't have given for just a few cold beers? *But where would it end? One beer would quickly turn into 10 pints, 10 pints would turn into a bottle of Scotch, a bottle of Scotch would turn into quaaludes and then quaaludes would turn into lines of cocaine. Maybe one day he would be able to enjoy a simple beer again, but for now he would have to take it one day at a time.* He was so tempted to get out of the car and walk into the pub, but he suddenly stopped himself. *It was not fair on his father, it was not fair on Cathy and more than anything it was not fair on himself.* It took all of the strength and courage he had, but from somewhere he managed to find it within himself to turn the car around and head back down the long driveway to the main road…

As he drove back through Gornal Wood towards Dudley, Micky Cole suddenly noticed a blonde woman who was walking on the pavement at the side of the road with a small boy. At first he could not understand why she caught his attention, but as he drew closer he realised why. It was Lucy Price, the first woman he had been madly in love with as a teenager and the child he had helped when he put them in a taxi to escape her abusive husband 18 months previously. She had been particularly grateful for his assistance and he slowed the car down to pull alongside her. It was a welcome distraction from the constant temptation of the pubs he was passing on the way home.

"Lucy, its me, Michael. Can I offer you a lift?" She turned around suddenly and recognised him straight away, but her eyes did not look happy to see him. She paused for a moment or two before nodding and climbing through the rear doors and into the back of the car with her young son. "Where are you going?"

"Ar live on the Wrenna now… It ay the best place to bring up a child but ar'm a single mom and I had to gew where the council put me." The last time she saw Micky Cole he had paid for her Taxi and given her money to leave her husband, but nothing had been seen or heard of her husband since and the police had assumed that he was either dead or had ran away on account of what had happened to his sadistic employer Cedric Tanner. Davey Price was a gangster, a nasty piece of work with no morals who had supported Cedric Tanner throughout his adult life and Micky Cole had no regrets over what had happened to either men.

"I see… Just tell me where to gew and ar'll teck you there… How yow been?" Cole felt a little awkward and tried to make small talk.

"My son keeps asking where his dad is…" The randomness of Lucy's comment surprised Cole and he said nothing. "Ar know you stayed at the house that day after you put me in the taxi and I know what happened to Cedric." A nervousness crept into Lucy's voice as if she knew she was talking to a killer. "Nobody could blame you after what Cedric did to you when yow were a child, but the way in which he died was absolutely sick." The details of Tanner's death had horrified many when they eventually came out due to their utterly barbaric and gruesome nature. "The thing is Mick, ar know that yow hated Davey too and nothing has been seen or heard of him since that day you put me in a taxi." She knew that she was in a car with her husband's murderer and she suddenly feared for hers and her son's safety, but she had a burning curiosity to find out what had happened to her husband and she needed answers.

"What does it matter? Davey Price was a piece of shit and he used yow like a punch bag and was even prepared to let yower son spend time with a known kiddie fiddler!" Lucy knew that Cole was right, but she still needed answers.

"He is my husband though Micky… Ar just need to know so I can move on with my life…" Lucy began to cry and Cole could see her tears in the rear view mirror as he drove through the deprived streets of the Wren's Nest Estate in Dudley. "Ar wake up in the middle of the night, sweating, crying, unable to get mar breath. Just needing to know where Davey is? Sometimes he was nice, sometimes he loved me."

"Yeah, and the other times he beat the shit aaht on yer!" Cole felt insensitive but it was true.

"Yes he did, but I still deserve the right to know what happened to him... Sometimes I wake up unable to breathe and paralyzed with fear in bed, worrying in case he comes back in and hurts me again... Sometimes I just feel lonely and believe it or not I miss him..." Lucy was confused as her crying became more intense and her little boy began to cry too at the sight of his upset mother. "I just need to get on with my life and only you can help me with that Michael." Cole pulled the car up outside the address that she had given him and felt torn. He wanted to help her find inner peace, but he did not want to admit his guilt and risk her going to the police. This had been an unexpected event and the last thing he needed in his battle with drugs and alcohol. "Look Michael, ar spent enough of mar life around low life gangsters like you... Ar know how it works an I ay about to grass if that's what yow'm worried about... I just need to know one way or another." Cole looked at the steering wheel for a whole minute and then turned around slowly.

"Ok... Davey woe be coming home no more... That's all I can say... Sorry." Lucy suddenly erupted into a dramatic sob, she screamed, hit the back of the seat on which Cole was sat and then grabbed her son.

"You monster!" She clutched her son tightly and rushed out of the car and up into her house as quickly as she could. Cole fumbled for a cigarette and shook as he put it into his mouth and lit it. *What had he done? Would she go to the police?* He cursed himself several times for his stupidity and then pulled away quickly creating a wheelspin as he went. *He needed a drink...*

Two days passed and Micky Cole sat in the side bar of the Haden Cross with Harry Scriven and Eddie Fennel and sipped a lager shandy. Despite his run in with Lucy Price the other day he had managed to hold off the hard liquor and had instead drank shandies. He was nervous and constantly worried about Lucy Price speaking to the Police, but he kept his mouth shut. Harry Scriven had gone through enough hassle thanks to him and didn't want to worry them with anything else. Harry Scriven had his own worries. He only had a few days left until 'Clubber' Clark wanted his drug money otherwise he was going to do Micky for the murder of Cedric Tanner! Killing a Police officer was wrong and against the 'old school' codes, but 'Clubber' Clark was more of a villain than anyone. Scriven was seriously considering the murder of the corrupt cop, though he worried in case there were other coppers in league with him who also had evidence on Micky Cole.

The only member of the drinking trio who was stressless and care free for the first time in weeks was Eddie Fennel. He was no longer making obscene amounts of money from drugs, but he still had his security firm and he had made more than enough cash to get by.

"So how's married life treating yer Harry? Yow'm a lucky bastard with a younger bird who looks like that! All the blokes raahnd here fancied Suzy." Fennel sensed that Scriven and Cole were a little tense and he wondered why so he tried to inject a bit of light-hearted banter.

"Yeah, good thanks Eddie… How's Teresa?" Scriven made polite conversation but he could not get his situation with 'Clubber' Clark from out of his mind.

"Her's alright thanks Scriv. Yow'm quiet ay yer Mick?" Fennel looked at Cole. He was starting to get frustrated with the sombre atmosphere and was thinking about going over to the 'Nep' to see his old friend Tummy 'Ducks'.

"Sorry Eddie, ar'm getting a bit fed up of drinking this bloody shandy!" Cole was only half lying, though the dominant issue on his mind was the situation with Lucy Price.

"Fuckin' hell mate, a pint of mild ay gunna hurt yer aer kid. But if yow start teckin' that shit again ar'm gunna tell Billy!" Fennel tried to make light of the situation but Scriven did not appreciate the comment. *Cole was his son and it had nothing to do with Billy Mucklow.!* Before he could say anything, an unwanted visitor arrived in the room.

"Well, well, well… Look at this, the three stooges." DCI 'Clubber' Clark came and sat down at the table without invitation and Scriven's heart sank. For a second Scriven considered throttling the man to death there and then but there would be too many witnesses and he wanted to hear what he had to say first. "I've been hearing things about you boys… I've got a name for you. A blast from the past." Clark had a smug grin on his face and the other men said nothing. "Davey Price…" Clark dropped the name and then left a long pause as Micky Cole especially began to discretely worry. "He worked for Cedric Tanner… A total fucking bastard… Just like you boys." Clark laughed but nobody else found him amusing. "Well a little bird tells me that one of you lot done him in just like you did Cedric Tanner in." Clark looked at Micky Cole and raised his eyebrows. "Now I can't afford to have my biggest earners go down for murder can I? But I am going to need something in return." Clark turned to face Scriven whom he perceived to be the boss. "First of all Harry, that number goes up to 20 percent…" Fennel and Cole turned to look at Scriven, they had no idea what Clark was talking about. "And I will also need you to tell me where Price is buried… His wife wants 'closure' and I'm coming under pressure to produce a body… Now if I continue to get my 20 percent, I can ensure that the murderer is never found… But if I do not get my money, then there will be a thorough and conclusive investigation." Clark continued to amuse himself and all three of the other men had burning questions they needed to ask each other once the cop had gone.

Clark wrote a number down on a small piece of paper, folded it and then pushed it across the table to Harry Scriven. "Once you have the money and can lead me to the body, give me a call on this number." Clark smirked again and stood up and walked towards the door. "Good evening gentlemen. I have a golf club function with the Chief Constable that I really cannot be late for." With that, 'Clubber' Clark left the room and the three remaining men looked at each other with confused eyes.

After several hours, total honesty and several rounds of drinks, the three men hatched a plan to deal with 'Clubber' Clark…

Chapter 20

Several scandals occurred in the late 1950s involving high-profile allegations of police corruption. The first of these was in Brighton in 1957 when Scotland Yard were sent to investigate Brighton Borough Police force. Soon after, several high-ranking officers were arrested. Another high-profile incident was in 1959 involving Nottingham Police which also led to the arrest of 20 local labour councillors. As a result, a commission known as the Royal commission was set up in 1960 with the instruction to "review the constitutional position of the Police throughout Great Britain." This in turn led to the Police Act of 1964 which updated legislation governing Police forces in England and Wales, constituted new Police authorities and gave the Home Secretary new powers to supervise local constabularies. However, despite the 1964 Police Act, corruption in the British Police force remained rife. In 1969 a Detective from Camberwell CID in London by the name of Jon Symonds was secretly recorded giving advice to villains. Symonds explained on tape that he would be unable to help a criminal if he was apprehended committing a crime outside of London. By the mid-1970s, not much had changed and Detective Chief Inspector 'Clubber' Clark was a classic example of a corrupt Police officer.

'Clubber' Clark got his name from his time spent as a Bobby on the beat in the 1960s. He would take any opportunity to use his police truncheon to hit or 'club' local kids for the simplest of minor disturbances. He would systematically seek out the 'toughest' kids in the neighbourhood and then invite them to fight him 'raahnd the back' of local shops. Then he would pull out his truncheon and proceed to give the youthful scallywag a damn good clubbing. He kept the streets clear from troublesome youths, but of course, when it came to the more seasoned criminals, he was open for business. Taking bribes had never been a moral dilemma for 'Clubber' Clark. If he had not done so well in the police, he would have been a villain, but why be a villain when he could feed off the success of other villains?

In the early days, Eddie Fennel had been one of 'Clubber' Clark's best customers. In the absence of Billy Mucklow, Fennel had been king of the local underworld and 'Clubber' Clark had been a valuable asset. However, as the criminal landscape changed and became more reliant on narcotics, and as Clark moved up the hierarchy of the police, he became substantially more expensive and his focus shifted to the lucrative world of drug dealers.

Micky Cole was one such 'businessman' who was ripe for the taking. Not only was he at the top of a drug ring that span the entirety of the Black Country, but he was also the chief suspect in a high-profile murder that had horrified the nation at Christmas 1973. Then there was Eddie Fennel who was now trying to pass himself off as a legitimate businessman! 'Clubber' Clark found this highly amusing. The reality was that owning a 'security firm' was an up to date and supposedly 'legal' way of operating a protection racket. Instead of the old 'cloak and dagger' methods of extortion that had been employed by the old boys like Willie Mucklow and Eli Davis, Eddie Fennel would offer pubs and clubs legitimate security contracts so that he could provide door staff. Of course, if the venue turned him down, there would be a series of violent disturbances and threats until the owners were bullied into taking on Fennel's firm. 'Clubber' Clark was not stupid. He knew exactly how it worked and it all worked in his favour. He needed Fennel's security network in place so that Cole could distribute his product and the latest Black Country 'Godfather' Harry Scriven could pay him his 20 percent. The only problem 'Clubber' Clark had was that the 'three stooges' as he liked to refer to them, had more morals than he did, and they wanted to get out of the drug business.

'Clubber' Clark sat in his office inside Old Hill police station and smoked a cigarette between sips of cheap blended Scotch from his hip flask. It was collection day, and he was eagerly waiting to hear from

Harry Scriven with regards to the 20 percent he was owed and the whereabouts of Davey Price's body. Clark desperately needed the money. He had been living well above his means as a police detective and he had serious problems with his gambling addiction. He sat back in his chair and thought about what he would do if Scriven did not make the call. He certainly could arrest Micky Cole for Cedric Tanner's murder, but then he would be losing his biggest cash cow. Much to his relief, the phone rang and he crossed his fingers in the hope that it was Harry Scriven.

"Hello."

"It's Scriven."

"Good… I was getting worried Harry. I was thinking about poor Micky getting locked up in jail." Scriven ignored the comment.

"Ar got yower money and we can show you where Price is…"

"Good lad." Clark could not help but patronise Scriven.

"Do you know the Wyre Forest? Near Bewdley?"

"Fucking hell Harry, it ain't that close!"

"Meet us there in an hour. There's a pub called the Duke William opposite the entrance. We will see you on the pub car park." The phone line suddenly went dead and Clark smiled and took another sip of whiskey. He would be getting his 20 percent and solving the disappearance of Davey Price. *Today was going to be a good day!*

'Clubber' Clark travelled alone in his red Ford Cortina 1.6L which had a black vinyl roof. He cursed Cole for burying the body so far away and as he sat in traffic at Kidderminster, he checked his watch frequently. He was going to be slightly late and he hated being late. Not that he minded making Harry Scriven wait, but he needed the money in his pocket as quickly as possible and he did not want to waste any more of his own time then was completely necessary.

Clark's Cortina pulled up on the car park of the Duke William 15 minutes after the agreed time and he parked alongside Scriven's

Mercedes. Micky Cole and Harry Scriven got out of the Merc and walked around to the Cortina.

"Just the two of you? Where's the third stooge?" Clark got out of the car and locked the front door.

"Eddie ay got nothing to do with this." Scriven lied.

"Yeah right Harry, the man is as much a gangster as either of you two and that bastard cousin of yours out in Spain… I don't suppose you two know anything about a drug dealer who was found with half his head blown off in the cut?" Cole and Scriven shook their heads and Clark asked no further questions, it was not in his interest.

The Wyre Forest near Bewdley in Worcestershire covers an area of 10.17 square miles and is one of the largest areas of semi-natural woodland in Britain. In the 14th century, hunting rights within the forest belonged to the Mortimer family who's patriarch held the title of Earl of March from 1328. They were the Overlords of much of Shropshire and hailed from the nearby village of Cleobury Mortimer which was partially named after the family. In the 17th and 18th centuries, the forest was used as a coppice to provide wood for the production of charcoal to fuel the iron forges of the nearby Black Country.

As Micky Cole led Scriven and Clark deeper into the forest, 'Clubber' Clark grew increasingly nervous. He had already considered that Cole and Scriven were very dangerous men who could quite easily be leading him to his death, but his greed for money was greater than his fear and he had issued himself with a CID pistol which he concealed within his suit jacket. After about 25 minutes of walking, Micky Cole suddenly stopped next to an old, abandoned stretch of railway line.

The Tenbury and Bewdley Railway company opened the Wyre Forest line in 1864, but with the increasing use of road traffic the railway fell into decline and was closed for good in 1965. The track ran straight through the forest, but by 1975 it had been disused and abandoned for 10 years.

Micky Cole stood at a patch of ground which was about 10 feet from the side of the track, and he picked up a large stick and drove it into the hard soil to create a marker. Clark smiled and made a mental note of the position. Despite it being late summer, it was cold in the forest due to the copious amounts of shade provided by the huge trees and Clark shivered at the thought of the decomposing corpse that lay beneath them.

"So… Have you got the money?" Clark was eager for his payment so that he could return to the station and get back to the spot with a team of bobbies and their shovels. Scriven turned to face the marker and almost ceremoniously held up a wad of notes high in the air so that they were clearly visible. As Clark put out his hand to collect the money, Scriven appeared to hold onto the cash for a couple of seconds and Clark assumed that the whole situation must have been hard for the villain and that it was grieving him to hand over so much cash. The thought amused Clark and he smiled. "Thanks boys. Maybe next month we can complete the transaction somewhere a little more local." The three men made their way back through the dark forest and not a single word was spoken due to a mutual hatred.

DCI 'Clubber' Clark returned to the forest early the next morning with three burly bobbies with spades and another one who had a police sniffer dog. They had to operate in a low-key capacity as the forest was outside of their jurisdiction and was within the force area of West Mercia Police. Clark was not overly concerned by this as the murder involved crime figures from his patch, but the last thing he needed was detectives from a rival force poking their noses into his activities. He led the party to the area at the side of the railway and pointed to the makeshift marker.

"Right boys, this is the spot… It's been there for 18 months so it's gunna stink!" Clark pulled a face of disgust in anticipation of their gruesome find and he stood well back and let the others get on with the digging. The dog handler stood nearby with the great Alsatian at his feet, but the dog seemed disinterested.

As the sun cast spectacular rays through the gaps in the huge oak trees, 'Clubber' Clark chain smoked and took regular sips from his hip flask. It was taking a long time and after about 2 and a half hours of digging one of the bobbies approached him with the news that they could not find anything.

"What do you mean you can't find anything? It's there next to the stick marker... It's a decomposing body, surely the dog should be able to find it?" Clark rushed back to the scene and climbed into the hole to search for himself. "Get that bloody dog back over here, it's here somewhere." The dog handler approached with the dog who was more interested in birds and squirrels.

"Gov, this is the best dog we've got, and he's been daahn there for the last hour and all raahnd the area. There definitely ay no bodies raahnd here ar guarantee it sir." The dog handler was convinced, and Clark believed him. He had originally thought that Scriven and Cole had been a little fast to give up the location and in his haste to get his 20 percent, he had fallen for it... 'Clubber' Clark was pissed off, he had wasted his time and he had been made to look a fool. "Right then... We better get the fuck out of here before the West Mercia lot turn up." Clark signalled for them to disperse and he frustratedly kicked trees and plants as he made his way back to his car.

Upon Clark's arrival back at the station, a rather attractive WPC on the front desk had a message for him.

"A Mr Harry Scriven has phoned for you sir... He said that it is urgent and can you give him a call back on this number." She handed him a piece of paper and Clark rudely snatched it as he made his way through to his office. He sat down in his chair, took another swig of whisky and then picked up the telephone.

"Hello." Scriven answered the call after just a few short rings.

"What the fuck is going on Scriven? Are you trying to make a fool out of me you bastard?"

"No... I can't talk on the phone. Come and meet me now... I will see you under the bridge on the cut next to the Neptune pub... Do you know it?"

"Yes..." Clark grunted and slammed the phone down. *Scriven better have a good excuse!* He thought to himself as he went back out to his car and drove the short distance from Old Hill Police station to the Neptune public house. He parked by the industrial units opposite the pub and crossed over Powke Lane and walked under the canal bridge.

"Hello Clarkie." Harry Scriven was stood under the bridge and Micky Cole and Eddie Fennel stood either side of him looking purposeful and menacing.

"What's going on?" Clark demanded to know what was happening but Scriven punched him hard in the stomach and then slung him forcefully against the wall and held him by the scruff of his neck. Scriven pushed his face into Clark's, his eyes lived and his mouth and teeth snarling like a rabid dog.

"Yow think yam so clever do yer... Well teck a look at these." Scriven looked back towards the other two men and Fennel produced a large blown-up photograph from his pocket that clearly depicted 'Clubber' Clark accepting a substantial wad of cash from Harry Scriven at the side of the railway track in the Wyre Forest. Clark groaned inwardly upon realisation that he had been well and truly set up. "You see, aer Eddie was there yesterday after all." Scriven enjoyed his moment of payback. "He's good with a camera is Eddie... I think it's time we negotiated a new deal Clarkie..." Clark said nothing. "This is how its gunna be from now on... We ay selling drugs no more and we ay paying you nothing. There will be no investigations involving my son into the murder of Cedric Tanner or the disappearance of Davey Price... Plus, there will be no investigations into the business ventures of Eddie Fennel... If these terms are met then we will keep hold of these photographs and they will not be shared with the Chief Constable... Ar doubt he would want to play golf with yer if he saw them pictures Clarkie..." Scriven smiled and intensified his grip on Clark's collar so that the corrupt copper could barely breathe.

"Ok Harry, you got it." Clark struggled to speak and he nodded as best as he could. Scriven suddenly let go of him and kneed him in the testicles with force. The Detective fell straight to the floor in pain and Cole and Fennel erupted into laughter as all three men stepped over the crooked cop and made their way inside the pub for a celebratory drink…

Chapter 21
July 1979

In the world of politics, 1979 was a ground-breaking year as Conservative leader Margaret Thatcher became the first female Prime Minister of the United Kingdom on the 4th of May. Trevor Francis became the first £1 million footballer when he signed for Nottingham Forest and he would go on to score the only goal in the European cup final as Forest defeated Swedish champions Malmo FF in a 1-0 game at the Olympiastadion in Munich. In Yorkshire, fear spread through the streets as Peter Sutcliffe, the Yorkshire Ripper claimed his eleventh and twelfth victims in Halifax and Bradford. In the Black Country, Harry Scriven, Micky Cole and Eddie Fennel had no more problems with DCI 'Clubber' Clark and the three 'businessmen' thrived outside of the drugs trade.

Eddie Fennel continued to run a highly successful security firm providing door staff and other forms of 'protection' throughout the Midlands. His business practices were not always 100 percent ethical, however 'Clubber' Clark upheld his end of the bargain and ensured that Eddie Fennel was free from police interference. Harry Scriven enjoyed semi-retirement with his wife Suzy. He had kept a holiday home in Spain and the couple spent much of their time on the Costa del sol with the Mucklows. Scriven had purchased two nightclubs in the Black Country area that had thrived under the management of his son Micky Cole. There had been the odd set back, but Cole had managed to more or less continue his abstinence from drug usage, and he enjoyed overseeing the management of his father's clubs. Cole had been gifted a generous stake in the business and this had been a great incentive for him to make sure that the clubs were thriving and that he in turn also became a very wealthy man. This was a shrewd move on Scriven's part as he knew that in giving his son a business opportunity outside of drugs, it would help to keep him clean.

July 1979 had been very dry with temperatures and sunshine slightly below average. However, by Friday the 27th the temperature had risen to over 30 degrees and as Micky Cole walked into the extensive beer gardens of the Sun at Romsley, he wore a short sleeved, silk shirt, white chinos, a pair of aviators and an elaborate, diamond encrusted, gold Rolex. Seated at a wooden bench, smoking cigarettes and loudly drinking beer were the crew. The men Cole had come to regard as his family, and he had a big announcement to make.

Seated around the bench and enjoying the intense summer sun were Eddie Fennel, Barry O'Leary and Harry Scriven.

"Where yow bin? Yer beers getting warm and we'm on our third pint!" Eddie Fennel teased and moved up so that Cole could sit down.

"Ar bin daahn the doctors ay I." Cole made the announcement and Scriven immediately looked over with concern.

"Why? What's wrong with yer?"

"Nothing. Ar was there with aer Cathy."

"Well, what's wrong with her then?" Scriven thought highly of his daughter in law and he knew that she was good for helping Micky to stay on the straight and narrow.

"Her's good, but ar've got an announcement to meck." Cole took a long drink of his lukewarm beer and smiled in anticipation. "Cathy's pregnant, ar'm gunna be a dad and yow'm gunna be a grandad!" Cole looked proudly at his father and Scriven was almost moved to tears. The men around the table were quick to congratulate their friend and Scriven sent Barry O'Leary into the pub to fetch champagne.

"Fuckin' hell Mick, its abaaht time ay it aer kid? We was beginning to think that yow was a jaffa!" Fennel patted Cole on the back and laughed.

"What's a fuckin' jaffa?" Cole was confused.

"A seedless orange!" Fennel burst out into laughter again and Cole took it in good humour as the three men laughed, joked and shared the banter. O'Leary came back with the champagne and four glasses and Harry Scriven poured them a glass each.

"Right. It's Friday night and ar'm celebrating. Ar'm tecking yer all in mar car to Lily's and we'm gunna get smashed. Champagne and cigars on the house!" Cole had christened the Dudley nightclub Lily's after his mother and he was eager to celebrate the good news.

"Me and him am fuckin' 60 years ode... We ay dancing ter that Disco shit." Scriven looked at Fennel and smirked.

"Hang on a minute Harry, ar bay 60 yet!" Fennel protested. "Ar'm up for it... Saahnds like a good night. It's yower club Harry."

"Ar know but ar dow gew in!" Scriven held up his hands and laughed. They were celebrating the news of his grandchild and of course he was going to take part. The four friends had another round at the Sun before piling into Micky Cole's white BMW E23 728i. The E23 was the first incarnation of the popular 7 series which was the flagship luxury vehicle in the BMW range. The other men left their own cars on the pub car park which was standard procedure as they would often be too intoxicated to drive and end up ordering taxis.

The car was luxurious inside and Micky Cole insisted on playing the latest cassette from Earth Wind and Fire. Cassette players in cars had become popular in the mid-70s and the album 'I am' was the 9th studio album by the popular R and B band. It was released in June 1979 and the first single was 'Boogie Wonderland' which Cole could not help but groove to as he threw the 7 series around corners.

"Yow got any Tony Bennett records Mick?" The older men in the car were not overly impressed with Mick Cole's choice of music, but it was his night and the cassette was only a taster of what they were about to get once inside the club.

As the BMW pulled up outside the nightclub, a member of staff came straight outside and took the keys from Cole and parked the car. The July night was hot and sticky and the sounds of greasy Disco burst out of the sweaty club; the floor was pulsating with the sounds of fat bass grooves and Cole could hear the inner thoughts of the old men as they complained inwardly.

Micky Cole led the other three men past the lengthy queue of revellers who were waiting to get inside and straight to the entrance where two enormous doormen were surprised to see their employer Eddie Fennel. They immediately straightened their ties and respectfully held the doors open so that the four men could go inside. Once inside the club, they were instantly greeted by 'Disco Inferno' by The Tramps and Harry Scriven actually thought that he was going to 'burn baby burn' as it was so hot in there. Cole clicked his fingers and an attractive blonde in a ridiculously short skirt brought over chilled champagne and cigars before leading them to an exclusive area that was reserved for VIPs. Cole thanked her with a slap on the backside and the men sat down to enjoy their perfectly cold drinks.

"It's a nice place yow got here Micky." Barry O'Leary lent over and congratulated Cole on the club, though he could be barely heard over the loud music. O'Leary was not a blood relative, but he had been a loyal servant since he was a teenager in the early 1950s and he still continued to do odd jobs for Harry Scriven. He also knew Micky Cole well from when they both worked for Dickie Hickman. In fact, it was Barry O'Leary who had introduced Cole to Hickman back in 1973, and from that point Cole had begun the process of trying to track down his real father.

"Thanks Bazza. If there's anything ar can get for yer, just let me know." Cole noticed two particularly attractive looking girls on the dance floor. It was always the shortest skirts that he noticed first. He was not much into dancing, but the least he could do was offer them a drink and then get chatting. He made his excuses and made his way over towards them as the other three looked on. Harry Scriven was still feeling uncomfortable. *He was too old to be inside a nightclub, even if he did own the place, and the music was definitely not to his taste.*

"We'm getting ode mate." Scriven looked over towards Eddie Fennel and tried his best to be heard.

"Yu'm only as ode as the woman yer feel and yower wench is a lot younger than yow!" Fennel enjoyed his cigar and did not feel out of place. He was used to being around nightclubs from his security firm and he quite enjoyed it. Before Scriven could respond he suddenly noticed some rather suspicious activity going on in a dark corner of the room.

"Did you see that Eddie?"

"See what Harry?" Fennel turned around and glanced in the same direction Scriven was looking.

"That chap over there, with the long hair. He just gave them chaps something and they paid him."

"What?" Fennel took the accusation very seriously. He was responsible for security and if his boys were letting dealers in or even worse, they were on the 'take' then something needed to be done about it. Fennel and Scriven continued to watch the long-haired man closely and they were not surprised to see him repeat the process several times. Scriven's heart sank. *Was Micky involved? Was he using the club Scriven had bought for him to sell drugs and launder cash?* Fennel and Scriven watched further and then saw that the long-haired man joined up with another who had black hair and a somewhat Celtic look about him. The second man passed the long-haired man something from out of his pocket and Scriven and Fennel had seen enough. Scriven instructed Fennel to keep an eye on them and then he got up and marched over to where Micky Cole was flirting with the two women.

"Mick, ar need to have a word with you." Scriven tapped his son on the shoulder and Cole immediately turned to face him.

"See you later girls." He gave the women a wink and they both giggled and went off to dance some more. "What's up dad?" In the last 12 months Cole had started referring to Scriven as dad and words could not describe how happy this had made Harry Scriven feel.

"Am yow selling drugs in this club?" The question surprised Micky Cole and he felt disappointed that his father had thought of it.

"Fuck off! I ay doing that shit no more!" Cole spoke the truth and Scriven immediately felt guilty for making such an accusation.

"Ok… Sorry aer kid… But there's some fellas over in the corner who look like they'm dealing."

"Where?" Cole looked around angrily. If he wasn't going to profit from the sale of drugs, then he certainly didn't want anyone else doing it in his club! Harry Scriven gestured over for Eddie Fennel to join them at the side of the dance floor and then the three men approached the two shifty characters in the dark corner.

"Hello gentlemen. Are you having a good night?" Cole spoke first and the short haired man shot him a suspicious look. His eyes were dark and aggressive, and his face was thickset and threatening.

"What's it to you?" The man had a thick Dublin accent and had no interest in speaking to Micky Cole.

"This is mar club mate… Would you two mind walking this way? I'd like to have a chat with you somewhere private." Cole's expression changed from friendly to insistent.

"What if we don't want to?"

"Then me and my two associates behind me will kick the shit aaht on yer here on this dancefloor and take whatever shit yow'm pushing for ourselves… But if you do as I ask then we can solve this a lot more discretely without causing a scene and you woe have to explain to yower boss how yow lost yer gear… Believe me mate, ar know how it works." Cole gave the Irishman no choice. He looked at the two men behind Micky Cole, *they were no Spring Chickens, but they still looked tough.* His long-haired accomplice was no fighter and he didn't fancy his chances on his own. He nodded reluctantly and followed Cole to an office that stood at the back of the club as 'Ring my bell' by Anita Ward rang out through the building.

Cole sat down at his desk in the middle of the room and poured himself a brandy from a cut glass decanter that stood on one side. He took a drink and then poured one a piece for Fennel and Scriven.

"Right… Ar'm celebrating tonight and the last thing ar want is to spend it in here with yow pair of pricks. We can do this the easy way or we can do this the hard way… Who are you working for?"

"Your feckin' mother!" The short haired dealer did not know that Cole's mother was in fact dead, but his words were like a red rag to a bull. Cole stood up and brought his face closer to the thuggish looking drug dealer.

"Mar mother's dead…" The dealer shrugged.

"Go fuck yerself Sassenach!" Sassenack was a derogatory term used by the Irish and Scottish to describe the English but Cole had no idea what it meant. He gave the word no further thought and quickly punched the man hard in the stomach and then brought his head down hard onto the desk and into the cut glass decanter several times. A mixture of blood, glass and brandy spilt out over the wood and dripped onto the floor and Cole turned to face the other long-haired dealer who looked on with fear. Cole had noted straight away that the skinny man with the long hair was probably the most likely to talk. Scriven and Fennel stood by and sipped their drinks as Fennel was feeling secretly worried in case his doormen had been in on it. The shorthaired man tried to move and Cole pushed his face further into the crushed glass and it made an horrendous noise as his cheek bones and torn tissue grinded and crunched against the broken pieces.

"If yow dow want this to happen to you then ar suggest yow tell us what we want to know!" Cole looked at the long-haired man again and then pulled a pair of pliers from out of his desk draw. He went back to the short-haired dealer who was barely conscious on the table and then turned him over so that he was facing him. Cole placed one hand on his neck to hold him in place and the brought the pliers up to his mouth and grasped one of the dealer's front teeth.

"Don't go too far aer kid." Harry Scriven suddenly stepped in. The episode was beginning to remind him of his encounter with Jimmy Danks back in 1955 and he was hoping that things would not escalate too far. "Ar'm sure our friend here is ready to talk now?" Scriven turned to face the long-haired man who had urinated in his trousers and it had proceeded to dribble down his leg and out onto the floor. "Who sent yer here kid?"

"We are from a caravan site. We are just travelling through… We won't come here again I promise." The long-haired man also had a strong Irish accent and Scriven assumed that they were gypsies. The last thing they needed was a feud with local traveller families and Scriven began to worry that the damage had already been done. "Micky, put the pliers down." Cole looked at him for a few seconds and then reluctantly put them away. The man on the desk wiped the blood from his face and Scriven handed him his own brandy. "Here. Teck a drink mate." Scriven took a £50 note from out of his pocket. "Listen boys, we are prepared to overlook this one mistake, but we will not have drugs in our clubs…" Scriven handed the short-haired man the money. "Sort your face out and buy a new shirt." The dealer snatched the note and grunted and Micky Cole could not believe what was going on.

"Just one question before you go." Eddie Fennel suddenly piped up. "Were the doormen in on it? Did you pay them?" The long-haired man shook his head and Fennel was relieved, the man was too nervous to lie and Fennel believed him.

As the two drug dealers swiftly left the club through a rear exit, Micky Cole turned to face his father with fire in his eyes.

"What the fuck was that? You heard what he said about mar mother?"

"He was just some dealer, he dow know yow from Adam Mick… Dow teck it personally, it's street talk… Surely yow know that?" Cole took a long drink of brandy. He knew his father was right, but he was still angry.

"If those boys are gypsies, and they definitely sounded like gypsies, then the last thing we want is some kind of war with them… You're gunna be a father soon Mick… Think about your wife and unborn child… Yer dow wanna gew around picking unnecessary fights." Cole nodded reluctantly. "Lock this room up and we'll get Barry to clean it up on Monday." Scriven put a reassuring hand on his son's back. He was beginning to show some of the leadership skills of his cousin Billy

Mucklow and he was not living in his shadow anymore. "Now lets gew and enjoy ourselves!"

Chapter 22

Teresa Fennel was in her late 50s but she still looked good. She was every young man's attractive 'older woman' fantasy and she knew it. She also loved her husband and had supported him through thick and thin. When Billy Mucklow went to prison and left Fennel to fend for himself, when Cedric Tanner had tried to muscle in on Fennel's manor, when Fennel was sent to prison himself for fraud and through the darkest days of the drug trade, Teresa Fennel had been there for her husband. Not only did she love him, but she also loved the lifestyle that he had given her. The expensive sports car, the detached house, the holidays in Spain, the expensive clothes. *He did go out drinking with his gangster pals nearly every night, but it was a small price to pay and it was the life that she had chosen.*

The previous night, Fennel had been out at the club celebrating the pregnancy of Micky Cole's wife Cathy and tonight was Saturday so that meant that Fennel was at the Neptune on Powke Lane with Tummy 'Ducks' and their old friends Homer and Tromans. Teresa didn't mind, she enjoyed her Saturday nights in front of the television with a bottle of Mateus Rose and a block of Cadbury's Bournville.

As she lay, scantily clad in a satin nightie on the leather sofa, she smoked cigarettes and drank her wine. She watched the Paul Daniels magic show, but she found it somewhat boring. Magic didn't really interest her. Her husband had been making other people's money disappear for the last 30 years and she found that fascinating, but magicians were not really her thing. She stretched her long legs out on the sofa, stood up and turned off the television before walking over to the LP collection. She scanned the titles and pulled out her favourite Dean Martin album. *Chocolate, wine, cigarettes and the silky-smooth tones of Deano would make her Saturday night perfect.* She pulled up the lid of the record player when suddenly she heard a loud bump come from upstairs. *Who on earth could it be?* The house was completely empty apart from herself and their Staffordshire bull terrier and he was old and asleep on the floor in front of the TV. She told herself that it was probably just a noise from outside and she took the record from out of the sleeve when suddenly she heard the sound again, but this time she clearly heard footsteps walk across the upstairs landing. A total and utter fear came over her as with horror she realised that she was not alone in the house. *What should she do? She knew that her husband had guns, but they were hidden upstairs in the study and she could not risk going up there.* The dog, though once strong and powerful, was now old and not so good on his legs so he would be of no great protection. She put down the record and began to panic. *She could telephone the Neptune pub and tell her husband to come home, but chances were the intruder would hear her and realise that she was on to him.* Her Lotus Europa was parked in the garage and she thought of driving over to the pub to fetch her husband, but then she realised that the keys to the garage were on Eddie's keys and he had those with him. *Was she being paranoid? Was there really somebody in the house with her? The front door had been locked the whole time and she had definitely not seen anyone pass her.* As she sat alone in the living room in her sexy attire, she felt vulnerable. The intruder could have easily got in through the back door or any one of the many open windows, as it was late July and the weather had been over 30 degrees the previous day. She pulled up her bare-naked knees and hugged them tightly as she buried her face into her legs. *Was he up there now? Listening to her heavy breathing? Ready to pounce at any moment?* She remembered the stories she had heard on the news of the Yorkshire Ripper and she began to feel even more terrified as she wondered if maybe he had travelled down to the Midlands from Yorkshire. It wasn't 'that' far away and being Irish she was not as familiar with English geography as she could have been. She listened hard again for more movement and she could feel her own heartbeat racing with fear. She downed her glass of wine, poured herself another and lit a cigarette to try and steady her nerves.

As she sat in almost total silence for another hour and a half she anxiously looked around the room for something she could use as a makeshift weapon. Whoever was upstairs had not made their move yet and as the minutes passed excruciatingly slowly, she hoped and prayed that the intruder would hold off so that her husband could get home.

Teresa Fennel had finished the wine and had chain smoked all of her cigarettes when she finally heard the familiar rumble of her husband's straight 6 Jaguar on the drive outside and she had never been so relieved to hear anything in her life. The key turned in the lock and Fennel walked in with a bag of sweets for Teresa and a bag of Jay's pork scratchings for himself.

"Eddie!" Teresa whispered over to him quietly and Fennel could not understand why she was whispering in their own home.

"What's the matter bab? Why you talking quiet?" Fennel had a few drinks in his system and he did not understand the need for subtlety.

"There's somebody upstairs, I heard them moving around. I've sat here for the last two hours scared out of my mind!"

"Yer what?" Fennel frowned and tried to comprehend what she was saying.

"There is an intruder in the house Eddie and they are moving around upstairs!" Teresa raised her voice slightly in frustration and Fennel finally got the gist of what she was trying to say.

"Yow'm fuckin joking bab?" Fennel felt instantly angry that his wife had been made to feel afraid and he marched loudly up the stairs without fear or concern for the potential consequences. He pushed open the door of the master bedroom which he shared with his wife, switched on the lights and then searched the room meticulously. It was empty so he moved back out onto the landing and into his daughter's old bedroom. She had since got married and moved out, and as he searched he found that the room was also empty. He quickly looked in the bathroom with no success before coming to the conclusion that if anyone was in the house, then they must be hiding in his upstairs study. At the back of his mind he was thinking that his wife had probably drank too much wine and that she was being paranoid, but he would look anyway. He crossed over the landing, into the room and switched on the light switch. The room remained dark. Somebody had unscrewed the lightbulb... As Fennel stood there in the dark room, he could hear heavy breathing in the blackness and just as he was about to lunge forwards into the shadows and tackle whoever was there, a small Tiffany lamp on his desk suddenly flickered on.

"Hello Eddie... I've been expecting you." Fennel recognised the voice straight away but it took him a few seconds to make out the face as the small lamp did not give out much light and the man's face remained in the shadows.

"What the fuck are you doing here? I haven't seen you in over 30 years!" Fennel was confused, angry and surprised all at once.

"I thought I'd pop in to see how my cousin was doing." Johnny O'Connor had not appeared to age much though he was clearly in his 50s.

"Fucking hell Johnny, you dow break into people's homes and wait in the darkness and scare the shit ahht on folks!" O'Connor laughed.

"I wanted to surprise you Eddie. Aren't you going to offer me a drink?" Johnny O'Connor wore a black suit and his eyes and features looked dark and menacing amongst the shadows of the room. Eddie Fennel went downstairs to reassure his nervous wife before returning back up to his study with a bottle of Bushmills Irish Whiskey and two glasses. He placed them down on the table and pulled up a chair opposite his Irish cousin before pouring the drinks.

"What are you doing here Johnny?"

"I had no choice but to leave Ireland. My father died a couple of years back and since then it has not been a safe place for me. Basically, I had to get out of Ireland or I would have been killed mate." O'Connor nodded a thanks for his drink and gratefully swallowed it down.

"Who could force you out though Johnny? I thought you were connected? A fully-fledged member of the IRA?" Fennel was confused.

"You're right... I was. But Sinn Fein don't take very kindly to the kind of business activities I was involved in and when my father died I lost all protection." O'Connor shook his head with disappointment. He was still devoted to his country and his political cause, but his greed and devotion to money was greater.

"What kind of business are you in Johnny?"

"You know me Eddie... Always ducking and diving, trying to make a bob or two. Like the old days back in Dublin when me and you were on the hussle... They were good old days weren't they Eddie?" Fennel nodded but a deep sense of dread began to fill his mind as he knew what was about to come next.

"So what business are you involved in now Johnny?" Fennel repeated the question.

"I'm in the drugs game now so I am... There's a lot of feckin' money to be made there mate... Only problem is, Sinn Fein don't feckin' like it. They prefer to see themselves as political activists these days and they can't have known IRA soldiers running around Dublin making drug deals!" Fennel shook his head disapprovingly.

"So why are you here? And how did you find out where I live?"

"Your wife Teresa has a sister in Dublin who she writes to. She gave me your address." O'Connor smiled and Fennel was kind of pleased to see him. They were cousins and had had fun together in Dublin in the late 1940s.

"But why are you here Johnny?"

"I heard that you were in the security business and that you control the doors of a lot of prominent night clubs in the midlands." Fennel could not believe what he was hearing and he knew exactly where the conversation was going.

"So?" Fennel's tone changed slightly.

"I also heard that you and your pals own a couple of popular clubs locally."

"I do not own them personally."

"These men are respected crime figures around here with a lot of influence, even with the Police? I could use friends like that myself... Harry Scriven and Micky Cole?" O'Connor took another drink of his whisky and spoke with confidence.

"Well, you certainly have done your homework Johnny." Fennel poured more whisky for his cousin.

"We can all make a lot of feckin' money together... I have a contact. He brings the gear into Ireland on a small boat... The Irish navy consists of a rubber dingy and two rubber rings so we don't get much trouble." O'Connor laughed at his own joke and Fennel couldn't help but smile. "Then I can get the stuff brought over here. I can manage that, I have the right connections. Then you and your boys come in and help me distribute the product... I heard that Micky Cole has particular talents in this area?"

"They woe have nothing to do with drugs Johnny... And neither will I." It was not the reaction O'Connor was looking for. "Wait a minute, did you send two of your boys into Micky's club last night?" Fennel suddenly remembered that the two men they apprehended in the club the previous night both had Irish accents. O'Connor smiled.

"Yeah... Those boys work for me. I have been staying with friends whilst I am in the country. The gypsies help me bring the stuff over from Ireland." Fennel sighed and downed his whiskey. "Your man Micky Cole has a wee bit of a temper so he does." O'Connor smirked.

"Yeah he fuckin' does and so does his ode man and they woe teck kindly ter yow pushing drugs in their clubs!"

"That's where you come in Edward. Me and my gypsy pals mean business and we are certainly not scared of those two!"

"Well, yer can count me out Johnny... My answer is no... Ar bay touching drugs again." Johnny O'Connor did not look impressed.

"You feckin' owe me Fennel!" O'Connor suddenly raised his voice in anger. "I saved your feckin' life back in Dublin and I also got a message to your feckin' wife so that she could join on that boat back to England... If it wasn't for me, you wouldn't have your lovely wife and you would be feckin' dead!" Fennel could not argue with the truth and he was grateful for what O'Connor had done, but he could not go back into drugs.

"What do you want me to say Johnny? Me and Teresa both appreciate what you did for us... But I will not go back into the drugs game.

"You disappoint me Edward." O'Connor downed his second drink and gave Fennel a look that was both intimidating and disappointed. "This isn't the last you'll be hearing from me Eddie... I do not give up... You owe me and I intend to collect..." O'Connor stood and walked around the desk until he stood menacingly over Eddie Fennel.

"Where are you staying? Can I offer you a bed for the night?" Fennel was not happy with Johnny O'Connor, but he was family and he had saved his life in Dublin in 1946.

"No... I'm with the travellers over in Balsall Heath, Birmingham." Fennel knew the area. There was a Tinkers camp and scrap car dump on waste ground near the red-light district in the inner-city slum of Balsall Heath. It was near to the Mount Pleasant School which was situated between Balsall Heath Road and Belgrave Road. "They are a very loyal bunch. I feel at home with them, they are like family to me." The dig was intended to offend Fennel but in reality he could not care less. He did not consider himself as Irish and he certainly had no time for drug dealers.

Johnny O'Connor said nothing more and he swiftly left the room, went down the stairs, out of the house and vanished into the night... Eddie Fennel stood routed to the spot and wished that the entire encounter had been nothing more than a bad dream...

Chapter 23

In the 1960s, lager was an upmarket drink in the U.K and only accounted for a tiny share of the British beer market. Lager was considerably more expensive than bitter or mild and many affluent drinkers began to drink it as a portrayal of wealth in much the same way that they would choose to buy a premium car such as a Mercedes, Jaguar or BMW. In the early 1970s, lager was around 35percent more expensive than a pint of best bitter, however, by 1979 lager was becoming more popular as the drink now accounted for 29percent of all beer sales. Traditionally, lager came from Europe and the word lager derives from the German word lagerbier. Eddie Fennel had gotten a taste for lager whilst holidaying in Spain where he had enjoyed San Miguel; but as he sat in the bar of the Neptune on a Friday afternoon, he drank Carling Black Label which was the biggest selling lager in Britain at that time. Carling was a Canadian beer that was brewed under licence in Burton on Trent and would eventually go on to become regarded as a British lager. It was cold and moist and quenched Fennel's thirst in the August heat, but compared to the European equivalents he had consumed in Spain; Carling Black Label was far inferior. *Any port in a storm!* He would often tell himself.

On a Friday afternoon in the Neptune, Paddy, the landlord who was really named Claude but was christened 'Paddy' on account of his military service in the Enniskillen Fusiliers, an Irish regiment of the British army; had a special licence that allowed him to open the pub early. This was so that a long-haired Asian man with particularly large teeth could collect copious amounts of beer to be taken to local foundries so that the workers could enjoy a thirst-quenching beer whilst performing their gruelling work inside the intense heat of the Black Country foundries.

Eddie Fennel would often take advantage of the extra drinking time and as he stood at the old wooden bar that had remained vastly unchanged from when he had drank there in the 40s, he thought about how he had not heard anything from his cousin Johnny O'Connor in nearly a week. *Maybe he had gone back to Ireland? Maybe he had moved to a different part of England?* Fennel didn't really care. He did not want to get dragged into drugs again, so no news was good news.

The back room was being used more for pool and cards and as Eddie Fennel now spent much of his time at the Haden Cross with Harry Scriven and Micky Cole, he tended to remain at the bar when he drank in the Neptune.

"Tummy 'Ducks' bin in?" Fennel lent on the bar and asked if his friend had been in the pub lately.

"I ay sid him all week bab." The barmaid replied as Fennel downed his beer. "Yow want the same again Eddie?" Fennel nodded.

"Ar… And one for yourself bab." The barmaid thanked him and poured a pint for Fennel and a large gin for herself. Fennel wondered where his friend was. Tummy 'Ducks' helped to manage the security firm and was well paid, but even though he was an old friend, Fennel did not always trust his honesty and he often wondered how much work Tummy 'Ducks' actually did for his money. "Ar bet he will be in later bab, it's Friday night!" The barmaid shrugged and offered her thoughts.

"Ar bet he will cus he knows ar will be up the Cross later with Harry." Fennel didn't believe that Tummy 'Ducks' was actually avoiding him, he had never done so before. Fennel still had the incident with Johnny O'Connor 6 nights previously on his mind and he was waiting for his Irish cousin's next move. Just then, a scruffy looking man in a black leather jacket, shaved hair and a vicious scar down the right side of his face entered the pub. Fennel had not seen him before and he watched him curiously.

"Pint of Guinness." The man had an Irish accent and for obvious reasons it instantly caught Fennel's attention. The barmaid poured the drink and the man paid her without thanking her. He sat down on a stool and turned to face Fennel who was at the other end of the bar. The Irishman had dark staring eyes that looked wild and intense and Fennel had a strong inkling that he was connected to Johnny O'Connor. The two made eye contact and Fennel smiled politely and went back to his beer.

"Your name Fennel?" The Irishman grunted and Fennel looked up.

"Who want's ter know?"

"My names Byrne... Liam Byrne. I work for Johnny O'Connor." Fennel nodded and took a drink of his beer. He was not surprised.

"What do you want Mr Byrne?"

"Johnny O'Connor says you need to reconsider his proposition." Fennel laughed.

"Fuck off mate... Ar bay interested." Byrne did not laugh. The intensity of his eyes grew stronger and the scar on the side of his face gave him an aggressive and menacing appearance.

"You have a nice wife so you do Mr Fennel." Byrne's face did not show a hint of feelings or emotion.

"What yow mean by that aer kid?" Fennel placed his pint on the beer mat and stepped closer to Byrne.

"I was just saying that you have a nice wife... I also heard that you have a nice daughter... It would be such a shame if anything were to happen to them."

"Like what?" Fennel was livid and it was taking all of his restraint to control himself.

"Maybe if you give Mr O'Connor what he wants you will not need to find out what happens to your wife and child Mr Fennel." Fennel said nothing. He diverted his eyes to the bar before suddenly swinging back around with an almighty right hook that smashed Byrne of his stool and onto the floor. Before the Irishman could react, Fennel smashed the three quarters full glass of Guinness into his face before pummelling his head into the hard wooden bar several times. Fennel then grabbed him by the scruff of the neck and pinned him to the bar before picking up a piece of broken glass and pushing it into Byrne's throat. He made a small cut that was dangerously close to the man's Adams apple and applied just enough pressure.

"Yow as much as look at mar wife and daughter the wrong way and ar'll cut yower fuckin' throat open and teck a piss in the hole!" Fennel was fuming but the injured gypsy remained calm.

"I'm just delivering a message Mr Fennel… Johnny says he will be in touch." Liam Byrne smirked and Fennel punched him hard in the stomach before throwing him across the room towards the door. Byrne stood up, wiped blood from his face and gave Fennel an intimidating wink before leaving the pub.

"Yow ok Eddie?" The barmaid brought him a whisky and Fennel downed it in one.

"Yes bab… Ar think ar need to gew and speak to Harry…"

Eddie Fennel still owned the same old red mk2 Jaguar he had owned for nearly 20 years and as he crossed the road from the Neptune and got into his car, he did not realise that he was being watched. A blue Ford Transit van was parked just down the road and inside sat Liam Byrne and two burly skinhead gypsies. They watched closely and as Fennel's Jag accelerated away the Transit followed. The Jag turned right at the island and headed towards Old Hill before turning left onto Wrights Lane to avoid the town centre. The Jaguar continued to the end of the road before turning right onto Beauty Bank Road and then left onto Halesowen Road past the Council building. Eventually, Fennel's Jag turned right into the driveway of a grand detached house and the Transit pulled up close by to watch.

"That's Harry Scriven's place." Byrne sat at the wheel of the Transit and chewed gum. "He's the boss… Johnny says that if Fennel is still telling us to feck off, we need to persuade Harry Scriven instead." Byrne grinned as his colleagues shared his violent thoughts.

"Harry, ar need a word." Fennel was lucky to catch Scriven. He was just about to leave for the Haden Cross where they were due to meet later that night anyway, but what Fennel had to say was urgent.

"What's up Eddie? Ar'm gewin up the pub in a bit." Scriven was surprised by the sudden arrival of his friend.

"An old friend, a relative has turned up out of the blue mate." Fennel was nervous and Scriven could tell.

"Here, have a fake aer kid." Scriven passed Fennel a cigarette to calm his nerves before lighting it for him.

"This fella is trying to move his drug business from Ireland to England... It was his boys in the club the other night... He wants me to get his dealers into the venues ar look after and he wants yow and Mick to set up your ode distribution network." Fennel breathed deeply on his cigarette and Scriven laughed.

"Tell him ter fuck off... We ay interested."

"That's the problem Harry... I did but these boys are serious. He's connected to the gypsy mob in Balsall Heath and the fuckin' IRA!" Scriven suddenly stopped laughing and realised that the situation was serious.

"Just keep telling him we dow wanna know Eddie."

"The guy, Johnny O'Connor, saved mar life years agew and now he thinks that he has some kind of hold over me... He reckons that ar owe him!" This was the last thing that Harry Scriven needed. He had had the perfect relaxing retirement in Spain and since his return to England it had been one drama after another. The last thing he wanted was for his precious son Micky Cole to get mixed up in the drug trade again.

"Right Eddie... Relax... Yow gew over the Cross and ar'll gew and get changed and see you up there in a bit. We can have a chat abaaht it up there." Fennel nodded and went back out to his Jaguar and drove off. As Scriven went back inside he did not hear the Transit pull onto the drive and the three men get out. They were all carrying tools: bats, knuckle dusters and crow bars... Harry Scriven would not make it to the Haden Cross that night...

Chapter 24

For the first three weeks of August 1979, 'I don't like Mondays' by the Boomtown Rats was the U.K. number one selling single. The song was written by the Irish band's singer Bob Geldof after hearing of a school shooting in America. 16-year-old Brenda Ann Spencer had fired into a children's playground in San Diego, California and had killed two adults and injured eight children. When questioned as to why she had committed the atrocious act, she had simply replied "I don't like Mondays." As Eddie Fennel sipped Harp Lager at the bar of the Haden Cross with Barry O'Leary, the song played on the jukebox and Fennel thought about how much he disliked it.

"Where's Mick and Harry?" Barry O'Leary suddenly spoke and Fennel looked down at his watch. *What was taking so long? Harry was supposed to be coming right over and that was nearly 2 hours ago!* Fennel shrugged.

"Ar dow know mate... Maybe Suzy is keeping him busy?" Fennel joked and O'Leary smirked.

"Her could keep me busy any day Eddie. She turned me daahn a few times." O'Leary laughed and looked out of the window for signs of Cole and Scriven.

"Yow must be the only chap hers turned daahn aer kid." Fennel laughed and took out his cigarettes.

"Dow let Harry hear yer saying that!" O'Leary took the comment in good humour and gratefully accepted one of Fennel's cigarettes. Fennel looked at his watch again. *Something was wrong... Scriven and Cole were never this late.* Fennel suddenly began to fear that Johnny O'Connor had maybe caught up with them. A sinking feeling came over him and he suddenly remembered that O'Connor had gotten it into his head that Harry Scriven was the boss who controlled everything. *Maybe he had paid*

Harry a visit? Before Fennel could think anymore, the pub door suddenly flung open and Micky Cole burst in with eyes of fire.

"What's up Mick?" Fennel feared the worst.

"Who's Johnny O'Connor?" Fennel had never seen Micky Cole look so angry.

"He's mar cousin… He's over from Ireland." Cole's eyes widened and he took a step closer to Fennel.

"So why has he sent a van full of chaps raahnd to my ode mon's and put him in intensive care?"

"What? When? Is Harry ok?"

"Just, whilst yow pair have been sat in here supping. I want answers Eddie and they better be good!"

"Hang on a minute Mick, dow yow threaten me! We'm on the same side aer kid! How's Harry? Where is he?"

"He's in Russell's Hall… He's stable but they gid him a good lampin."

"How'd yow know it was Johnny O'Connor?"

"Cus that's the name he managed to give me whilst he was being carried out to the ambulance." The barman brought a large scotch over and Cole necked it in one. "What's gewin on Eddie?"

"Johnny O'Connor is a drug dealer, he's in with the gypsies. He wanted me ter gew in with him and give him access to the clubs… Ar told him ter fuck off."

"What's that got ter do with mar ode mon?"

"O'Connor knows that your ode mon owns some clubs and he's got it into his head that ar run the security firm for Harry."

"If anything happens to him then ar'm gunna hold yow responsible Eddie!" Fennel slammed his glass down onto the bar and squared up to Micky Cole.

"Fuck off Mick! I ay done nothing wrong!" Cole closed his eyes and turned to think for a minute.

"Yow pair fighting bay gunna solve nothing lads." O'Leary offered his advice but it wasn't really necessary.

"Right, we hit back hard… Where is this Johnny O'Connor?" Cole beckoned for the barman to bring him another scotch.

"He's staying with the gypsies over in Balsall Heath, the place will be a heavily armed fortress Mick." Fennel had previously been a highly experienced and effective soldier and he knew if targets were realistic or not.

"Its Friday night, them Paddy's will be aaht on the piss raahnd Brum somewhere I guarantee it." Cole was determined.

"A load of gypsies have been getting in the White Oss in Harborne… Mar wench lives over that way and ar gew in there sometimes… I even had a drink in there with Northfield Ronnie Hall! Me and Harry put him in a wheelchair back in the 50s. He can walk now but he dow half limp." O'Leary offered an interesting suggestion but the other two were not interested in his trip down memory lane at this time.

"Harborne… Is that close ter Balsall Heath Eddie?" Cole was not overly familiar with Birmingham geography.

"It ay that far Mick, abaaht 3 miles?"

"So it could be O'Connor's lot gewin in the White Oss?" Cole knocked back his second Whisky.

"Ar suppose so?" Fennel was not convinced, there were a lot of pubs in Birmingham; however, he had to show willing in case his lack of enthusiasm was mistaken for some kind of loyalty towards Johnny O'Connor.

"Right, lets gew! If they'm in there we will hit back tonight!" Micky Cole led the other two men out to his 7 series BMW that gleamed in the rich summer evening sun. "Get in! We'm gewin' hunting!" The three men got into the large car and Cole slammed the auto box into drive and screamed off the car park at full pelt. They sped towards Halesowen and then turned left up Mucklow's hill till they got to the Stagg and three horseshoes at the top where they carried on towards the Kings Highway in Quinton. Eventually they came out on the Hagley Road in Birmingham and Micky Cole drove like an absolute hooligan as his tyres screeched and smoked as he applied the handbrake to get the powerful rear wheel drive car sideways.

Barry O'Leary was in the back seats of the BMW and he was relieved when they finally pulled up outside the White Horse pub on York Street, Harborne. He had been genuinely worried that he was going to be sick from the particularly aggressive driving.

Cole flew out of the car and instantly pulled a pistol from out of his pocket.

"What the fuck am yer playing at Mick?" Eddie Fennel could not quite believe what he was seeing. "Am yow trying to get us all nicked before we even find them? We dow even know if Johnny is in there, he could be in any bloody boozer in Brum and that's a lot of fuckin' pubs!" Cole reluctantly nodded and slid the gun back into his pocket. "Let's just gew in there, order ourselves a pint each and see who's abaaht." Fennel's cautious approach made sense and Cole knew it. Micky Cole had always been calm, calculated and precise in his use of violence, but he was not used to having family and he felt particularly protective over them.

The Victorian region of Harborne was a middle-class suburb of the city of Birmingham; with parts of the area, known as Harborne village, dating from Anglo Saxon times. Harborne became known for its pubs and the famous 'Harborne run' pub crawl. This was in part due to the lack of pubs in nearby Edgbaston and Bournville as Harborne was a distinctly non-Quaker area of the city. The White Horse on York Street was a popular and prominent public house in Harborne and it first became a pub in 1861 when a Thomas Warden became its first licensee. The area had traditionally been under the control of the now deceased Isiah Boswell and the Brummie boys and as a result, Eddie Fennel, Barry O'Leary and Cole were not overly familiar with the location.

"Just stay calm Mick, ar'll let yow know if ar see O'Connor in there, but only if yow promise not to react straight away?" Fennel stroked his somewhat impressive beard that he had grown over the last twelve months and waited for a response.

"Ok Eddie, but meck sure yow tell me who he is, I ay never seen the bloke."

The three men strolled into the smoky, sweaty Birmingham pub and wondered how they could possibly find anyone in there. It was crammed full of people and Cole, Fennel and O'Leary pushed their way through to the bar. Fennel looked across the counter and was impressed to see that the selection of beers was broader and more cultured compared to what they were accustomed to.

"Three pints of Stella Artois please bab." Fennel eventually got served and thoroughly enjoyed his drink. He was nearly 60 years of age and he would much prefer to stand there and sink several pints of Stella as opposed to going after his cousin Johnny O'Connor. "So Harry is going to be ok Mick?" Fennel suddenly realised that he had simply assumed that Scriven would be ok, he found it hard to believe that someone as tough as Harry Scriven could not be ok.

"Yeah, he should be fine in the long run Eddie, but that ay the point... Where's that bastard O'Connor?" The pub was cramped and loud and Micky Cole struggled to make himself heard. Fennel had a good look around the main part of the bar and could not recognise anyone; but then he noticed that at the back, the room went around into a kind of L shape. He moved through the crowd and positioned himself at the edge of the bar where he could look around to the left. Fennel had been hoping that O'Connor would not be there, but to his disappointment, there he was sat in the corner at a circular table wearing a smart black suit surrounded by huge, menacing looking thugs. *What should he do? Tell Cole and risk a blood bath? Or say nothing and get accused of protecting Johnny?* In his own mind, Eddie Fennel was quite clear that his loyalties lay with Harry Scriven and Micky Cole; but Johnny O'Connor was still his cousin and had saved his life and enabled his wife to come to England... It was quite a dilemma but Fennel decided to let Cole know discretely.

"Mick... Johnny is around the corner, but he is surrounded by a load of heavy looking gypsies... They got a lot more blokes than us and yer cor move in here let alone have a scrap." Micky Cole thought very carefully about his next move. His initial thoughts were to casually walk over and shoot O'Connor in the head at point blank range; but the room was full of witnesses and he had to think about his pregnant wife and unborn child. Cole and Fennel moved to the other side of the bar so that they could see into the corner.

"Yer see that flash git sitting at the table? Black suit, dark hair, drinking champagne with a Jameson chaser?" Fennel tried to discretely describe O'Connor without blatantly pointing him out.

"Ar, looks like a fuckin' leprechaun!"

"That's O'Connor, look at all them big blokes around him Mick." Cole looked and could not deny that they had no chance that night. He did not want to give away their intentions in some botched pub brawl. He glanced at the table and saw that it was littered with a vast assortment of empty glasses and bottles and the Irishmen appeared to be more than worse for wear. Cole suddenly had an idea.

"Hey Eddie!" O'Connor suddenly recognised Fennel from across the crowded room. "Come on over and have some champagne mate." O'Connor gestured for Fennel to come to the table. "Bring your friend, the wines nice and cold."

"Seems very cosy to me?" Cole gave Fennel a suspicious look.

"Fuck off Mick, he's trying to get me into business with him. He needs my security firm, that's his goal." Fennel turned back to face O'Connor. "Shove it up your arse hole Johnny… Ar know what yow did to Harry!" Fennel shouted back and O'Connor smiled.

"It's just business Eddie… Nothing personal." O'Connor laughed at his own godfather pun and gestured again for Fennel to come over.

"Let's get the fuck aaht on here before ar shoot that prick!" Cole turned to walk away and much to Johnny O'Connor's disappointment Eddie Fennel followed him. Barry O'Leary was at the bar and as Cole and Fennel walked past to leave, Fennel nudged him and told him it was time for them to go.

The drive back towards the Black Country was relatively silent. Fennel sat and worried that Cole did not trust him and Micky Cole said nothing. He was deep in thought about the next course of action. They dropped O'Leary off first at his house in Old Hill and then came back on themselves so that Fennel could get in his Jag which was still on the Haden Cross car park. Fennel wondered why he was being dropped off last when it made more sense to drop him off first and he prepared himself for an attack from Cole.

"Right Eddie, this is the plan." Cole suddenly interrupted the silence and Fennel waited in anticipation. "Ar'll meet yow tomorrow morning by the cut at the bottom of Powke Lane at 5:00 AM... Bring some tools... Me and yow am gunna hit the camp site whilst they'm sleeping off their hangovers... We will leave Barry at home, he's fat and slow and will be a liability. I have another friend I will be bringing along." Fennel groaned inwardly and nodded. "Ar'm trusting yower loyalty Eddie... Dow let the family daahn." Fennel felt disappointed that his loyalty was even being questioned. *He had been a loyal servant to Willie Mucklow, Bill Mucklow and Harry Scriven since well before Micky Cole was even born...* He got out of the BMW and walked over to his Jaguar with the same nervous anticipation he had felt the night before he took part in the Normandy landings in 1944.

Chapter 25

Eddie Fennel glanced enviously at his wife as she slept peacefully alongside him. He had struggled to sleep the entire night and now it was 3:30 AM and he was due to meet Micky Cole in an hour and a half. The August rain beat against the window and Fennel wished that it's hypnotic rhythm would help him drift into a numb and dreamless slumber where his anxieties would cease to exist. He had spent the whole night thinking of what the next morning would bring. *Who was Micky Cole's friend who would be accompanying them? How many men would they be up against? Would he have to hurt his own cousin? Did hardcore Irish gypsies even get hangovers?* He sat up in bed and then got out. *It was no use trying to sleep now and he had tools to get ready.*

Fennel quickly got dressed and crossed the landing into his study where he opened up the draw of his old Victorian desk. He pulled out the trusty old Lugar and felt the cold steel in his hand as he wondered if he should take it or leave it at home. He certainly did not want to get hurt through lack of fighting back, but the penalties for being caught in possession of a firearm were understandably harsh and if it were to go off in the excitement of the day and somebody were to be killed, then he would spend the rest of his life in prison. Eddie Fennel desperately did not want to go back to prison. He had been in jail before and he certainly was tough enough to hack it, but he was nearly 60 years of age now and he was looking forward to a peaceful and relaxing retirement in the sun with Teresa. He had had enough of the drama, the scams, the fighting, the violence. In just a few more months he intended to sell his security firm and use the proceeds to buy a villa in Spain. He had it all worked out and the last thing he needed was to end up dead or worse still, a slower prolonged death seeing out his days away from his beloved wife and without the comforts and luxuries he had worked so hard to achieve. HE SIMPLY COULD NOT GO BACK TO PRISON! He sunk into the soft leather armchair that stood in front of the desk and stared aimlessly at the gun. *Why did Johnny O'Connor have to come over and stir up all this trouble when he (Fennel) was so close to retirement? Why was Micky Cole so intent on such a bloody and brutal revenge?* Fennel had even considered selling his security firm directly to Johnny O'Connor, but his own morals would not allow him to do it. As much as he wanted out, he simply could not hand it all over to a greedy drug dealer who just wanted to use it as a front for drug distribution. Sure, Fennel had been no saint in his life. He had defrauded many faceless credit companies and strongarmed wealthy night club owners into giving him lucrative security contracts, but he still retained a strong sense of ethics when it came to the drug trade. He always remembered his encounter in Homer Hill Park with the father who had just lost his daughter due to drugs and the freak snowfall had helped to make the day stand out in his memory. When it came to narcotics, Eddie Fennel had no problems in making the positive choice between money and morals.

Fennel made sure that the gun was not loaded and then pushed it into his jacket pocket. He glanced around the room and then walked over to the far wall where he picked a large Japanese Samurai sword from off the wall. It was ornate and authentic and Eddie Fennel would regularly ensure that it was sharpened and ready for use in the event of another intruder in the house. He stared at the impressive weapon for a full minute before placing it back on the wall and picking up a cricket bat and a small knife instead. He then walked sadly back into the bedroom and kissed his wife on the cheek as she lay sleeping. He almost had tears in his eyes as he thought of their retirement together in Spain. *Would they make it? Would he see her again? Was he too old for all of this? What would Micky think if he didn't turn up? Would Micky still go alone? If anything happened to Micky would it be his fault for not backing him up and how would he face Harry again?* Questions continued to fill his mind and eventually his sense of loyalty towards the men he regarded as family dissuaded him from getting back into bed with his wife…

Micky Cole sat and listened to the rain pepper the roof of his BMW as he smoked a cigarette. It was five to five and Cole had absolutely no doubt that Eddie Fennel would be there. In truth he had no questions over Fennel's loyalty, but he understood that his friend and distant relative was in an awkward situation as Johnny O'Connor was his cousin. However, he also knew that Fennel had a passionate hatred for drugs and family or no family, he would not go down that route again. Micky Cole on the other hand was only interested in personal revenge for the attack on his father.

Cole had been clean from drugs for over 4 years, but he still understood that there was a huge market for them. He had read about the American prohibition between 1920 and 1933 with much interest and he regularly had it at the back of his mind.

Prohibition was the nationwide constitutional ban on the production, importation, transportation and sale of alcoholic beverages in America. It had been quite a significant failure and had helped to ensure the greater financial success of organised criminal groups such as the Cosa Nostra who had profited from the illegal production, transportation and sale of alcohol. The gangsters established underground drinking establishments known as speakeasys where all members of the local community including police officers and politicians could engage in the illegalities of drinking alcohol. As a result, the government lost out significantly on the taxes that were to be gained from alcoholic beverages and the money went straight into the criminal hands of the Jewish and Irish gangs and most notably the Cosa Nostra.

Cosa Nostra is an alternative name for the Italian/American Mafia. Cosa Nostra translates in Sicilian to 'our thing' and is a highly organised crime syndicate that originated in the Italian region of Sicily in the 19th century. Over time, the group grew significantly and separated into individual 'families' who all followed the same organisational structure and code of conduct. It's members call themselves 'men of honour' and the act of becoming an official member of a family is referred to as becoming a made man. Only men who's ancestry can be traced back to Italy can become made men though others who operate within the family are regarded as associates.

The Mafia would go on to become highly established in America with the prohibition period allowing them to get an even stronger foothold in the country. By the 1970s the City of New York was overrun with Mafia activity and almost every element of society was controlled by them as part of a multibillion-dollar business.

Micky Cole figured that one-day certain narcotics would eventually become legal anyway and then the people whom he considered to be the biggest gangsters of all- the government- would be able to profit from high taxes. In his mind he would often wonder: *Why shouldn't I cash in on this whilst I still can?* He was expecting his first child and as he sat in his car on this rainy August morning, he thought that he wanted to *provide more and more wealth for Cathy and the baby.* The fact that O'Connor had ordered the beating of his father was all very inconvenient. *Maybe they could have done some good business together?* Cole's father-in-law, Bobby Murray, had now completely retired and after Cole had suddenly ended their previous arrangement, he would not be able to ever ask for the same favour again. In reality, Murray had actually been pleased when Micky had cleaned up his act for the sake of his daughter Cathy.

As Cole glanced down at his watch again, a sudden and wicked thought entered his mind… He instantly felt guilty for thinking it but it would not go away… *The biggest obstruction to his involvement in the lucrative prohibition of drugs was Eddie Fennel… Harry was retired and could be shipped out to Spain, but Fennel was fiercely anti-drugs. If something was to 'happen' to Eddie, then it would make life a lot easier…* He quickly dismissed the thought from his brain with guilt and tried not to think of it as he wiped condensation from the windows of his car.

Eddie Fennel's red Jaguar pulled up alongside Micky Cole's BMW bang on 5 o'clock and Fennel got out, opened up the boot and pulled out his rather sinister looking cricket bat. Cole got out of his car and shook the man's hand whilst still feeling an element of guilt.

"Morning Eddie. Yow alright mate?"

"Ar will be once we've sorted this lot aaht and we'm back in the bloody boozer aer kid." Fennel locked his car. "We gewin in yower motor Mick?"

"Ar, jump in the front." Cole nodded for Fennel to walk around and get in.

"Where's the other fella we'm teckin instead of Barry?" At that moment in time, Eddie Fennel wanted nobody other than Billy Mucklow himself to be backing them up... *The whole situation and assault on the gypsy camp would be perfect for Bill.* Cole smiled and opened up the rear door of the 7 series.

"Meet Max, he's mar best mate..." The biggest Rottweiler Fennel had ever seen jumped down onto the floor and as a dog lover himself he instantly fell in love with it. He was huge, aggressive looking and Fennel didn't know whether to hide or stroke him. "He's friendly, but when the shit hits the fan he gews psycho on command!" Cole smiled and patted his pet lovingly. Fennel looked at the canine and could not help but think that he did actually look remarkably like Billy Mucklow. *Maybe he had got his wish after all?* Cole ushered the dog back into the car and the two men climbed into the front. "Right, lets teach these motherfuckers a lesson!" Cole grinned and once again slammed the auto box into drive.

Micky Cole parked the luxury vehicle in Balsall Heath discretely around the corner from the gypsy camp.

"Yow cor leave a car like this raahnd here mate... I hope yow got insurance aer kid." Fennel looked out of the window at the poverty-stricken slum.

"This is mar fuckin' insurance!" Cole pulled his pistol from out of his glove compartment and loaded it.

"That the gun yow used to shoot Cedric Tanner with?" Fennel was intrigued.

"Dow talk saft Eddie." It was no secret between the men that Cole had murdered his former father who had abused him as a child. "Ar watched the fucker burn!" Cole grinned again and Fennel shared the enthusiasm. Cedric Tanner had threatened Fennel's family in the 60s and he had every reason to hate Tanner, though not as much as Micky Cole did.

As they got out of the car, an Indian girl in a tiny leather mini skirt approached them and Cole was distracted.

"You want business?" She smiled at them and offered her services.

"Maybe another time bab." Micky Cole slapped her backside and gave her a wink. Fennel waited for the stick thin prostitute to walk away and then spoke.

"Yow should pack them in Mick. Yow got a kid on the way and yer can catch all sorts off a whore." Fennel offered his worldly advice.

"Yow telling me yow ay ever had one Eddie?"

"Course I have, when me and Billy Mucklow escaped in Africa during the war and in Hamburg after the war, but once ar met aer Teresa all that stopped mate." Cole had forgotten that Fennel had been a gifted soldier during the Second World War and he figured that his experience would be useful. He opened the back door and attached Max to his chain lead.

"So what do you reckon Eddie? How am we gunna teck these fuckers daahn soldier boy?" Fennel looked in deep thought as he grabbed his cricket bat and surveyed the area.

"Lets be realistic Mick… There's gunna be loads of blokes in there and believe me them gypsy fellas can fuckin' fight mate. Plus they've probably got more angry dogs, or dags as they call them, than yow've had pox infected whores!" Cole half smiled but he knew that Fennel was right. He had been angry and reactionary the previous day but this morning he had become realistic in his expectations. Plus, at the back of his mind he had ideas of a potential 'business deal' with Johnny O'Connor further down the road. But before this could happen, he would have to first avenge his father's beating. Fennel pulled out a pair of binoculars and took a closer look at the gypsy camp and the junkyard that stood next door. "Ar suggest we hang abaaht outside and catch a couple of them on their own... We give em a good seeing to and leave um as a message to Johnny?" Fennel hoped that Cole would consider his suggestion, it was less dangerous and much more realistic.

"Yeah... Ok Eddie. That will send um a message and make things even." Fennel was surprised that Micky Cole went for it but he did not know that Cole had more lucrative plans on his mind.

At the side of the camp lay a junkyard that was full of rotting old cars from the 1950s and 60s and Fennel and Cole walked Max along the edge whilst they kept their eyes open for men who were gypsies. Dogs from within the camp barked nearby and every time they sounded Max would stop and his nostrils would flare up as he sniffed the air. After 20 minutes of walking, two men appeared from around the corner and walked towards them.

"Hey! What the feck are you two doing in here? You can't come on here nicking from our scrapyard!" As the men got closer, Cole recognised that they were the same two men they had caught dealing drugs in the club over a week ago. The gypsies suddenly recognised Cole and Fennel too and they turned to run back towards the campsite to alert their colleagues.

"Max fetch!" Cole yelled in a hoarse tone and the giant Rottweiler sprung forwards and caught up with the two travellers in no time at all. He grabbed the long-haired dealer's arm and pulled him to the ground before pinning him there and barking and growling aggressively in his face. The other dealer looked like he was about to get away and alert the camp, but Cole dropped onto one knee, aimed and fired a shot from his pistol that ricochet into the man's right leg. He fell to the floor in agony and Cole and Fennel knew that they only minutes to dispense their 'justice' before the other gypsies arrived to investigate the gunshot.

Cole apprehended the long-haired thug who was still pinned to the ground by Max. He kicked him several times in the chest, breaking a couple of ribs and then slapped him hard across the head.

"Max, bite!" Cole held the dealer up by his hair and then watched with vengeful satisfaction as the Rottweiler went to work on the man's face. Blood decorated the floor and the drug dealer's face would never look the same again; the price he paid for supporting an organization that had ordered and carried out the beating of Micky Cole's father.

Eddie Fennel walked over to the other dealer who lay on the floor with blood pouring from the bullet wound in his leg. *Fennel knew that he had to make a bold statement to Scriven, Cole and Johnny O'Connor and he knew that he had limited time in which to prove his loyalty. He almost felt apologetic as he went about his brutal work, but just like in the old days, he was simply acting upon the orders of others.*

"That looks nasty aer kid." Fennel gestured to the gaping wound in the man's leg.

"Feck you!" The injured man was full of defiance.

"Oh dear..." Fennel was sarcastic as he raised the cricket bat to the wound and proceeded to push the bullet in even further before wiggling the torn flesh back and forth with the end of the bat. The gypsy screamed in absolute agony and Fennel applied more pressure. "Now, yow be a good lad and give Johnny O'Connor a message from me... If me or mar family get anymore problems from yow lot then ar'm gunna cut his fuckin head off!" Fennel dropped to his knees and produced a rough, rusty and jagged knife from out of his pocket. He held the injured dealer up by the hair and then put the blade to the side of his mouth... In a motion that was half pushing and half sawing he used the rusty blade to cut a rough line from the edge of the man's mouth right back to his ear. Blood cascaded everywhere and Fennel's hands were covered as he repeated the same brutal, cold blooded action on the other side. The man could not move from the bullet in his leg and he passed out from the agony of the smile that would haunt him for the rest of his life. Fennel jumped up, blood covering his beard and camel coloured Crombie and walked back towards Micky Cole who was still looking on as he fed the long-haired dealer's face to the rottweiler. Cole eventually pulled the dog off and both men were left with permanent facial injuries and disfigurements that they would never get over…

"Now let's gew and have some fuckin' breakfast." Fennel placed the bat over his right shoulder as if he were a soldier marching with a gun and Cole and Max followed as they went back to the car and sped off.

Micky Cole and Eddie Fennel cleaned themselves up before heading into Cradley Heath High Street where they went into 'Stevens' café for a full English breakfast. They ordered three large breakfasts, one each for themselves and one for Max who ate from the plate on the floor. Some of the locals looked on with disgust as the men ate their black pudding, sausage, bacon and beans and the huge dog did the same as he obediently lay at the foot of the table. It was Max's breakfast and he deserved it!

"Them fuckers am gunna shit themselves now mate." Cole laughed and as he passed additional sausages to his beloved dog. They had had their revenge and now he hoped that there was room for business to be done, but Fennel was not as optimistic. *He knew exactly who they were up against and he knew that today's random acts of violence would not deter Johnny O'Connor and the gypsies in the slightest, but at least Cole had had his revenge!* Fennel placed a ridiculous amount of English Mustard onto his breakfast and continued to enjoy it.

"Yow lot cor last 5 minutes on yower own can yer?" An imposing voice suddenly sounded out of nowhere and it was tinged with humour and sarcasm as the door opened and the stranger walked in.

"Billy! What am yow doing back?" Fennel looked up from his breakfast with mixed emotions as Bill Mucklow walked into the café.

"Ar thought I'd find yow in here at this time of the day Eddie." Mucklow sat down at the table and helped himself to a slice of bacon.

"Ar got a phone call from aer Suzy last night… Her told me that Harry was in hospital so I got on the first flight back… Fuckin' hell lads, Harry has always been the bloody same. He needs me to come back and sort him aaht every 5 minutes!" Fennel and Cole looked at each other. Fennel could not help but feel relieved, but he also knew that the war with Johnny O'Connor had suddenly just become more intense!

Chapter 26

On Saturday the 1st of September 1979, the Pioneer 11 robotic space probe became the first human made device to encounter Saturn as it passed the Saturnian System just 13,000 miles from the surface of the planet. In Balsall Heath, Johnny O'Connor sat in the caravan of the head of the camp, Paddy Dunne and the pair drank whiskey.

"Listen Johnny, I can't have this sort of thing happening to my boys! My sister's lad had a feckin' dog maul his face off and that cousin of yours has cut Hughie Keenan's face from ear to ear!" Dunne was angry and as he spoke he used his finger to help make his point. "Now I don't care if you are some feckin' tough guy IRA gangster man, I will not have this sort of thing happen to my boys... Their families want instant retaliation, and I can understand why Johnny. I'm struggling to hold them off on your say so, just let me strike back!" O'Connor shook his head calmly.

"Do you want retribution Paddy? Or do you want to be feckin' rich?"

"Well of course, I wanna get rich, but you ain't the one with members of your family getting cut up!" O'Connor nodded sympathetically.

"I understand your situation Paddy, I really do. Just bear with me my friend. We must be patient... Good things come to those who wait." O'Connor savoured the whiskey in his mouth and oozed confidence.

"Those men out there." Dunne pointed towards the other caravans in the vicinity. "They are chomping at the bit for their revenge and if I don't do something soon I am gunna have a feckin' mutiny on my hands!"

"We can keep trading punches with these boys, or we can take decisive action... They think they are equal now after what we did to Harry Scriven, so now we make the deal..."

"Feck that! I don't wanna deal with those feckin' English bastards. They are sick sadistic sons of bitches and I want them dead! Do you hear me O'Connor? Dead!" Dunne began to raise his voice, but Johnny O'Connor remained calm. Paddy Dunne was an overweight man in his early 50s who had a fearsome reputation as a bare-knuckle boxer.

"Paddy, you remind me of just about every wannabe Fenian tough guy I've met over the last 50 years, and believe me mate, I've met a lot of them. If you're so bothered about it just feck off to Belfast and fight them loyalist boys... Believe me I've been there, but you reach a point where you think, feck it, I just wanna be rich!" Dunne sighed and looked down at the whiskey in his hands. "Without access to the night clubs, we will not be able to shift our product." O'Connor spoke in a persuasive tone. "Eddie Fennel and Micky Cole have access to and knowledge of a drug distribution network that can make us both extraordinarily rich. Without them on board, we will struggle." O'Connor left a deliberate pause and gave Dunne time to take in what he was saying. "You know where the funding for our drugs came from don't you Paddy?" Dunne's demeanour suddenly changed and he lowered his head and nodded. "Do you want to explain to the boys in Dublin how we took their buy money but have no return to show for it?" Dunne shook his head. Paddy Dunne knew that if he and O'Connor could not show a healthy return on the Dublin gangster's investment, then they would end up dead alongside their families. Dunne shrugged.

"So how do we convince these English bastards to make a deal then?" Dunne took a long drink of his whiskey and waited for an answer. O'Connor smiled.

"Excuse the quote from the movies, but I'm gunna make Fennel an offer he can't refuse..." Dunne grunted and almost laughed. "Go and fetch Liam Byrne. He's a sick, twisted little fecker. He will do a grand job..."

Micky Cole sat on a wooden bench outside the Crooked House pub near Himley and relaxed in the late summer sun with his beautiful wife Cathy. She was in the early stages of pregnancy and a small bump was beginning to show above her short denim skirt that showed off her long perfectly tanned legs.

"What do yow think we should call the baby Mick?" Cathy hooked her shapely thigh over husband's knee and stroked his cheek.

"Ar dow know bab." Cole took a sip of his Harp lager and watched a wasp that was trapped under a glass on a nearby table. It reminded him of Davey Price who had suffered a similar fate and Cole made a mental note to himself that he would release the insect before he left. He hated to see creatures suffer undeservedly. "Ar was thinking maybe we could give it a double-barrelled name?"

"What do yer mean Mick?"

"The baby's surname could be Scriven-Cole? Ar reckon mar ode mon would love that and technically it should have been mar name too." Cathy nodded approvingly.

"Ar reckon Harry would be med up with that bab… Ar cor see Suzy being happy being a granny though!" Cathy laughed but Cole didn't catch her last comment. He was deep in thought as he lay back and enjoyed the sun on his face. Cathy had often noticed this lately; he would drift off into little moments and she would have no idea what he was thinking about. She allowed him to sit quietly for about 5 minutes before she finally broke the silence. "What's important to yow Mick?" The randomness of her question caused him to suddenly sit upright in surprise.

"Yer what bab?"

"Ar mean it Mick, seriously, what is important to yow in yower mind?" Cole thought seriously for a few seconds and then turned to face her.

"Well, yow and aer babee of course!"

"Yeah, and what else?" Cole smiled and relaxed back into the sun.

"Being rich! Money, and fuckin' lots of it!"

Harry Scriven sat upright in bed and smoked an expensive Cuban cigar that Billy Mucklow had bought over from Spain. He had just been released from hospital on strict orders that he had to take it easy and continue to recuperate at home. His bedroom was large and the vast bay window overlooked Haden Hill Road which ran adjacent to the house and Coombs Road ran to the right that went up the hill. On chairs within the bedroom sat Billy Mucklow and Eddie Fennel who had come to wish their injured friend well.

"What am we gunna do with yer Harry?" Mucklow interrupted the silence. "Yow cor do nothing without me can yer aer kid?" Mucklow's remarks were meant in good humour but they instantly annoyed Scriven intently. *Who had set the business up in Spain? Who had returned to England, got married and set up a nightclub business? Surely he had proved that he could do his own thing without Billy Mucklow?* And then in that moment it suddenly occurred to Harry Scriven that maybe it was Bill who needed him more than he needed Bill? *All of these years he had been living in the shadow of the great Billy Mucklow, when all along it was Mucklow who needed him? Maybe Mucklow needed to be needed? After returning from the Second World War maybe he needed to find purpose in protecting his family?* Harry Scriven could not believe that it had taken him the best part of 60 years to realise this and he almost felt pity for his cousin... Bill Mucklow was definitely not a man to be pitied, but as Scriven watched him in the natural light of the room he saw a man who was beginning to show his age and a vulnerability suddenly seemed to appear from him that Scriven had never thought could exist... He said nothing.

"So what do yow reckon we should do about these gypsies Bill?" Fennel still looked up to Billy Mucklow more than anyone else in the world. The man had been his commanding officer throughout the hardest and most unimaginable times during the Second World War and he had total and utter blind faith in him.

"Wait and see Eddie... From what yow told me the ball is in their court... But remember this aer kid!" Mucklow suddenly got ultra-serious and Eddie Fennel gave his complete undivided attention. "Always hit back harder, as harshly as yow can... Just look at Hiroshima and Nagasaki! It forced the Japanese into surrender and ended the war." Fennel hung on Mucklow's every word and he nodded enthusiastically.

Hiroshima and Nagasaki were two Japanese cities which on August the 6th and 9th 1945, the United States forces dropped two nuclear bombs killing between 129,000 and 226,000 people, most of whom were civilians. There were plans to drop further bombs and this in turn influenced the Japanese decision to surrender. If these bombings had not taken place, then the Allied forces would have had to make a full scale land invasion of Japan which would have cost many lives, therefore, the harsh severity of the atomic bombings had prevented such an invasion. These events had always remained fresh in Bill Mucklow's mind and he had always maintained such an outlook. Violence was bad for business, but when there was no other option, it needed to be done properly and seriously... Harry Scriven lay in his bed and listened to the same talk he had heard so many times and he simply wished that he was back in the Mediterranean sun with Suzy and having no involvement in the current events.

Liam Byrne had been given his orders by Johnny O'Connor and he drove a white Ford Transit van towards the Black Country. As he drove, he allowed his depraved imagination to explore his options and he also had a thirst for revenge after two of his fellow gypsies had been badly disfigured. Even though it was a Saturday, the traffic wasn't good and as he drove, he smoked cigarettes and listened to the radio. He followed the Hagley Road out of Birmingham and then drove onto Halesowen high street where he followed Stourbridge Road past the Halesowen Town football ground and then on into Colley Gate. The Transit then drove down Windmill Hill and then turned right onto Furlong Lane where Byrne parked up near the bottom of Talbot Street where Harry Scriven had been born and brought up. Liam Byrne then squinted and looked further down Furlong Lane to see if he could see a red Jaguar. Johnny O'Connor had given him directions to Eddie Fennel's house, and he had also strictly informed him that he was to wait until Eddie Fennel had left for the pub before he carried out his evil deeds. The Jaguar was not present and all Byrne could see was Teresa's Lotus that was parked on the drive. He put the van into gear and drove slowly down the road to the house before reversing onto the drive in front of the Lotus sports car. The time had come for the gypsy's revenge!

Chapter 27

The Heath hotel stood near the Worcestershire town of Bewdley. The Victorian building was constructed in 1886 and had always been used as a prominent luxury hotel. The town of Bewdley lies on the River Severn and is about 3 miles west of Kidderminster and 22 miles south west of Birmingham. The town was a popular tourist destination and was known for its bridge that was constructed by the Scottish engineer Thomas Telford in the late 18th century. When in Britain, Bill Mucklow had taken to staying at the Heath hotel as he was away from the hustle and bustle of the Black Country and Birmingham. It was also a safe haven as it was a less obvious location for his historic enemies to find him.

In the 1950s, Bill Mucklow had carried out a high-profile robbery of a jewellery warehouse that had belonged in part to several prominent Jewish gangsters from London. Mucklow had served his sentence in prison for the crime, but he was still wary of potential acts of vengeance from the many underworld figures he had stolen from. Billy Hill and the Kray twins had guaranteed his safety, but the twins had been in prison for over ten years and Hill had long since retired.

Billy Hill was one of the most significant underworld figures in London from the 1920s through to the 1960s. He and his gang carried out many robberies and defrauded London's high society out of millions of pounds. He ran smuggling operations and was also known for his extreme violence and a high-profile war with fellow London gangster Jack Spot Comer. Early in their criminal careers, Reg and Ron Kray worked for Hill and he served as a mentor to them as he coached and advised them in their chosen career path. When Bill Mucklow went to prison in 1955, it was on the orders of Hill, but in return, he and Harry Scriven were allowed to keep their ill-gotten gains from the robbery and the safety of their families was guaranteed. By staying out of the Black

Country over night, Mucklow could sleep easier in his hotel room as he waited and yearned for the current situation with the gypsies to 'blow over' so that he could return to his wife in Spain.

'That's life' was one of Frank Sinatra's most popular songs and was taken from the album of the same name which was released in 1966. Bill Mucklow had always been a huge Sinatra fan and as he lay and relaxed with a single malt Scotch before bed, the song span on a record player and Mucklow thought about how the song's lyrics could be related to his own situations over the years. He had known good times and bad times, but he always got himself up and got back in the race! But part of him was beginning to get tired of it all. *Why did Harry have to come back to England? They were all happy, safe and relaxed in Spain, why did Scriven have to bloody spoil it? Eddie Fennel is big enough and ugly enough to sort out his own problems! Why couldn't Harry stay in Spain with me? He could have even brought his kid!* The current situation with the gypsies irritated Mucklow. It was Eddie Fennel's problem and Mucklow could not understand why Harry Scriven had been dragged into it... Despite his annoyance, Mucklow had never once in his life questioned his devotion to Harry Scriven... The man was a brother to him.

There was a sudden knock at the door of Bill Mucklow's hotel room and he almost spilt his drink in surprise.

"Who is it?" Mucklow glanced around the room for anything that he could use as a makeshift weapon.

"It's me Eddie." Fennel sounded distressed and Mucklow walked over to the door and opened it. Mucklow had left Fennel at the pub a couple of hours previously after they had visited Harry Scriven at his home.

"What's up Eddie? It's half bloody twelve aer kid!" Mucklow pointed to his solid gold Rolex.

"They've took her, they've fuckin' took her!" Fennel was irate and his eyes were filled with panic.

"Right, calm daahn mate... Who's took who?"

"The gypsies and Johnny fuckin' O'Connor, they've took mar wife Teresa and left this note." Fennel handed Mucklow a handwritten note that he had found on his arrival home from the pub.

"Eddie, we have your wife, unless you want her face cut like what you did to one of ours, you need to make the deal with the boss. We can reach you and your family at any time." Mucklow read the note aloud and it angered him. *Back in his day there were rules, people respected families and civilians. Now it was one big dangerous free for all and Mucklow was glad that his wife and children were out of it.* He shook his head and handed Fennel his whisky. Fennel needed it more than he did.

"Just sell yer business to O'Connor, get yer wife back and then come to Spain with me." Mucklow looked at the floor and Fennel had never thought that he would hear such a defeatist attitude coming from Billy Mucklow… *What happened to 'hit back as hard as you can?' Was that just whisky talk?* Fennel took a few seconds to try and comprehend what he had just heard before he eventually spoke.

"What? Just give everything I have worked for to drug dealers? Let them take over our old manor? What about the kids? What about the good honest people whose children are being taken by drugs? Kids that am dying from overdoses and addiction?" Fennel became animated and passionate. "It ay safe for mar ode mom to walk daahn the streets on her own cus some kids on drugs will mug her to feed their addiction. Yow have parents here too Bill." Fennel downed the whisky and shook his head in disbelief. "These are the people we fought for in the war Bill, the people our comrades fell and died for…" Mucklow suddenly felt an intense self-loathing as Fennel's words rang true. *What had he become? Years sat drinking in the Spanish sun had softened him and made him selfish; but he was 60 years of age!* "Well, I'd never thought that I would ever see the day that I'd see the great Billy Mucklow lost for words." Fennel did not try to hide his disappointment, but he had more pressing matters on his mind. Mucklow stared at the floor and thought intensely for a minute. *He could not let the ordinary people from the place that he regarded as his home down…*

"Yeah, ok Eddie… Yow'm right aer kid." Mucklow slipped his shoes on and grabbed his jacket. "Yow got any tools?" Fennel nodded.

"A boot full outside in the Jag."

"Where is O'Connor?" Mucklow asked as the men walked out of the hotel room and into the corridor and he turned to lock the door behind him.

"He's staying on a gypsy camp site in Brum, but it's full of blokes, we woe get in there without getting noticed and that will meck um hurt mar wench!"

"Ok. We will drive over there and watch to see what comes in and what comes ahht of the camp. Did your neighbours see anything?" Mucklow looked deep in thought.

"What do yer mean?"

"Your neighbours, did they see who took Teresa or did they spot anything that might give us a clue?" The pair continued to walk down the corridor towards the main entrance hall.

"Ar dow know Bill, ar come right to yow?" Mucklow nodded and wondered when other people would stop being so reliant on him. He had escaped this life and he wanted to enjoy his retirement, though the thought of not being needed at all was even worse.

"Right, lets swing by yower place and ask the neighbours." Mucklow and Fennel went out to the car park and climbed into Fennel's Jag. The engine fired instantly and the straight 6 rumbled as Fennel pulled off the car park, turned right towards Franche and Wolverly and then carried onto the Stourbridge road towards the Black Country.

Eddie Fennel hammered on the front door of his next-door neighbour's house and gave no thought to the fact that it was pitch black and well after 1 AM in the morning. He was worried about the safety of his wife and anxious for her return.

"Who is it? What is the meaning of this? Do you know what time it is?" Fennel's neighbour was a doctor and he was particularly annoyed by the banging on his front door at such an unsociable hour. He opened the door and recognised his neighbour straight away. "Mr Fennel... What on earth do you want?" The neighbour's obnoxious tone annoyed Fennel and he stepped into the doorway and resisted the urge to grab the man forcefully.

"My wife was abducted earlier this evening... Did you see or hear anything out of the ordinary?"

"Oh my goodness me! I am sorry to hear that Mr Fennel... Have the police been informed?" The neighbour showed genuine concern.

"Do not contact the police!" Fennel raised his voice. "Did you see or hear anything?" The neighbour thought hard for a few seconds.

"I'm so sorry Mr Fennel but no I did not."

"What about your wife?"

"She's not here at the moment. She is staying with her family in Manchester." The truth was that the neighbour's wife was having an illicit affair and she was in a hotel room with her lover, but the doctor could hardly bare to admit this to himself let alone to his ruffian neighbour.

"Eddie?" Bill Mucklow suddenly appeared from the direction of the neighbour's house on the other side. "Them next door saw a white Ford Transit parked on yower drive earlier... Apparently the driver had a black leather jacket and a nasty scar down the right side of his face." Fennel turned around to face Mucklow.

"Liam Byrne..." Fennel said the name with a mixture of anger and fear of what could potentially happen to his wife. He had met Byrne previously in the Neptune and Fennel was pretty sure that it was Byrne and his cronies who had put Harry Scriven in hospital.

"You know him?" Mucklow gestured for Fennel to go back over to the car and away from the prying ears of the neighbours.

"Ar met him once... He's a nasty piece of work Bill..." Fennel got back inside the car and Mucklow climbed in alongside him.

"Ar'm sure he ay as nasty as us Eddie!" Mucklow spoke with gusto and Fennel began to feel a slight sense of reassurance that the true

Billy Mucklow was returning. "Now lets gew and park up by the gypsy camp and look ahht for a white transit." Fennel started the Jag and it roared off into the night. "Yow sure yow got some tools Eddie?" Fennel nodded.

"Oh yes Bill… I've got plenty of tools…"

Chapter 28

Eddie Fennel slept and felt the breath of his wife on the back of his neck. He could sense her presence and he drew comfort from the knowledge that her body was next to his... Suddenly, thoughts of their past life together filled his mind and a thousand happy memories whispered through his brain.

First, he was back in Dublin in the 1940s and he had just come round from the beating he had received in the IRA bar. He looked into the eyes of his beloved for the first time once again and they drew him in. Within seconds he was back at Our Lady and All Saints Roman Catholic Church in Stourbridge and was looking into the eyes of his Irish angel as they were married. Then, he was holding his new-born daughter in his arms as Teresa looked on and smiled. The memories had been the happiest times of his life and the abduction of his wife was no longer a prominent feature of his thoughts. A moment later and he was relaxing on a sun lounger next to a perfect turquoise swimming pool in Andalusia. He drank a perfectly chilled glass of Spanish lager and smoked his favourite cigar as he watched his wife smouldering in a bikini whilst playing with his daughter by the pool. It was a special moment that would always remain in his memory, a perfect day, a perfect family. As he enjoyed the memory, his family suddenly began to physically move further and further away from him, as if his sun lounger was being pulled backwards into darkness. He called to Teresa frantically and as she moved further away, he felt complete and utter despair as she could neither see nor hear him. The vision of his wife and daughter slowly faded away and his world descended into total darkness. He suddenly became aware that he was dreaming and he turned over and tried to wake himself up, but he felt her bony fingers move across his face and he knew that they were dead...

"Wake the fuck up Eddie!" Bill Mucklow shook his friend who was sat next to him in the driver's seat of the old Jag. Fennel stirred and slowly came to his senses.

"Sorry Bill." Fennel woke up and remembered where he was and the sudden remembrance of what had happened to Teresa hit him like a hard gut-wrenching fist in the stomach. The nightmare he had suffered played with his mind and he feared the worst.

"Its yower wife and we'm supposed to be finding her, not gewin' ter fuckin' sleep!" Mucklow spoke harshly but in reality, he had allowed Fennel to sleep for several hours. At least one of them would have their wits about them and Mucklow had become used to putting the needs of his men before his own during the Second World War. Eddie Fennel had accompanied Bill Mucklow through many a torrid time and against the odds they had always made it through. At Torbuk, during the disastrous battle of Gazala, during their escape through Africa and then throughout the invasion of Europe, Eddie Fennel had been at his side, one of the best. A loyal and brave soldier who was also a blood relative. Bill Mucklow had no choice but to support his friend during his darkest hour.

"Have yow seen anything Bill?" Fennel felt guilty for falling asleep whilst watching for clues about the whereabouts of his wife.

"Nope... Nothin' has come in or ahht of the camp." Mucklow nestled back into the worn leather seat, his sleepless eyes still focused on the entrance to the gypsy compound. *When he returned to Spain, he would sleep for a week!* "Yow got any fakes?" Mucklow had smoked all of his own cigarettes and cigars.

"Here Bill." Fennel opened up his cigarette case and both men took one and lit up. Mucklow looked at his watch and saw that it was 8:30 in the morning. *If they had not heard anything by 10 he was intent on walking straight into the camp and using whatever tools Fennel had on this guy O'Connor to make him talk.* Deep down he knew that this would be incredibly dangerous, but he was sleep deprived, irritable and he had had enough.

"Thanks for helping me with this Bill." Eddie Fennel drew back on his cigarette and realised that he had not shown any gratitude to Mucklow for his support.

"Dow talk saft Eddie... Yow'm family ay yer? But if ar get bloody killed sorting this shit aaaaht with Johnny O'Connor then ar'm a gunna come back from Hell and teck yow daahn with me!" Mucklow was only part joking but Fennel was in no mood to take offense. He had more important issues to worry about. He felt the tobacco smoke slide down into his lungs and he savoured its calming effect. He could not get the dreams from the previous night from out of his mind and as he sat and smoked, he tried to make sense of them. *Was Teresa dead? Or were his subconscious fears playing tricks on him?*

Another half an hour passed by and suddenly something emerged from out of the gypsy camp that instantly caught both Mucklow and Fennel's attention.

"It's the white transit!" Fennel spoke first and he instantly turned the ignition key and the Jag fired into life.

"Right, dow drive up his arse Eddie, we dow want them ter know we'm following them!" Mucklow offered advice.

"What if she's in the camp though? Am we just leaving her?" Fennel suddenly paused.

"We ay got no chance of getting' in there on our own Eddie... Let's grab the transit driver and meck him tell us where she is..." Mucklow gestured for Fennel to drive off and follow the van. "If we find aaht she is in the camp we will come back with some of yower boys and storm the place like we did at fuckin' D-Day mate... Fuck em!" It made perfect sense and Fennel emerged onto the main road and followed the transit van at a safe distance.

As they drove, Bill Mucklow could feel the adrenaline rising inside of him. The same ultra-aggressive desire to fight that had dominated and defined his life. He had been thinking that he had lost his edge, that the years spent in prison and then living in luxury in the gangster haven of the Costa del sol had softened him. But as they pursued the Transit through the back streets of Birmingham, he could feel the intense energy flow through his veins. It made him feel relieved. In his opinion, the only way to survive a war was by getting your head down and throwing your whole being into the fight. Those that were scared or lacked dedication to the cause, hesitated and wound-up dead. *It was like diving into a 50-50 tackle in a football match. If you pulled out at the last minute or relaxed the intent, then you were certain to get injured.* The rush of anger, the total desire for violence was greater than any thrill Mucklow had ever received from sex, alcohol, nicotine or cannabis; and as they drove on, he enjoyed the thrill of the chase and the anticipation of the fight…

The Transit continued to drive back towards the City Centre where it got onto the Hagley Road and headed towards Halesowen. In Quinton, it turned left into a petrol station and Fennel pulled the Jag into a nearby road to watch the gypsy get out of the van to fill up. Fennel scratched his beard and strained his eyes to see if he could recognise the gypsy.

"Its him! Its fuckin' Liam Byrne!" Fennel went to climb out of the car, *he was going to seriously hurt Byrne there and then and beat his wife's location out of the man!*

"Wait…" Bill Mucklow was ready for violence, but he was not as emotionally involved as Fennel and was thinking more rationally. "Think abaaht it Eddie… Why is the Byrne chap heading towards Halesowen?" Fennel was in no mood to think, he wanted to tear Liam Byrne's head off and he was seriously debating on dousing the Irishman with petrol from the pump and setting him alight.

"Ar dow know Bill?"

"Cus he's probably holding yower Mrs over there… Why would they teck her back to the camp when they can hold her closer to the abduction site? Yow ever met a gypsy wench? They wouldn't be happy bout their chaps holding a female hostage on the campsite… Maybe Byrne is going to check on the hostage?" Fennel thought about it, it made sense. "We might as well follow the van and see if it leads us to Teresa..." Mucklow finished his cigarette and threw it out of the window. "If it dow lead us to her then we can grab this Byrne and teck him to yower lock up on brickhouse and meck him talk!" Fennel liked the sound of Mucklow's plan. He got back into the car, shut the door and watched impatiently as Byrne paid for the fuel, got back into the transit and drove off.

Fennel and Mucklow continued to follow the transit as it made its way through the outskirts of Halesowen on the A456 Hagley Road. Much of the road originated in Medieval times, though the bypasses came along much later. In 1753, the section of the road between Birmingham and Blakedown was improved in order to improve links to the market house in Stourbridge. At this time, Blakedown was part of Hagley and this would lead to the road becoming known as the Hagley Road. The Halesowen bypass was built in the 1950s due to rising traffic levels and the growth of the town and as the red Jag continued in its pursuit, they finally reached the top of Hagley Hill and then followed the van right at the island towards Wassell Grove and past the Old Halesownian's Rugby ground.

Halesowen was recorded in the Domesday book of 1086 as being bigger than Birmingham. It was originally known as Hala from the Anglo-Saxon word Halh before the town was gifted by King Henry II to the Welsh Prince David Owen. It was at this point that the town became known as Halas Owen. Halesowen was originally a market town but during the 18th century it developed rapidly as part of the industrial revolution with the manufacture of nails particularly providing a strong income for the town. The town was also known for its iron production and collieries and when at its peak in 1919, Halesowen had 130 working mines. It was during these heavily industrialised times that Halesowen would become known as being a 'gateway' to the Black Country from the nearby city of Birmingham and the rural regions of Worcestershire.

The Old Halesownians Rugby football club was founded in 1930 and played their home games at Wassell Grove which lay just off the

Hagley Road. As Fennel and Mucklow passed the rugby ground, Bill Mucklow recalled past memories of his youth as a Halesowen grammar school lad playing rugby. He had always preferred the game of football, though he enjoyed the rough physical contact of rugby.

"Where the fuck am we gewin Bill?" As the car continued through the country lanes towards Colley Gate, Eddie Fennel began to worry that maybe they had been spotted and the transit was taking them on a wild goose chase. He needn't have worried… The van pulled off the country lane and then descended down a rough track that led to an old, abandoned farmhouse. Fennel stopped the Jag out of sight and he and Mucklow watched as the van stopped outside the house. "Do yow reckon that's where they've got mar Mrs Bill?" Fennel was still anxious to make a move, but years of following orders from Bill Mucklow kept him in check.

"Maybe… But if she is not there, it will be a nice quiet and secluded spot for us to meck this Byrne fella talk." Fennel smiled at Mucklow's words and hoped that his wife was alright. "Lets teck a look at yower tools then Eddie." The Jag was concealed behind a high hedge and the two men got out and walked around to the rear of the vehicle. Fennel popped the boot and Mucklow cast his eyes over a wide selection of weapons. Fennel pulled out his Lugar and a vicious looking axe and Mucklow picked up another handgun and the Samurai sword that had previously hung on the wall of Eddie Fennel's study.

"Yow ready Bill?" Fennel gritted his teeth and looked at Mucklow.

"Ar… Bostin aer kid. Lets gew!"

Chapter 29

Two heavily built gypsies sat and played cards at an old, abandoned wooden table that stood in the middle of a run down and dilapidated kitchen. The farmhouse had not been lived in since before the Second World War and there was no running water, gas or electricity. The house was morbid and forbidding and in dark shadowy corners lay poignant and slightly disturbing signs of past lives that served as a thought-provoking echo of the people who once lived there. In the hallway stood an old Victorian pram which was covered in dust and had been mostly eaten by moths. Inside lay a porcelain doll whose eyes were staring and haunted and both men, Riley and Docherty would never have admitted to each other that they found the doll slightly unnerving. In the kitchen, an old grandfather clock stood firmly against the wall, its time forever showing 25 minutes past eleven, the time from which the entire house had stood permanently still. In another corner of the room was a small Edwardian table and upon on it stood a dust covered and rusted pair of spectacles. The two men had spent the entire night there and they were both eager to get out. At their sides, they each had a loaded 12 bore shotgun which was needed to help them guard their hostage…

Suddenly, the kitchen door flung open and Riley and Docherty anxiously grabbed their weapons.

"Calm down yer feckin eejits!" Much to Riley and Docherty's relief, it was Liam Byrne who had entered the room. "It's just me… Where is the feckin' bitch?"

"She's upstairs Liam. She's tied to the chair. She ain't going nowhere." Riley spoke as he rested his gun back down on the floor and went back to the cards.

"Neither of you have touched her have you? I know she's getting on a bit but she's a cracking bit of stuff for an old girl!" Byrne had his own plans for Fennel's wife, but he had been strictly ordered by Johnny O'Connor not to touch her until Fennel had been given the opportunity to make a business deal. Of course, Byrne wanted to make money from drugs as much as anyone else, but a niggling part of him wanted Fennel to continue to reject all offers so that he could have his wicked way with his wife.

"No, we ain't touched her Liam. My Mrs would go mad for sure!" Docherty and Riley shook their heads and Byrne was confident that Teresa Fennel had not been interfered with in anyway.

"So, how long have we gotta keep her here for Liam?" Docherty finally spoke and Byrne shrugged.

"I don't know. Johnny said to keep her until her husband agrees to help us."

"For fecks sake Liam, we were sat here all feckin' night and we've drank all the feckin' whisky!" Riley could not hide his annoyance and neither men fancied another night sat guarding the hostage.

"Don't worry lads. Paddy Dunne and Johnny O'Connor are gunna send over another couple of guys in the morning… Yous can go home then." Byrne placed a plastic bag on the table that was filled with snacks and another bottle of cheap Irish whiskey. "This lot ought to keep yers going for a bit… Give the bitch some of this water too… If anything happens to her O'Connor's gunna go mad." The two guards went back to their cards and Byrne rested against the wall and lit a cigarette. "She's very quiet up there?"

"Yes Liam, we had to feckin' gag her cus she kept moaning and it was getting on our nerves." Byrne laughed. "She kept going on about how her husband is gunna do this and that." Riley and Docherty laughed too.

"Well, now that you've got your supplies I best be getting off… I'll be back tomorrow with the new boys." Byrne moved as if to leave when they were suddenly startled by a loud hammering outside on the side of the van.

"Who the feck is that?" Riley picked up his shotgun and moved as if to run outside and investigate.

"Wait…" Liam Byrne put a hand across his friend's path, stopping him from going out. "Whoever is outside is trying to draw us out by banging on the side of the van… It's what they want lads, lets not fall for it."

"Were you followed here Liam?" Docherty grabbed his shotgun.

"No, of course I wasn't." Byrne answered the question but was having second thoughts. He had had a heavy session on the booze the night before and he had not been paying attention during the drive over… *It was perfectly possible that he had been followed.* He cursed himself silently and took a look out of the glassless window. He looked towards the Ford transit, but he could see nothing out of the ordinary. The sky above suddenly became eerily dark, and the trees began to sway as the wind got up. There was no lighting inside the old, abandoned house and the shadowy kitchen became even darker. The three men looked at each other and a loud and sudden crack of thunder sounded overhead. Byrne looked out of the window again and a dense, black rain cloud descended upon them. The rain spots were thick and intermittent to begin with, but they soon became more intense as a flash of lightning lit up the sky and another crack of thunder sounded just a few seconds later. There was a muggy atmosphere in the air and the men could smell the rain as the birds and local wildlife scurried to find protection from the storm.

"Maybe the sound we heard was just the thunder?" Riley offered his thoughts, but the other two men were not convinced.

"It definitely sounded like somebody hammering on the side of the van to me so it did." Docherty clenched his gun tightly and tried not to show any fear. "Is this Fennel guy dangerous?" There was a long awkward silence and Riley eventually spoke.

"You could say that… Apart from being a WW2 veteran you saw what he did to two of our lads didn't yer?" Docherty shook his head. "He cut one of them from ear to ear, gave him a Chelsea smile." The tense atmosphere within the room began to build.

"What did they do to the other lad?" Docherty was intrigued but he could not let his tough gypsy persona be compromised.

"They fed his face to a feckin' Rottweiler!" Riley laughed nervously. "Lovely fellas, and we've got Fennel's feckin' Mrs upstairs!" Byrne shook his head in annoyance and pulled out a machete from out of his pocket.

"Stop acting like a couple of feckin' fairies!" He held the knife in his right hand and moved out into the hallway and then onto the open doorway to the old house.

"Who's there?" He shouted defiantly, the rain lashing down violently on the muddy ground and hammering off the roof of the nearby transit. A foggy haze filled the air and Byrne could see no signs of anyone outside. He turned and went back into the kitchen. "It's probably just kids fooling around, but we can't risk them running back and telling their parents who will phone the law... If they have been out there the whole time, then chances are they will have heard everything we have been talking about."

"What shall we do then Liam?" Docherty remained anxious.

"Like I said, it's probably just kids. If we can't find them then we are gunna have to move the bitch someplace else. We can't have her whereabouts compromised. O'Connor has too much at stake on this." Byrne glanced outside at the heavy rainfall again and the storm continued to rage overhead as violent streaks of lightning cut jagged lines in the dark daylight sky. "We are gunna have to go outside and look for them." Liam Byrne did not fancy going out in the storm. Since childhood he had held a secret fear of thunderstorms. He had been brought up in a strict Catholic environment and he had been made to believe that the storm represented god's wrath upon the evil of men... *He was an evil man and his evil deeds were justly punishable by the anger of the Almighty... What would Holy Mary Mother of God have to say about his vicious actions towards women? Did this storm portray the anger of God towards his own actions?* Liam Byrne was a relatively young man but he feared death with an intense obsession that led him to drink. He was a god-fearing man and he knew that his sins would send him straight to hell upon his final breath. He accepted this and wished for the eternal sufferings of hell over the judgment of his Lord.

"But its feckin' throwing it down outside! And we could get struck by lightning!" Riley protested but Byrne was not listening.

"Don't be such a fairy. Riley, you check the field behind the house and Docherty you go into those trees over there." Byrne pointed to a dark woodland area to the right of the house. "I'll stay here and watch the prisoner."

"Typical! You stay here in the feckin' dry!" Docherty was not impressed.

"Well somebody needs to do it. If we are all out there then Fennel and his boys could just come in and snatch the woman. Do you wanna explain that to Paddy Dunne and O'Connor?" Riley and Docherty shook their heads and reluctantly picked up their shotguns.

"This is feckin' bollocks mate." Docherty made his feelings known one final time and the two men trudged out of the building and into the dark forbidding rain of the thunderstorm.

A crash of thunder sounded with such intensity that the foundations of the old farmhouse seemed to shake. Byrne was relieved that the men had gone, he no longer had to hide his fear of the storm. He reached for the whiskey in the bag, cracked the seal and then felt it's hot peaty flavour fill his mouth and seep down his throat, burning his gullet as it went. Liam Byrne said a silent Hail Mary and sat down at the table. A flash of sheet lightning illuminated the room and he caught a glimpse of the many snails and spiders that decorated the dust and filth covered walls of the deserted room. He could hear rats squeaking and moving in other parts of the house and he assumed that they were also startled and taking shelter from the storm. He took another gulp of whiskey and listened to the rain that fell upon the remnants of the old roof. He knew that he should probably go upstairs and check on the woman, but fear gripped him and he remained routed to the spot. Byrne knew that his feelings of fright were irrational and childish, but he had an overwhelming and unshakeable feeling of impending doom. *What had hammered on the van? Why had the storm arrived at that exact moment? Had it been forecast? Was it time for his eternal judgement?* Liam Byrne closed his eyes to the storm and continued to take down swallow after swallow of the whiskey until he realised that Riley and Docherty must have been gone for at least half an hour. *Where were they?* He told himself that they would be back at any minute and he lit a cigarette. The red glow in the dark room gave him a strange comfort and he smoked and watched it burn until it was just a stub in his hand. It burnt his fingers and he reluctantly flung it to the floor and extinguished it with his foot. *He had delayed the inevitable for too long… He would have to venture out into the storm and find out where his associates were.* He picked up the machete from off the table and then walked out to the front doorway. Part of him longed to jump back into the transit and drive away as fast as he could, but what would he tell Dunne and O'Connor? He said another Hail Mary and plucked up the courage to step out into the rain… The hypnotic rhythm of the downpour beat heavily upon his head and it felt strangely refreshing as he sweated from the muggy atmosphere and his own fear.

Liam Byrne looked towards the dark woodland, but *he could not go in there!* He ventured to the rear of the farmhouse and began to walk across the muddy field. An old, abandoned tractor rotted silently to his right and a decrepit barn looked as if it was about to give way at any moment from the force of the weather conditions. Various wild birds continued to crow and scutter their protests and fear at the ongoing storm, *but God did not listen…* As Byrne ventured past the old barn and rusted tractor, he felt that his judgement was upon him. *Who's eyes were upon him? Who was watching him stumble in the godforsaken rain? He should have listened to the teachings in the holy bible, he should have listened to his mother and led a wholesome and good existence… Was it too late?* He made his way further across the field and his feet sank further and further into the sodden, mud infested ground. It was as if the fires of hell were beckoning and were tearing at the souls of his feet, pulling him underground to his final destination.

A dark shape appeared ahead of him and at first Byrne thought that it was an animal lay on the ground through fear of the storm. As he drew nearer, he realised with horror what it actually was. A human body lay face down in the mud with pools of crimson rain puddles building either side... Byrne knelt, shivered with fright and a bird shrieked amongst the sound of the ever-present rain and thunder. He hovered over the body and eventually found the nerve to turn it over and reveal the victim's face...

It was his gypsy associate Riley. His lifeless head was twisted in terror and a clear and deliberate cut was evident across his thick throat... His Adams apple had been obliterated and blood continued to pour violently from the fatal wounds and mix with the pools of rainwater... Byrne closed his eyes and said another Hail Mary. What was most disturbing was that Riley's eyes had been gouched out forcefully with a sharp blade and the sockets now wept blood from the torn and sightless holes that would forever remain burned and indented into Liam Byrne's mind. Byrne vomited and wondered if Riley's eyes had been removed before or after his death. He hoped and preyed that it had been after, but somehow, for some reason he just knew that this had not been the case... Byrne took a deep breath and stood upright. He had known Seamus Riley for many years. He knew his wife and he knew his children... This cruel fate was not deserved, and Byrne took some comfort in his sudden anger and desire for vengeance. He temporarily forgot his fears and began to march back towards the farmhouse, the machete still clenched tightly in his hand.

As he neared the old tractor, a loud gunshot sounded out which was clearly identifiable amongst the sounds of the storm. Byrne could instantly tell that it was a shotgun and a feeling of relief came over him. *Nice one Docherty mate, you have killed the bastard!"* Byrne quickened his pace and made his way towards the woodland. The shot had come from the direction of the trees and as he crossed the field at the rear of the house, he no longer felt fear. *His friend had fired a shot and Riley's killer would be dead.*

Byrne arrived into the woodland and the trees and foliage provided a slight shelter from the incessant rain. He listened to the raindrops as they crashed into the leaves and ran down the trunks, giving the trees much needed nourishment from the dry summer atmosphere.

"Docherty?" Liam Byrne called out into the woods, but there was no reply. "Paul, its me Liam... Where are ya?" There was still no reply and Byrne moved deeper and deeper into the woodland. He stopped at a slight clearing in the trees and glanced up at a distant light that shone from a country house that must have been about a mile away. It was daytime but the darkened clouds and the shadows of the woods made it feel almost like night and Byrne took some comfort from the nearby house. He turned to his right and smelt a rather peculiar smell. It was a metallic smell, a smell that he had smelt before, but at first he could not think where. He moved slowly towards the right and he felt the sound of rain intensify as he moved back into the cover of the trees. The sound of rain upon the leaves was almost deafening and the mysterious smell became richer. He walked towards it and misjudged his footing as he tripped on a branch and found himself lying face down in the muddy rainwater.

Byrne sat upright and wiped the mud from his face, but it was not brown, it was not mud coloured. At first, he thought that he had injured himself in the fall, but there was so much blood... It covered his face and hands and he suddenly realised that the stench of raw meat reminded him of freshly slaughtered livestock that he had cooked and eaten in the past. The smell of death hung pungently in the air and as Liam Byrne rose back to his feet he saw something truly awful before him... An arm... An arm that had been severed cleanly and smoothly in one swift movement and now it wept copious amounts of blood into the slippery and sodden roots of the woodland. Byrne could not be sure who the arm belonged to and he walked on until he came to the next gruesome discovery.

Paul Docherty lay facedown on the wet woodland floor. Whatever rain escaped the cover of the foliage beat down on his lifeless carcass and there was just enough light for Liam Byrne to identify that several of his limbs were missing. His right arm had been hacked off and so had his left foot. As Byrne turned the body over to face him, the indents of a vicious and heavy implement were clearly visible on the remnants of Docherty's face. It had been chopped in several places, collapsing parts of his skull and creating a truly horrific image. Byrne clasped the machete even tighter in his hands and looked all around him as rainwater and blood continued to fill his eyes and make it hard for him to see. *He had been right... He had spent his life fearing the conviction of his Lord and he had known all along that the violence of a storm would signal his judgement...* In that moment, Byrne no longer cared about the wishes of Johnny O'Connor or Paddy Dunne. He cared for his own salvation and he simply had to get away. He reached into the sodden pockets of his jeans for the keys to the transit, but they were not there... *Had he dropped them somewhere?* He then remembered that he had left them on the table inside the old farmhouse and he would have no choice but to make his way back over there and pick them up so that he could make his escape. He took one last look at Docherty's dead eyes and then began swiftly back towards the edge of the forest. He did not look left, he did not look right and he did not look behind him. He had one simple task and that was to escape the forest, retrieve the van keys and get the hell out of there!

Flashes of sheet lightning illuminated the sky and as Byrne neared the farmhouse he pushed rainwater from out of his eyes and squinted to see that the Ford transit was no longer there! *Somebody had taken the keys from off the table and driven away. Maybe he would not be judged upon this day? Maybe the reapers of death had escaped with the hostage and he would be given a second chance?* As he grew closer to the house, the sense of relief began to build... It had cost his associates their lives, *but this would be a lesson that he would learn from.* His life to date had been shrouded in evil and he had not been a good man... Upon this dark thundery day, he had been delivered from evil and his redemption was beginning to fall into sight… *He would learn from this… He would be a good man and he would turn his back upon the evil in which he had been brought up… A confusing evil. An evil that had constantly lectured him upon the teachings of Jesus Christ and his Holy Mother, but that had also committed forbidden sins…* The confusion ebbed away and as he neared the front door, the rain had all but washed away the darkness from Liam Byrne's soul. *He had been given a second chance…*

The van was gone and there was no other method of escape. Byrne figured that Fennel's wife was probably gone, but just in case, he would check and potentially carry out his first act of righteousness. If she was still there, he would free her and offer her comfort and apologies. A light shone in the tunnel of darkness and it was all clear to him now…

Chapter 30

Liam Byrne made his way back into the farmhouse with the soul intent of checking on the welfare of his prisoner. The day had been truly horrific, sobering and enlightening as he had 'found himself' and would now spend the rest of his life trying to redeem himself for his previous criminal acts. He no longer felt fear as his soul had passed into the light and as he climbed the stairs of the old farmhouse a sense of purpose entered his mind.

He reached the top of the stairs and he pondered which room Teresa had been put in as rain trickled through the holes in the roof and he began to feel the chill from his sodden clothes. He kicked open the first door and ventured inside, noting that the floorboards were particularly unstable and he could see the room which lay below through the holes in the floor. The upper room was completely empty so Byrne went back into the hallway before turning left into another room that seemed darker. In the middle stood a stained and stinking chair where Teresa Fennel had been held and tied for hours. She was no longer there but the sight of the chair made Byrne instantly begin to further repent the action of her kidnap.

"Well, well, well... Mr Byrne... We meet again." Liam Byrne instantly recognised the voice and the man from the Black Country stepped out of the shadows. He wore a smart three-quarter length jacket, a cream-coloured tie and in his hands was a long bloody axe. His beard was red and stained with the blood of Byrne's friend and his eyes were wild and furious.

"Mr Fennel, where is your wife?" Byrne's concern was genuine. The rain eased slightly but the thunder continued to rip through the fabric of the house.

"She's safe now... Away from yow bastards." Fennel looked at the blood-stained axe within his hands and Byrne could see the whites of his eyes that rolled around his murderous and vengeance obsessed head. Byrne said another Hail Mary, but he was no longer afraid. *Would Fennel spare his life? Would he be massacred? Either way, he had seen the error of his ways and he had repented. His judgement lay in the hands of God now and he would accept and rejoice in the decision of the Almighty.*

"Ar told yow what ar would do to you if yow ever laid a finger upon mar family day I?" Fennel moved closer to Byrne, the axe still firmly in his grip. "After that, yow beat up mar cousin Harry Scriven." Fennel touched the blade of the sharpened axe and did not flinch at the pain as it pierced his skin. "Then after that, yow put yower hands upon mar wife and brought her to this stinking place." Byrne could not argue with the truth, but he had seen the error of his ways. "And on top of all that, yow and that bastard Johnny O'Connor want to flood the area with yower filthy drugs! So that mar mother cor walk down the streets safely, so that all the kids raahnd here get their brains polluted with that shit..." Liam Byrne could see further rage building within Eddie Fennel as he spoke.

"Forgive me father, for I have sinned." Byrne got down upon his knees and threw himself at the mercy of Eddie Fennel.

"What the fuck yow on abaaht?" Fennel was confused by Byrne's actions and he did not trust him.

"I have done wrong in my life... I know that. I accept my judgement, but I ask of you this Mr Fennel..." Byrne paused for a few seconds before continuing. "Allow me this opportunity to truly repent. I know all about Johnny O'Connor's drug smuggling. I will give evidence against him in court. I will come with you now to the Police station and we can stop the drugs... I wish to make good a life of sin." Byrne spoke the truth and the distant thunder still rolled as Fennel stroked the dampness of blood and flesh as he stroked his beard.

"Then throw down that machete and push it away." Fennel gestured to the weapon that was still in Byrne's hand and the Irish traveller obliged and looked up at him with hope filled eyes. Fennel muttered something under his breath and slowly became louder as he chanted. "Bitte vergib mir... Bitte vergib mir..." Byrne had no idea what Fennel's Germanic chant meant, but he figured he would soon find out... The intensity of Fennel's gaze was truly frightening and after he repeated the phrase several times he stopped and looked back at the axe. "Do you know what that means Liam?" Byrne shook his head.

"So what about it Mr Fennel? You and me go down to the Police and tell them about Johnny O'Connor? I won't mention what happened to Riley and Docherty I swear..."

"Its German..." Fennel had no interest in what Byrne was trying to say. "It means please forgive me..." Fennel cast his piercing gaze back towards the gypsy. "When me and Billy Mucklow helped to liberate the concentration camp at Bergen-Belsen, the guards and staff there knew the severity of their crimes... As they stood amongst the piles of rotting flesh of the countless men, women and children they had massacred, some of them uttered Bitte vergib mir... Bitte vergib mir... Please forgive me..." Fennel shivered at the memory. "Every inch of every one of us British soldiers wanted to kill them, to punish them for their unforgiveable crimes... But we showed restraint. That was our orders." Fennel stroked his stained beard again. "How fuckin' dare yow touch mar wife... How fuckin' dare yow threaten mar family... And now, you kneel there, and yow ask for forgiveness?" Fennel was almost amused. Byrne said nothing and the rain finally stopped. An intense ray of sunlight pierced through the holes in the roof and finally light filled the room. "You filthy piece of meat... You filthy stinking dead meat..." Fennel's eyes were intent on murder. He had warned Liam Byrne and he would not show forgiveness. He looked down upon the retched individual who knelt before him and raised the axe high into the air. "Ar told yow Liam... Ar fuckin' told yow, do not touch mar family." Fennel was cold to death. He had massacred and maimed many a man on behalf of the British Army and their opponents had done exactly the same to them. That was business, but this was personal... He brought the axe down upon Liam Byrne's neck in one smooth and brutal movement and the gypsy was decapitated.

His headless torso went into instant shock and shivered and shook violently as the head rolled upon the floor and it's eyes circled madly within its condemned head... As he died, Liam Byrne looked on as he watched Eddie Fennel carry out the horrendous final action of his promise. He drew out his penis and proceeded to urinate upon the lifeless torso, paying particular attention to the severed neck... *A promise was a promise.*

Upon completion, Fennel picked up the severed head of the man who had dared to abduct his wife and carried it down the stairs and back up the track towards his car... This would all end now, upon this day of reckoning...

Bill Mucklow sat in the front seat of the transit van and tried to comfort Teresa Fennel. He was supposed to have driven her home whilst Eddie Fennel carried out his final act of vengeance. The two men had worked together on Riley and Docherty. Fennel had taken the axe into the woods whilst Mucklow had used the Samurai sword in the field... Both men felt no remorse for three less drug dealers in the world.

Mucklow had led Teresa to the van and was supposed to be taking her home where they would meet up with Eddie, but he had parked the transit behind the Jag and he sat and waited for Fennel. He did not know anything about this Liam Byrne and for all he knew, the gypsy could have killed his old and valued friend! As he sat and tried to comfort Fennel's wife, he anxiously looked out of the transit window and waited for his friend to appear... Eventually, Fennel appeared. He was walking back up the drive, but he was carrying something and Mucklow strained his eyes to try and see what it was. As Fennel got closer to the two vehicles, Mucklow realised exactly what it was that he was carrying and he did his best to shield it from the eyes of Teresa. He needn't have worried, she was still far too traumatised to understand what was going on.

Fennel walked over to the boot of his Jag and placed the severed head inside.

"What the fuck am yer doing Eddie?" Bill Mucklow jumped down from the van and walked over to confront his friend. He noticed that Fennel was dripping in the blood of Liam Byrne, his face and beard were red and he looked truly demonic.

"This ends today Bill... Ar'm gunna stick this bastards head on a fuckin' spike aahtside of O'Connor's caravan... Fuck em... They dow know who they'm fuckin' messin' with!" Fennel was ranting and not thinking clearly.

"Eddie, when the cops show up they'm gunna find three dead bodies... It ay the 50s no more mate, we ay gunna get away with this... There's a fuckin blood bath down there mate and yow've got blood all in the boot of yer Jag!" Mucklow was not impressed. "We agreed that we would get Teresa and then gew straight to yower house and get yower passports... We fuckin' agreed mate." *Fennels actions were going to get them both sent down! He had done his time in prison and he did not want to go back there for the rest of his life!* "We would have been in Spain before the cops even found the bodies."

"I have to do this Bill. Ar cor just roll over and give everything I have worked for to them drug pushing bastards." Fennel wiped blood from his face.

"That dow matter now Eddie... There's nothing yow can do. Let's hide the head and burn the Jag. Kids burn aaht cars over here all the time, no one will ever know." Wassell Grove had always been a hotspot for burned out cars that had been stolen in town. Thieves would joyride them out to the country and then set them on fire. It was a regular occurrence.

"Ar'm tecking Byrne's head to O'Connor... He's my cousin. Its personal, it's between me and him..." Foam began to appear around Fennel's mouth and covered the edge of his beard as he gritted his teeth in anger. "Yow teck Teresa home, sort ahht the passports and ar'll meet yer there in a bit." Fennel was resolute and there was nothing Mucklow could say or do to change his mind. Bill Mucklow was certainly not scared or threatened by his friend, but he came to the conclusion that he would probably do exactly the same thing if he was in Fennel's situation. He shrugged and walked back towards the transit…

Fennel wiped away the remaining blood from his face and walked over to the passenger window of the van where Teresa sat. She looked at him and erupted into tears. She threw her arms around his neck and she felt an immense sense of relief. Her emotion brought tears to his own eyes and this made him become even more intent on delivering his final message to Johnny O'Connor.

"I love you so much Eddie." She embraced his head and held on to him tightly.

"I love you too Teresa…" Fennel clung to his sweetheart and Mucklow glanced over at him and raised his eyebrows. Time was tight. *If he was to deliver his message to O'Connor, return to the house and then set off for Spain before the Police caught up with them, then there was no time to waste.* He pulled away and affectionately raised her chin to speak to her. "Bill is going to take you home and I will meet you there…" Further tears entered his eyes as he smiled. "Then we'm gewin to Spain baby… Everything we ever dreamed of… Me and you together in the sun." She smiled and looked at him with love filled eyes. "Then, we will send for aer Tina and she can come and visit us." Fennel kissed the tears away from her pretty adoring eyes and stroked her chin. She loved him so much, they had done so much together and she kept her gaze firmly upon his. *It was over, he had saved her and now they would ride off together into the sun…* Mucklow could wait no more. He started the Transit, put it into gear and as he drove slowly away, Teresa and Eddie kept their eyes upon each other until the very last second…

As Fennel raced back along the Halesowen bypass, he could think of very little else other than his beloved wife… *Was he making the right decision? Did he really need to take Byrne's severed head to Johnny O'Connor? What would the men who died next him in Normandy have achieved with their lives?* He pushed down hard on the accelerator and the straight 6 raced on. He had punished the men who had abducted his precious wife, but the war was lost. He had no choice but to run away to Spain. *Was he a coward? What difference would taking Liam Byrne's severed head to O'Connor make?* The sun had now intensified and he pulled down on the sun visor to aid his vision. *It would be one final act of defiance...* He reassured himself. *He may well be running away, but he would stick two fingers up at the enemy one last time before he went...*

It was a significant event. Eddie Fennel was the last of the 'old school gangsters.' The likes of Billy and Willie Mucklow, Eli Davis and Harry Scriven... The men who looked after their communities and made sure that the streets were safe for their grannies to walk. In leaving, Eddie Fennel was passing on the reins to a new breed... It was the dawning of a new era. A new breed of crooks who were only interested in selling drugs to fund their own excesses. The 1980s were on the way. Edward Fennel was a throwback, a relic and he had been beaten by criminal progress and his masculine desire to wreak blood thirsty vengeance upon those that had threatened his loved ones... All that mattered to him now was his family and as he drove onwards, he looked forwards to their future together in Spain...

As the faded red Jaguar hit the roundabout at the bottom of Manor way, Eddie Fennel was distracted by thoughts of his wife and the intense sun that shone directly into his tear-filled eyes. He pulled out onto the island and did not see the massive articulated lorry that ploughed into the side of his Jaguar and sent it plummeting across the road and rolling as it went.... As it rolled, Teresa Fennel stayed constantly within her husband's thoughts until the very last second...

Epilogue

Eddie Fennel lay upon his sun lounger and watched his wife as she dazzled in the intense Andalusian sun... He smoked his cigar and enjoyed his perfectly chilled Spanish lager... It was perfect... It was Heaven...

But, did Eddie Fennel deserve to go to Heaven? Did his great great grandfather deserve to be sent away from his family on a prison ship to Van Diemen's land? All because he had stolen chickens to feed his starving child... Did the ruthless men who sold drugs with no thought for anyone other than their own criminal wealth deserve to live as free men?

"Come on Eddie... The Judge is ready for you now." Fennel's solicitor tapped him on the shoulder and woke him from a dream that he did not wish to be woken from... Eddie Fennel had been found unconscious in the obliterated wreck of his Jaguar mk 2. The police had been particularly interested in the severed head that lay in the boot and it was later linked to three dead bodies in nearby Wassel Grove. Not even 'Clubber' Clark could help him out of this one! Fennel's eyes flickered open and he straightened his tie and adjusted his war medals before making his way up into the dock to be sentenced...

In nearby Birmingham, Micky Cole sat in a lavishly decorated caravan and looked into the wild eyes of Johnny O'Connor... *Bill Mucklow was in Spain, Eddie Fennel was in prison and his own father Harry Scriven would let him do whatever he liked...* O'Connor winked and pushed a glass of Irish whiskey across the table... All that was left for Cole to do now was to ask himself one question... *Money or morals?*

Also available by Thomas J.R. Dearn.

Once upon a time in the Black Country.
A 1950s Gangster Novel.

Once upon a time in the Black Country Part II.
Ghosts.

Once upon a time in the Black Country Part III.
Money and Morals.

Coming soon…

Costa del Criminal.
An English Villain in Spain.

Once upon a time in the Black Country 1934.
A 1930s Gangster Novel.

Author and musician Thomas J.R. Dearn was born in the Black Country area of the West Midlands and has a strong interest in early to mid-twentieth century history. He studied Music at Wolverhampton university before embarking upon a long and successful career as a schoolteacher. Thomas now lives in Worcestershire with his wife, three children and Rottweiler/German Shepherd cross. He enjoys football and is a supporter of Aston Villa and Halesowen town football clubs. Thomas is also a classic car enthusiast and collector of vintage guitars.

Check the website, Facebook or Twitter for news of future releases:
www.onceuponatimeintheblackcountry.com

Printed in Great Britain
by Amazon